Life Erupted

Life Erupted

a novel

Mary Stanik

Published by Mary Stanik

For my mother, Virginia Gill Stanik Phillips, who believed in me and supported me even when all logic and reason told her not to.

Chapter One

Jenn stared out her ground floor office window in the Mayo Building at the snowflakes swirling and clustering outside. She had a ton to do, but her mind wandered to the weekend. Mostly. Would she go skiing at Trollhaugen in Wisconsin with Toni and Brandon? Ice skate with Elaine and her kids at the Milwaukee Road Depot downtown and then be the children's heroine because she would buy them the large and not budget-sized hot chocolates? Or would she talk Emily into going for a facial at the pretty expensive new salon and maybe convince her that just because the Red Dragon's Wondrous Punch had at least six shots of liquor in it didn't mean they would become comatose afterward? She was certain that this sort of mental wandering is what kept her mostly sane. But then she realized that her first choice, slaloming down the Troll's small but still rolling hills, was out of the question because she was on call this weekend. Again. She was considering this when the phone rang.

"Jenn, do you know a TV crew is up here?"

Her brain kicked in after hearing the stark bark sans greeting. The bark belonged to Laurence, nursing chief of station 89, the most intense of the hospital's intensive care units and someone Jenn thought should be on a continuous intravenous drip of anti-anxiety medication.

"No, I did not know anyone was up there," she replied, taking a deep breath, which she often had to do when talking to Laurence.

"I'll be right up."

"You know ... you know the rules ... why does this keep happening?" Laurence screeched.

"As we've discussed before, Laurence, if they get past the desk, and if security doesn't catch them, and if they don't call me ahead of time to tell me they're coming, and if the patient doesn't call me, I can't stop something I don't know is going to happen."

"Fine, then ... just get up here now and get rid of them."

Jenn put the phone down and wondered whether she had been solicitous enough. Laurence had sent at least three explosive letters to her boss over the past two years, complaining that Jenn acted more like a crusading reporter than someone "paid to protect our hospital." Jenn's boss, a former wire service reporter himself, would just call and remind Laurence that Jenn needed to put on reporter airs in order to better manage the reporters.

Jenn didn't hate being compared to reporters; well, the real ones, anyway, who could write and find Bolivia on a map without assistance. But not the ones who just appeared to do hair, makeup and wardrobe upon occasion, painfully pausing to report some real news from time to time.

Jenn ran out of her office and into a stinging breeze; she wanted to get to the hospital before things got worse. She was literally running, despite wearing a slightly tighter and shorter skirt than she normally wore to work, along with expensive four-inch heels she had bought in Rome when her father told her to get some good walking shoes. She thought that even she, Jenn Bergquist, age 36, of Minneapolis, Minnesota, deserved a tiny bit of élan in what she considered an often all too very average life, frequent trips to the intensive care unit notwithstanding.

Of course, élan was not a characteristic most Minnesotans, including Jenn's own thoroughly Norwegian-Minnesotan architect father, thought useful. They tended to favor a life that probably should be quite unassuming if it were to be productive.

She stopped at the information desk to see if the receptionist had seen any television reporters. Although she always asked the same question whenever she was on her way to catch any rogue journalists, this sort of query usually only resulted in something like an "Oh, which station? I just love that Ken Davidson on Channel 8 ..." remark from the elderly, innocent and heavily perfumed volunteers who usually staffed the desk.

After finding out that, as usual, no one had seen anyone or anything untoward, she ran on to the elevator and almost charged right into the chest of Dr. Yuki Atagari, the center's very short yet unquestionably powerful chief of surgery. Jenn liked him; he was one of the relatively few doctors at the hospital who understood why major medical centers needed people like Jenn on staff.

"Jenn! Jenn, my dear girl, what could cause you to be running again? I don't see any rain," said Dr. Atagari in his carefully cultivated Queen's English British accent (an accent that didn't really seem all that incongruous despite the fact that he had been born and raised in Tokyo). "You are always on the run. One might think you were in some sort of trouble."

"Well, Dr. Atagari," she said as she jumped off the elevator. "I just may be, as there are more outlaw reporters on 89."

Wearing his customary tie with patterns reminiscent of fine geisha kimonos, Dr. Atagari laughed more loudly than he normally might as the elevator shut. Jenn turned to find a reporter and photographer who clearly were not from the local group she knew, and, for the most part, that she either respected greatly or had learned to tolerate. The female reporter's hair was not so much haystack as it was perhaps missile silo, colored a garish yellow. The photographer seemed much more servile and outfitted in a more businesslike fashion than the local photographers, most of whom considered wearing clean jeans dressing for success.

"You must be the P.R. lady," cooed Silo Hair. "I am sure you can clear things up here with this dedicated nurse ... what is your name again, sir?"

Laurence stood next to the station's main desk stacked tall with purple and pink folders, hands planted firmly on his squishy hips. Jenn laughed to herself as she realized Laurence's hair wasn't very much different from that of the reporter, although maybe his yellow was closer to that of smudged old highway line paint rather than taxi exterior. Too bad they are getting off to such a bad start, Jenn thought.

"Jenn, these people just came up here and marched into Ms. Fiona's room," he snapped, his eyes twitching in a sort of unison with his eyebrows. "Now they have to leave this second or I will have to take further action with security and your superior."

Jenn took several deep breaths, just as she would at yoga. Did she really enjoy watching heart transplant surgery, or the thrill of mostly understanding articles in the *New England Journal of Medicine*, enough that she was willing to be smacked about so often by people like Laurence? She'd have to ask herself this question again later when she had time.

"Laurence, I am going to take care of this situation," she sighed. "I am just as concerned about this breach of security as you are, I assure you."

"Now listen here, we did not know about your rules," said the reporter in a far testier voice than her previous coo. "And Ms. Fiona invited us here and she wants us here and I would think that you would respect the patient's wishes."

Jenn had been in so many of these sorts of confrontations that she almost thought she could write a manual that every public relations person in North America would buy. She'd name the manual: *It Helps to be a Masochist: The Art of Subduing Staff Along With Reporters.*

"Laurence, I am going to escort the journalists out now," she said with what she hoped was some measure of calm authority. "Everything will be fine. I will talk with the patient later." Laurence slowly walked back behind the main desk and gave hard looks to his staff nurses who had been listening the entire time. It didn't appear as if he believed a word Jenn said, and as that was his usual reaction, she figured everything might be just fine.

"Well now, I don't believe we've been properly introduced, but I'm Jenn Bergquist, the hospital's media relations director," she said to the reporter in a way she felt conveyed the basic information as well as how mad she was that she not only had to run over to deal with someone with such terrible hair, but that she had to take abuse from Laurence yet again.

She made her introduction while purposefully walking past some gurneys and toward the elevator, forcing the reporter and photographer to follow her off the station if they wanted to hear her out. "It's true, photographers and reporters may not be present on intensive care units without prior authorization from my office, the patient's physician, and the nursing staff. Even if the patient wishes it so," Jenn said with what she knew was more than a touch of sarcasm but the silo was bothering her more than the attitudes or hairdos of most reporters. The photographer was another matter, as he seemed to be a kind person with rather gentle eyes, albeit one who did not speak.

"Well, Ms. Bergquist, I'm Nadine Jackson from Action News 3 in San Francisco," the reporter said without offering her hand. "We have flown a hell of a long way, we haven't even checked into our hotel yet, and we came here to interview Bianca Fiona and we are not leaving until we do so."

Jenn immediately realized that Bianca Fiona would not be like one of the many adorable small children who happened to need an organ or bone marrow transplant or some other medical intervention the likes of which was only available at world-renowned medical centers such as the University of Minnesota. Television stations didn't tend to send this sort of reporter to cover a mere child's sad story. No, when they sent harpies like this Nadine Jackson (Jenn's own strong feminist beliefs notwithstanding, she did like the word Jacqueline Kennedy Onassis used to describe detestable female reporters), the patient involved was someone famous, infamous, rich, or all three. Jenn was quite accustomed to celebrity patients. Laurence also thought he was very accustomed to celebrity patients. At least this patient wasn't a former first lady, like the one who had been at the hospital the year before, complete with her own professional salon standing hair dryer and small army of Secret Service agents.

Nadine pursed her heavily shellacked lips in the way a prostitute might if she was told she wasn't worth her asking price. Jenn decided it would be best to just keep taking deep breaths and to think hard before she said anything she might regret.

"Ms. Jackson, I do understand your situation, including the flying, but I have to enforce the hospital rules," Jenn said as she guided Nadine and the photographer into yet another elevator. "Let me find out what is going on with the patient. If her caregivers think it is okay for Ms. Fiona to be interviewed, I will let you know as soon as possible."

The elevator stopped at the lobby level. Jenn waited many moments in silence, with Nadine standing there, lips still pulled tight, before she and her photographer realized Jenn wasn't going to give in. Nadine fished into an enormous gold leather tote bag to pull out a card that she handed to Jenn with more than a little disgust.

"Here is my cell phone number, so call me or text me as soon as we can get to the patient," Nadine sneered. "Tell Ms. Fiona we are sorry her hospital of choice has kicked us out."

The photographer bowed his head of longish, dark brown hair. Jenn could have sworn he rolled his eyes. It was no wonder Jenn's diaphragmatic breathing was so excellent, as she had ample opportunity in this job to breathe deeply and think very carefully before talking.

"Ms. Jackson," she said in a cadence most people reserved for small children. "I'm sorry you see my actions as kicking you out. I'll talk to everyone involved as soon as I can and I will get back to you immediately. I'm really not here to be an obstacle, even though I know you might consider people like me to be just that."

Nadine gave Jenn a frozen stare. "Okay, we are out of here," Nadine clipped and turned away. Jenn watched them walk out, noticed Nadine carried none of the photographer's equipment as he wrestled with his camera, lights and all of the gear he needed to make aging celebrities look reasonably good. Jenn, too, turned and went back to the elevator.

When she got out at 89, Laurence was still behind the desk, although he didn't appear quite as ticked off. Maybe Jenn would avoid having another Laurence Love Letter sent to her boss today.

"So, I suppose you want to know about Ms. Fiona," Laurence said without any emotion. "She's in room 14. I'll take you there."

Jenn followed him, being careful to not click her heels too loudly and to stay a few steps behind. She let him use the sanitizing solution first and then was dutiful in slathering it on her hands so he could see she was observing infection control protocol.

"Ms. Fiona," Laurence announced in an almost too loud voice and door rap that Jenn thought shouldn't be used anywhere in a hospital, much less on intensive care units. "Our hospital P.R. girl, Jenn Bergquist, is here to talk with you about those reporters. I'm sorry she had to send them away, but our rules are firm."

Jenn didn't have time to be insulted that he'd called her a "P.R. girl." When she entered the room, she could scarcely believe she was in a hospital, much less a place for the quite critically ill. The normally dull aqua and beige walls had been almost entirely obliterated by a mass of paisley silk bedspreads in colors usually visible only after dropping acid, although a sort of purple seemed to dominate. Several large brass urns lined the tan terrazzo floor and were filled with hordes of silk flowers, in shades only slightly more restrained than those of the bedspreads. A large poster of what looked to be an unlikely collision of Saturn and the moon was mounted above the bed's headboard. There was what Jenn swore was a distinct patchouli scent that seemed to grow stronger the longer one stayed in the room.

Ms. Fiona herself fit right in. Jenn knew severe illness could put years on even the most beautiful people, so she could not always guess a patient's true age, but she appeared to be in her late 50s. She did have the yellow-tinged skin and eyes common to those with liver disease and resulting high bilirubin counts but she otherwise looked almost energetic. She was wearing a caftan that exactly matched one of the bedspreads. Jenn estimated at least a pound of gold jewelry was affixed to her ears, wrists, neck and fingers; it looked far more Cartier than street bazaar cart. Her mostly dark brown hair, darker than Jenn's own, reminded her of Elizabeth Taylor's, although Elizabeth Taylor's had been far better groomed.

Jenn fought hard to stifle an enormous laugh. Given the room's decoration, she figured Ms. Fiona had to be a psychic or medium of some sort, and probably wanted the TV people in there to promote her latest book or video. She couldn't believe how many New Age stereotypes Ms. Fiona brought to life, all the way down to the caftan, the planets in motion, and even the patchouli. Jenn wondered how often she would have her equally royal purple nails done each week, and if Laurence would allow a manicurist wielding acetone to come onto the floor without also doing his nails.

Ms. Fiona kept a serene look as she listened to Laurence, and Jenn was too busy taking in Ms. Fiona's aura to hear exactly what he was saying. When he seemed to be finished expounding on the importance of rules and why they had to be obeyed, Ms. Fiona raised her hand, kind of like how one would expect a great prophet to do when dismissing someone, and flitted it Laurence's way.

"I believe I can take care of things with Ms. Bergquist here," Ms. Fiona said in a voice that reminded Jenn of those of the good fairies of film. "She looks to be someone who understands priorities."

Laurence gave Jenn a look of rebuke as he left the room. Ms. Fiona's eyes might have been blue at one point, but now they just looked sort of tinged with ocean green as they fixed upon Jenn, although it was a little hard to really tell with the amount of extremely dark eye shadow she was wearing.

"I take it you don't approve of my interior decorating," Ms. Fiona said with a kittenish grin, moving a huge silk pillow near Jenn and motioning for her to sit down on the bed. "That's okay. We have a lot of time to work on you. What's important now is to deal with those people, even though so many journalists are so artless, as I believe Alexandre Dumas once wrote. Still, I do imagine my friends want to know if I am going to move on to the next plane of existence soon."

Jenn wanted to laugh some more but she also realized this might be one of those moments when a patient, even a seeming loony like Ms. Fiona, would want to talk. Jenn knew all too well that many patients didn't really have anyone at all to talk to, or they did not have much in the way of family who weren't focused on totally flipping out because their mother or husband or whoever was very ill and likely to die. Few nurses were as constantly angry as Laurence, but most of them were just too busy setting up IV lines or doing nine million other things to be able to listen very much.

"Ms. Fiona, I'm glad you realize the need to handle the television people," Jenn said in what she realized was a voice almost exactly like that of Ms. Fiona's, although she wasn't at all sure why she suddenly was sounding like Ms. Fiona. The last thing she wanted was to become yet another patient confidante, much less to someone who might tell her, for example, that she had actually been a sexually frustrated young milkmaid in 13th century Scotland. In 21st century Minnesota, she didn't need to be reminded that she was just carrying on as usual.

"If your doctor says you may have reporters in your room, and if Laurence agrees—and even Laurence agrees at times—well then I just need to have you sign this consent form giving me permission to talk publicly about your condition and then we can make arrangements for them to return," Jenn said. She wished Ms. Fiona would stop looking at her with an almost angelic but still creepy stare. She just didn't want any grief about the need to sign the form; she suddenly remembered the news release she needed to write for the human genetics people when she got back to her office.

"So Laurence is charming at times, that is lovely to know," Ms. Fiona said as she fumbled on her bed table for a filigreed gold fountain pen. "I just don't want to tolerate the kind of bad energy he seems to radiate, not now. But you won't have any trouble with Yuki. I mean Dr. Atagari—I've been calling him Yuki forever. He has a delightful soul, despite what he may have to display at times."

Jenn handed Ms. Fiona the form and before she could ask if she had any questions, and before Jenn could think about Dr. Atagari having a delightful soul, the paper was filled with some of the most interesting penmanship she had ever seen. To say it was like calligraphy wouldn't be quite accurate. But it did remind Jenn of the way people wrote centuries ago, beautifully flowing yet sturdy like Thomas Jefferson's Declaration of Independence hand, although she doubted Ms. Fiona was quite as concerned about liberty and justice.

"Thanks," Jenn said just a tad hurriedly. "I'll get in touch with Dr. Atagari, and Laurence, and if they say okay, Nadine can come on up."

"That sounds wonderful, sweetie," Ms. Fiona said as she adjusted more vividly colored silk pillows behind her back. "Then we'll talk about your soul. So very, very much turbulence in one who has traveled so far for so long."

Jenn looked down at the floor for a moment, and then stared vacantly at Ms. Fiona for a few seconds, before she stammered thanks and a promise to talk again soon. She walked quickly to the elevator without even pausing to look at Laurence.

When she got back down to the lobby, she could still smell the desk volunteer's lilac perfume, although for some reason the odor didn't really bother her. Maybe it was a relief from all the patchouli.

She ran once again across the now snow-covered cobblestone courtyard to her office and stopped to tell the story of Bianca Fiona to her co-worker Caroline, the office manager and executive assistant to the boss. Although she was now well past 50 (Jenn was sure she was at least 60), Caroline looked and acted more like a former Las

Vegas showgirl. Well, one who had regular access to an extraordinarily advanced plastic surgeon than a very capable Midwestern medical center office manager.

"So, I bet this woman probably had a patchouli candle burning under her bed—that had to be where the scent came from," Caroline snickered in her throaty voice while frowning hard at the office's latest budget reports. "Or else she's smoking pot and trying to hide it. I think it's great, Laurence is going to be so pissed when he finds out, no matter if she's burning pot or incense or even kerosene. Caroline laughed loudly and in a rather hard way, like some cigarette-addicted nightclub singer, though she did not smoke, and Jenn didn't think she had ever sung in a nightclub. "If she's burning pot, Laurence is going to want some, you know that."

"Caroline, Jesus Christ himself could appear on that station with a joint and a camera and say he was doing a story on medical uses for marijuana and Laurence would still be pissed, okay?" Jenn said, taking a moment to stretch out on one of the red velvet lounge chairs that Caroline had bought herself. She appreciated the idea that Caroline would spend her own money to buy things she found beautiful for the office rather than live with the "Appalachian gray" or "Sonoran beige" stuff from the hospital's furniture warehouse. "Although, to tell you the truth, and you know how much I detest Laurence, but I can't really blame him for wanting that reporter off of the station. If you meet her, you'll see and hear exactly what I mean. You would not believe that hair! I am not making this up—it had to be a foot high."

Caroline laughed and then ordered Jenn to get the hell back to work (with just the slightest shadow of a smirk) so she could justify her salary in the budget. Jenn rolled her eyes, forced herself out of the soft velvet, and went to her own more prosaic chair. A small miracle had occurred in that she had no phone, text or email messages. She started to think about how she was going to make inborn errors of metabolism sound fascinating to the general public when her damn phone rang again. She had to get that news release written and she was not particularly interested in helping Nadine at the moment.

But it was only Dr. Atagari.

"Jenn, I hear you have just met with Ms. Fiona," he said. Although many others in the hospital were happy to yell at her on any given day, he wasn't going to be one of them. "She truly is a beautiful person, even though she … well, she lost her way somewhat when she was younger. And that is why she is here with us now."

"Oh, okay, I suppose lots of people in this same situation have had troubles," she said in a way to let Dr. Atagari know she wasn't going to specifically ask if a patient abused alcohol or drugs in order to get on the liver transplant candidate list.

"She did have a difficult life," Dr. Atagari said softly. "I have known Bianca for years, ever since I roomed with her brother at Berkeley when I first came here from Japan for my undergraduate education. My English was even more BBC then than it is now, if you can believe it. He never once made fun of me. He was always the smart one in the family. No one was as good at math or physics or chemistry, or anything, as Tony Fionarello. He's a rather famous volcanologist now … but I'm always worried sick that Mount Kilauea is going to get him some day."

"Oh, I suppose it had to be tough to compete with such an accomplished sibling," Jenn said, while suddenly realizing she was actually interested in hearing this patient's story. "And her real last name is Fionarello? I guess Fiona is sexier and more suitable for the stage than Fionarello."

Dr. Atagari just laughed softly. "Yes, I suppose Bianca Fiona has better rhythm," he said quietly. "When you talk with her again, and you will, you will learn more about the things she has endured and how she finally found some peace. A lot of people scoff at what she does, but Jenn, you must know this, that we are not just the personalities we portray here in this life. We are all souls on a long journey, and Bianca has just learned how to connect with our souls better than the rest of us."

Jenn was ready to tell Dr. Atagari that she would be more than willing to learn more about how Bianca Fiona found peace, thinking he would say nothing, but then she sensed he really did want to keep talking. One thing she learned early on in her career at the hospital was the fact that when a doctor, and especially a powerful department chair such as Yuki Atagari wanted to talk, you had better shut up and listen.

"I'm just thinking here, Jenn, about all Tony and I and Bianca have gone through together all these years," he said in a way that made him sound almost like a regular person who was enduring the serious illness of a good friend while memories of better, happier days loomed poignant and large. "Bianca was still in junior high, or maybe she was a high school freshman, when Tony and I set up our quarters in that old dormitory at Berkeley. I remember she carried several of Tony's boxes of books so carefully and I thought, wow, this guy really has his little sister trained well. He could be Japanese." Dr. Atagari then laughed in a most American "guy" way, a manner Jenn found both surprising and rather attractive.

"Tony was only 18 and he already had graduate-level volcanology books in his possession," he said in his more customary voice. "And here I thought I would be the brilliant one in the room. I remember Bianca would take the bus in from San Francisco by herself, just to get away from her parents for a little while, wearing false eyelashes and some horrendously short miniskirt that was sure to get her in trouble with both school officials and boys. Tony and I would take her out to this hippie pizza place. And if you can believe it, we'd all have a cigarette. Or two or three. And wine. And beer. Sometimes too much beer and wine. They didn't card people in those days. When I would go to the Fionarellos for Thanksgiving and Christmas because I could only get back to Japan once a year or so, Bianca would help her mother serve all of this great Italian food. I didn't know where all of this talk about Americans eating turkey for Thanksgiving came from because we'd always have octopus or chicken cacciatore or some delicious pasta in marinara sauce. I used to tell Bianca that she would make a fine teahouse hostess. She used to tell me to shut up."

He laughed again, in that same ordinary guy way. It was evident that though Dr. Atagari was pained at the fact that his great friend's sister was now his very sickly patient, he also was clearly very happy to have gone on this small trip back in time.

Although Jenn enjoyed hearing Dr. Atagari's stories of Tony and Bianca, she could hardly believe what he was saying. It seemed so uncharacteristic of him. She did know he was a Buddhist, and while being a Buddhist might permit him to have more sympathy than other physicians for someone like Bianca Fiona, he was still a scientist. She was certain he would never talk this way at international surgery conferences.

"Okay, Dr. Atagari. I will talk some more to Ms. Fiona," she said. "I take it you have no problem with any reporters interviewing her?"

"No, let Bianca have as many reporters as Laurence will allow," he said, while laughing once again. "That way you won't have too much work to do. And I've already talked to Laurence about this particular television station, so you are spared at least one verbal lashing for this week."

"Thank you so much, Dr. Atagari," she said, all too audibly relieved. "I wish everyone in this hospital understood."

"Go and talk with Bianca," he said. "Speak slowly, and don't run to her room, walk. I know you can walk. You never know, she just might understand you a bit, too. And make sure you really listen. You are good at that."

Chapter Two

The garlic was already well cooked in the hot extra virgin olive oil and the tomatoes were chopped and ready when Jenn's father walked into the airy kitchen that looked as if it had been ordered in full (complete with immaculate stainless steel appliances and gleaming planked maple floors) from the showroom of a very upscale Scandinavian outfitter that specialized in the sparely elegant look many Americans thought typical of modern upscale Scandinavian design. He peered into the pan but was careful not to get too close to Jenn while she was near the hot stove. She knew he was going to ask her to please think about adding a few more tomatoes.

"Oh boy, spicy pasta yet again," sighed Olaf Bergquist, a man who had spent the bulk of his rather distinguished architectural career designing beautiful but austere Lutheran colleges, churches, and high schools. "Now, if your mother were still alive, we'd be sitting down to a nice roast turkey hot dish, being that it is Thursday."

Jenn looked up from the stove and wondered how many more years her father was going to tell her what her mother cooked for dinner each night. Christina Bergquist had been dead for four years, and despite the fact that Jenn was pretty sure she wouldn't return in the flesh and to the kitchen anytime soon, her father still wanted talk about what he might have eaten on any given day if her mother had not been so impertinent as to die on him.

At moments like this, she sometimes wished the stork she and

millions of other only children had believed in so strongly (although in Olaf's version, the stork summered in outer Australia and was unable to fly all the way to America very often) had brought her the little brother or sister she had wanted so much throughout her childhood. It would be really useful to have another sibling around at times like this, especially a younger and maybe more pliable one. She felt she could say to this possibly kind and sensitive brother or sister "here, you take him for a week and boil him some mush, you listen to this 'I'm so lonely, what did I do to have life be so miserable?' parental theater."

Jenn knew her father would never stop complaining about pasta, or food in general. But, as she was not going to prepare her mother's cream of mushroom-soaked dishes (unless she was having a truly depressed day, and then yes, the sodium and fat might do the trick), she accepted the fact that as long as she was going to be nice and make dinner for the man every week or so, the food fighting would never end.

"Dad, give me a break. You know very well that Mom would not complain if someone were cooking pasta for her," she said with a forced airiness, anything to get her father to lighten up and not dampen yet another evening with mordant ruminations. "And you know that garlic is supposed to be good for your health, you know that, I'm not just inventing this stuff to torture you."

Olaf just gave her a sort of bemused look as he sat down at the teak table that he had set himself with fine precision, complete with the real silver and the good French white linen napkins and tablecloth.

"Yes, yes, I know what those doctors say," he muttered. "It just could be that the Italians have it right ... just look at Marco, 92 years old and still flying off to see the pyramids."

Marco Leonardo had been her father's graduate school advisor and later, when he tired of the academic life, the senior partner at Olaf's architectural firm. Despite the fact that Marco loved lots of wine, whisky and other liquor and definitely was not Norwegian (and therefore couldn't be a proud member of the Sons of Norway, as Olaf, his father, grandfather, and great-grandfather had been), Jenn knew that her father greatly admired his design genius and still-un-quenched desire to have some adventure in his remaining years.

"Of course, Marco had his wife until he was 88, he didn't have to lose his at a young age like I had to lose your mother," he said with pained determination as he scanned about the table to make certain everything was lined up just so. "So we don't know for sure if it is all that wine and garlic that keeps him going or not."

"Well, Dad, you know, you might have a woman around your-self if you just would cut some of them a little slack," she said as she quickly plopped shrimp into the skillet and then worried that she had probably put too much Dijon mustard into the salad dressing. "In fact, what about that one you went out with last month, the one who wanted to go to that Irish bar on University Avenue to hear Celtic Hurricane? What was wrong with her?"

Olaf just glared at his crystal water goblet.

"What was wrong with her" ... he stammered ... "Her name was Colleen, if you please, and well ... you know very well that ... I don't care to go to such places ... there's just too much noise, and ... I think they wanted something like $40 a person to get in." His stuttering left Jenn unconvinced of Colleen's unworthiness. "Plus, I only told you this because, one, you are my only child, and two, you like to hear such sordid things, you obviously got your cavalier ways from those very Celts who consorted with our Viking ancestors. You are certain of that fact, are you not? Anyway, she put that negligee on right in front of me, with no warning whatsoever. Which she should not have done—she said she just wanted to have a cup of coffee."

Jenn thought she might drop her plate

"Dad, I cannot believe how naïve you are, being almost a man of the world," she said while trying to neatly arrange the shrimp, tomato and garlic mixture over the pasta, much to her father's unfeigned disgust. "You know it was after two in the morning when she invited you over, you know you don't drink coffee that late at night, and you told me, don't say you don't remember telling me this, but you said you couldn't believe her negligee was so full of wrinkles. You should just admit it, it was the wrinkles and not the fact that she wanted you that turned you off."

"I cannot believe I am having this conversation with my daughter," Olaf said. "But, as long as we are talking about problems with the opposite sex, well, my darling daughter, you are now 36 and it could be said that your 60-year-old father is the one who is having more fun. So now, why don't we just eat and maybe you can think about having coffee with some guy at two in the morning."

Jenn carried the salad to the table in silence, knowing that if her father, who hated most talk that even skirted the topic of sex, bothered to bring up the fact that she wasn't enjoying a scintillating social life, things had gotten pretty bad. But she was not going to try to explain her situation, lest he fix her up again with one of the sons of his Sons of Norway buddies. Caroline still teased her brutally about one of them, a lawyer who acted like King Olav himself in front of the group's mostly elderly members but in reality was kind of a lush, especially when it came to vodka. On their first date he had asked Jenn if she owned the hat portion of the Norwegian national costume and suggested it would be fun if she wore the hat and nothing else when having sex with him in his new Land Rover. Jenn actually didn't mind the hat suggestion so much, as she did own one, but sex in a Land Rover on a first date during a Minnesota winter—even with the heater blasting—might be kind of coarse.

She set a bottle of Chardonnay before her father, although he motioned that he only wanted a little splash. She was well aware that Olaf almost never drank to the point of being even remotely influenced by alcohol.

Jenn thought it was time to change the subject. "So, Dad, we've got a really strange patient at the hospital now," she said brightly, picking up her fork, only to see her father's look of reproach as she once again failed to remember to say grace. Olaf said a short prayer while Jenn kept her eyes fixed on the food.

"Anyway, I had a talk with this patient today from San Francisco, a psychic, I guess she's pretty famous, so these television people are following her story," she said while her father tried to poke his fork among the pasta as if to make certain he didn't eat any loose pieces of garlic. "She is big-time weird, and this reporter was pretty bizarre too. You would not believe the hair on this so-called journalist, Dad, it was a feat of truly monstrous architecture. You and Marco would be completely appalled."

Olaf grinned just a bit. He liked it whenever his daughter made even the slightest reference to his profession and the high standards he tried to uphold. Good design was as important to him as good manners.

"I'm always amazed at the interest people have in these psychics," Olaf said, while gently spearing some tomato pieces. "Of course, in a place as strange as San Francisco, I suppose anything is possible. I'm just glad I don't live in California anymore, as it was awful enough to go to graduate school in Los Angeles, and that was before the place became truly crazy."

"Yeah, Dad, well, I was born in Los Angeles while you were in graduate school, so it couldn't have been all that awful, and, I also should note we are drinking California wine tonight and so far no one has keeled over," Jenn said with just a little bit of a smirk. Her father cracked a somewhat larger smile than when she mentioned architecture.

"Whatever ... the woman's name is Bianca Fiona," she continued. "Isn't that a great name for a psychic? And, get this, she's also a friend of Dr. Atagari's ...her brother is some big shot volcanologist who went to Berkeley with Dr. Atagari as an undergraduate. He's got a more normal name, I think it is Tony, something like that, Tony Fionarello, I believe."

Olaf appeared to look through Jenn, which was odd; Olaf Bergquist seldom went blank. He then took a very small drink of wine, although it seemed as if he experienced some trouble swallowing the sip.

Jenn wasn't totally shocked to see her father go rather blank but seeing him do so set her off just a tad, even though she knew her father had never liked to talk much about the time he and her mother spent in California. Marco liked to talk about California, but Marco liked to talk about any place that wasn't Minnesota, even though Jenn knew he had been willing to put up with, as Marco put it "beastly winters and people who need much more beast about them," when he moved to Minnesota to help turn a rather dour little architectural firm into one of the nation's largest and most innovative creators of all manner of stylish buildings. Even though she had known Marco for as long as she could remember, she still had trouble reconciling the fact that he and her father were so close. Or why her father had not taken on more of Marco's traits, though Olaf and Marco did share a taste for costly clothing. It was just that most of Marco's clothes were representative of the best of the most current Italian design (although he admitted to making an "enormous error" as one of the first people in Minneapolis to wear leisure suits in the late 1970s). Olaf wore the best American prepster threads money could buy. His regular sales associate at Brooks Brothers even thought it was time for Olaf to leave the 1962 rich Yale frat boy look behind, though he was jealous of the fact that Olaf still had a 32 inch waist. Maybe Olaf didn't like the California wine Jenn picked to have with dinner and maybe that is what made him seem somewhat blank, or even kind of sullen.

"Yes … that is indeed quite interesting," Olaf said in an almost murmur after another long pause in the conversation. "It's a pity the sister couldn't have put her energies, as it were … see, your old father gets it … I said energies, but it's too bad she didn't apply herself as properly … as did her brother." Jenn thought he appeared even more uncomfortable as he continued to speak. "If she's a patient of Yuki

Atagari's, I suppose it's a safe bet that she's in for either a kidney or a liver transplant."

"Liver," Jenn replied warily. "She's been pretty open about having a real problem with booze in the past, before she figured out how to manage the cosmos and make a buck from it at the same time. And now, as long as we are talking about alcoholism, don't get going with me again about how we should not do transplants on alcoholics or other people who willingly abuse their bodies. I'm just not in the mood to hear about it tonight."

"I see," Olaf said quietly. "I'm not either."

Oh man, she thought, time to change the subject yet again, although she was just a touch troubled by her father's agreement to not get into a biomedical ethics argument. He did love philosophy and arguments that didn't become too heated. She knew he greatly admired Dr. Atagari, who he knew from the south Minneapolis cocktail circuit. The circuit, held in many houses that were much like Olaf's, didn't include too many cocktails, as most of the party guests were nice Norwegian Lutherans like Olaf, with a few highly accomplished people of other ethnicities like Marco and Yuki and Yuki's wife, the internationally renowned painter and Marco's wine club buddy, Miki Suganuma Atagari, thrown in for a bit of garnish. Jenn sometimes wondered what sort of mildly fascinating scientific paper a family counselor could write about her need to keep things very calm whenever she was with her father (or people at work, a related tome), as if there were an emotional seismograph within him that would break when things got even a little agitated or … tinged with garlic. Because Jenn had practiced this sort of emotional control her whole life, she really didn't think all that critically about her peacekeeping role, except maybe when her father would mention her need for a boyfriend or a husband. Then it was she who wanted to change the subject and keep the peace.

At some moments like this she knew where she had received the training she needed to breathe deeply and think long and hard before talking and possibly saying something really stupid. She had to admit that she was not completely ungrateful that Olaf had taught her to rein in some of life's rawer emotions. She knew people who would burst into tears at the thought of Christmas without snow, or martinis without olives, and she was indeed very glad she wasn't so overwrought or maudlin.

"Dad, we have thawed blueberries and angel food cake for dessert. I hope that's not too wild for you," she teased as cheerfully as she could before downing the rest of her wine.

"No, thawed blueberries are not too wild for me," Olaf said as he looked out the window at the snow now coming down in larger clusters than those that fell the other morning while Jenn was daydreaming. "You know, last week I even had tiramisu when I had dinner with some clients from New York, so there."

Jenn smiled widely as she shook her head and poured herself more wine.

"Give me a little more of that too," Olaf said. He looked as if he were almost ready to have either the rare good time or an equally rare temper outburst. "What the heck. Fill it up to the top, my dear."

Chapter Three

Nadine's Action News hair didn't seem so stratospheric today. In fact, strangely enough, it seemed almost flat. Jenn figured it must be because she couldn't get to a hairdresser she could trust to put 70 or 80 pounds of pressure in it. The photographer looked even more interesting than at first sight, and he also seemed to know what he was doing with a camera. Jenn suddenly thought it strange that she should consider it notable that someone could be both attractive and competent. All the same, she had been around enough good photographers to know that this particularly handsome specimen had done an excellent job of lighting the small room so the ceiling fluorescent lights, combined with the glare from Ms. Fiona's shiny silk wall hangings, wouldn't make people's faces look like those of plastic baby dolls.

Still, smaller hair and proper lighting aside, the look that came through Nadine's face plaster made it painfully clear that she was not the star of the show. And she knew this necessary refocus on who was the real celebrity here would really bother Nadine. She had dealt with this type before; there were lots of reporters who had finally made it to a large local television market and were just waiting for the break that would shoot them up to one of the networks. Nadine was obviously looking at this story as a way to get some good promotional pieces for her station to use during the next sweeps month. Something like "our Nadine Jackson goes to the most remote and faraway locations to bring you the stories you care about and need right now."

But today's star was Bianca Fiona herself. As it were, Jenn smiled at the tiny bit of weak humor that she felt sure maybe only Dr. Atagari would have thought of as well. Jenn still couldn't get over Bianca's fulfillment of the most outlandish ideas people might hold about psychics. She was wearing another caftan, this one in a swirly aquamarine print. She had on just as much annoying jewelry and pancake makeup and waved her hands around so furiously that Jenn thought maybe someone should get her some bread dough to knead so she could put all of the motion to good use.

"Of course, even 20 years ago I started to think I was drinking too much … but you know, I was young and thought I was partaking of the proverbial cup of life," Bianca said in a more elevated good fairy voice than she had employed the day before. "I think I thought if I drank and got drunk, maybe the pain would ease, maybe my third husband really would become a decent guy, the world would become more exciting, everything dark would become light … you know what I mean."

Nadine kept popping her mouth open like a giant mackerel, revealing incredibly overbleached teeth with each pop, only to have each possible word be muffled by yet another Bianca Fiona sound bite.

"And then there was the whole San Francisco scene in the 1970s. It really shaped me, you can't believe it, well, one had to just revel in the whole thing, eat that whole damn pan of brownies, dance naked until the sun rose. I just felt I had to LIVE and let life course through me," Bianca said breathlessly, although Dr. Atagari's very worried look made Jenn realize that Bianca's breathlessness was not entirely due to nostalgia for free love and brownies.

"Okay then," Nadine said, butting in with a shriek that made Bianca stop talking in mid-sentence and shake her head so her earrings clanged like cymbals. "So, when did you stop drinking and start realizing you were psychic? Were you married at that time?"

Nadine's interruption made everyone else in the room just turn and look squarely at her as if it were somehow completely absurd that she should want control of the interview.

"Well, I had just divorced my third husband around the time I realized I had a gift that should be developed, and then used, to help people," Bianca said in a suddenly stern way, almost as if she were sentencing Nadine to detention. "But I was still drinking. I only stopped drinking entirely around three years ago, though I've been in therapy about my drinking for many more years. Is that important?"

Dr. Atagari moved out from the room's corner, positioned himself right next to Nadine and put a firm hand on her heavily padded shoulder.

"I know we all would love to keep talking with you, but as Ms. Fiona's physician, I must insist that we stop this interview now, just because I sense my patient is becoming very fatigued," he said in the starchier accent Jenn had heard only a few times before, a voice he reserved for those he utterly despised. "What's important is that she rest and that a liver donor becomes available sooner rather than later. I am certain your viewers back in San Francisco want the same thing for someone who has done so much for so many of them."

Damn, he is so very good, Jenn thought while giving Nadine and her photographer a bit of a smile that the photographer returned but Nadine did not. Dr. Atagari just bowed to Jenn, Bianca, and the photographer and then walked quietly out of the room. Bianca silently propped herself upon more caftan-matching sheets and assumed a queen-like yoga pose, complete with carefully folded hands. As impressed as Jenn was with Dr. Atagari's performance, she knew it would be a real waste of his surgical talents as well as his financial acumen to have him become a hospital spokesperson.

"If you need help packing up, or carrying your tripod, just let me know," Jenn said in a genuinely pleasant voice to the still unnamed photographer, knowing that as smooth as Dr. Atagari was, he was just providing the opening for her to continue everyone's politely strained exit.

"I think Mark will do just fine, thank you so very much," Nadine snapped as she hoisted her huge tote bag and almost jumped out of the room. "I just want to get the hell out of here and shoot this story back to San Francisco in time for the six o'clock."

Laurence gave his customary glare as all of them clattered past the main desk, and Jenn then realized that a few other pieces of equipment were still sitting in Bianca's room. Jenn also thought this was the first time Mark was going to say more than hello or thank you and that he was sure to be in enormous trouble with Nadine for speaking up, and to the hospital flak lady of all people.

"Ms. Bergquist, do you know anyone over there? I think it is Channel 12, do you think you could you call someone and see if they'll let us come over right away? They might want us to come at a different time," Mark said as they all made a fast halt at the elevators.

Jenn looked at Nadine. Her left false eyelash was drooping.

"Of course, I know all the people over at 12. I can call them as soon as I get back to my office. I'd be happy to help," she said while smiling even more widely at Mark. "I'm sure there won't be a problem as long as you can work with their schedule. But I think you and I had better go back and get your equipment. Nadine, feel free to wait downstairs, we'll meet you in a few minutes."

"Fine," Nadine said. She had realized her eyelash was loose and was trying to pat it back down with her long, acrylic nails. "I just want to have this story on tonight's six, okay, no excuses, maybe we can even make the top of the news."

When Mark and Jenn got to Bianca's room, she had strapped a huge blue gel eye mask—the kind intended to reduce puffiness, not aid with sleep—on her face. She didn't actually see Mark and Jenn come in the room to take down the remaining lights. But she heard them clearly enough and took the mask off as Mark rolled the extension cord being held on the other end by Jenn.

"So, young man, you seem just much too talented to be dealing with such boring stuff as affiliates and the six o'clock news and extension cords," Bianca said playfully while trying to tousle her hairspray-stiffened hair around and around her fancy gold pen. Jenn thought she must have been pretty damn good at the pickup game, alcoholism and brownies aside, to manage three husbands. She wondered if it was possible that she was now trying to hit on Mark, who appeared to be somewhere in his 30s (but as with really sick people, Jenn also found it hard to gauge an exact age with really handsome men). Mark was intent on getting his equipment packed up as quickly as possible.

"Oh, I don't know, the local news bit is a good gig sometimes, and it lets me live in San Francisco," he said in a far more confident tone than Jenn had heard him voice when Nadine was around. "But you're absolutely correct, there are parts that can be a real drag at times." Mark paused. "That's why I really only work part-time on news so I can do a lot of freelance work, nature stuff, documentaries, work that takes me all over the place. Maybe you might think some of that is more interesting than local news?"

Bianca disentangled the pen from her mass of hair and pointed it Jenn's way. "Why yes, I do indeed. Don't you agree, Jenn? When you are done documenting my decline into physical ruin, Mark, what do you think you'll do next?"

Jenn blinked. Did Bianca's eyes just twinkle like purple lights? Jenn tried to think of a way to pick the equipment up even faster so she wouldn't have to witness this flirting prowess and so she might have a chance to talk to Mark herself, although even the thought that she wanted to engage in such talk made her very anxious. She had learned through painful experience that it was a dumb idea to try to hit on handsome out-of-town photographers or reporters, since most of the ones she had met were either married, very gay, or too fanatically heterosexual. She had gotten into big trouble the one time she did go out with one of them, a Canadian Broadcasting Corporation guy who probably should have gone into real politics, as all he wanted was to get her drunk on rum and Cokes so she would let him into the lab of a scientist who had previously said no Socialist foreigners would ever enter there. But she did get drunk, she did let the foreign photographer into the lab the next day (although she did not know for certain if he was a real Socialist or not), and then she did get into trouble.

"Well, funny you should ask, Ms. Fiona, but *National Geographic* is working on a new documentary on volcanoes—volcanoes all over the world. I've done some stuff with them in the past and so I am pretty sure I'll be working on this one too," Mark replied offhandedly while looking about carefully to make sure the floor was free of the duct tape photographers seemed to use all the time.

"If I get the job, I'm going to Iceland quite soon. In fact—and you probably know this already—but the reason I agreed to come here with Nadine was to try to get to know you a little bit because your brother is one of the scientists who will be getting major feature treatment in the program. I was reading his biography the other day and I thought, oh man, this guy must be insanely brilliant. I'm just guessing it probably was real hell for you when you were kids to have to live in the same house with such a brain."

Jenn sensed an awkward delay in Bianca's response. "Well, that is indeed curious," Bianca said slowly in a much lower voice than Jenn had yet heard her use. "If that is the case, then you had better read everything—and I mean everything—you can get your hands on about volcanology. Tony is a demanding taskmaster, although I love him completely. He's been a great brother to me while I was screwing up my life and he was ascending into the intellectual heavens."

Bianca suddenly appeared confused as she looked at Mark and Jenn. She clutched one of her pillows tightly to her chest, which made Jenn think she might be in some real pain.

"Do you need anything Ms. Fiona?" Jenn asked abruptly.

"Oh…no," said Bianca. She turned to Mark. "I think I did know Tony was going to Iceland pretty soon, but I forget about some things these days, as you can imagine," Bianca said while pressing against her pillow harder and looking out the window as if searching for something she had lost.

"And, you know, Tony does live a very exciting life, of course, you both must realize this, but that is the life he chose for himself this time around," she said, adopting her usual good witch voice with her concentration seemingly restored. "But he's not always had such an enjoyable time."

Jenn looked at Mark as if to say "Can we get out of here, and is it too early for cocktails?" Without such fortification, Jenn wasn't ready to get into a past lives discussion with this famous psychic from California. Suddenly she then started to think that maybe it wasn't right to focus on cocktails and a man when she was in the room of a woman who was going to need a new liver due to too much alcohol. She struggled to zip up one of Mark's duffel bags as he lifted most of the rest of his equipment and signaled to Jenn that he was ready to leave.

"Well, Ms. Fiona, it's been an honor and a pleasure, and I hope we can see you again before we leave town," Mark said in a way that made Jenn think he, too, could do effective hospital public relations, not that he'd pass on photographing exploding volcanoes in order to do so. "And, if I'm not mistaken, you might want to check, but I think your brother is already in Iceland. I go back to San Francisco tomorrow and that's when I hope I'll find out if I have the job. If you believe in luck...well, you know... I would be grateful if you'd wish me some."

Mark smiled in a way that made Jenn feel a bit flushed. Thank God her father was not around. She knew she'd be going out with him socially before he left town. She was certain of it. Bianca knew it too. And Mark probably knew it too. He looked like the type who knew exactly how attractive he was to so many women.

Bianca looked at Mark and then at Jenn in the way the cardinals might look at a newly anointed pope. "Oh, I do believe in luck, but in your case, there's no need for luck. You will get the job," Bianca said, while turning to smile demurely at Jenn. "Trust my inside knowledge on this one, just this once, okay? And when you arrive in Iceland, you must not tell Tony about how sick I look; I don't want him to get really upset. The world needs to know what Tony knows about volcanoes, and he can't share it properly if he is worried about me. Promise me you'll tell him I look ready to go dancing on Park Avenue."

Jenn started to giggle just a bit, given that Bianca's caftan might just work in some parts of the world, although probably not on Park Avenue when the sun and the Pradas and Chanels in BMWs were out.

"Don't worry, I'll be discreet," Mark said while laughing with Jenn. "Besides, you really do look just fine."

"Thank you," Bianca said while leaning back into the rest of her pillows, in which she now looked very comfortable. "I do hope you and Jenn will have some time to talk before you go to Iceland. Your auras, among other things, are in nice harmony. I know you don't believe any of this yet, but it's quite true."

Mark and Jenn took this mention of harmonic convergence to be the sign that they should say goodbye and get downstairs to a Nadine who was likely to be ready to explode, especially if she happened to be completely out of eyelash glue.

"We'll be seeing you, Ms. Fiona," Mark said. "And I promise I'll have only good things to tell your brother."

"Thank you, love," Bianca said while looking directly at Jenn. "Jenn, can you stay here for a minute or two? I had hoped to have some time to talk to you when everyone was gone."

Jenn felt as if she were the one now being held for detention at fairy finishing school but she maintained her best poker face.

"Certainly Ms. Fiona," she said quietly, while thinking how rotten it was of Bianca, who had already had three husbands, to try to make sure she couldn't have any time alone with Mark, even a few seconds in an elevator before she had to go back to her other work.

Jenn looked toward the door. "So Mark, you know the way downstairs, I'll call you as soon as I have those affiliate arrangements for you," she said in a way that she hoped said, hey, please call me, I would like to talk to you about more than affiliates and I am pretty sure I can be more charming than this reformed alcoholic psychic.

Mark gave her a faint smile and mouthed what Jenn thought was "be careful" and "I will call you" as he turned to leave. Bianca placed yet another big pillow on her bed's corner, and Jenn now knew that when Bianca put a pillow on the bed, it meant you had to sit down and listen, no matter how much work you thought you might have to do when you got back to your office.

She sat down on the pillow in proper charm school fashion while Bianca reached for a thick paperback book from her now completely crowded bedside table.

"Dear girl, I know you have a lot of work to do and I know, I do know, that this job is never an easy one for you, but I'd like to give you my latest book," Bianca said while lightly patting the jacket sleeve of Jenn's properly corporate pantsuit. "I like to think of it as the compilation of much of my life's work. I thought that if you could give it a read, you might understand me a lot better, maybe even understand yourself a little more, and things might just go very nicely for us from that point on, since we are likely to be together a fair amount over the next few weeks or so."

Jenn accepted the book as if it were a delicate flower (she had watched Yuki Atagari accept business cards that way and thought it was something she should emulate) and was startled to realize she had seen it displayed in the bestseller sections in the bookstores. The almost sleep-inducing blue hue and hypnotic patterns the publishers used on the cover jogged Jenn's memory. If Bianca Fiona really was a flake, well then she was a flake of some renown; her books were sold at the big superstores and read and bought by a hell of a lot of people.

Jenn was now glad she hadn't laughed out loud when she saw Bianca's room but then she remembered that Bianca had commented on Jenn's disapproval of the décor at their very first meeting. She was not yet ready to admit that Bianca might have some real extrasensory ability but she did figure that she had just better be ready for things to get even weirder. Bianca was definitely going to be one of those patients who would make life more than a little mental.

"Thank you for the book," Jenn said politely but probably a little more stiffly than required. "I think I've seen it in the bookstore before … I will read it right away."

"It's not a school assignment," Bianca said, looking approvingly at Jenn's decidedly less corporate black suede slingbacks. "I don't want to turn this into a session, or an amusing recitation of clichés you think you've heard people like me say before on infomercials, but I sense quite strongly that you spend a lot of time in this job trying to be the nice girl to everyone. And sometimes, sometimes, you try so hard that you end up pleasing no one, and none of it is your fault."

Jenn's first instinct was to think, right, look who's talking about performing for a living. But as much as she didn't want to admit it, she was really quite gratified that Bianca had said out loud (even if what she said wasn't all that much) what Jenn seldom said to anyone, except maybe to Caroline when they were going over the budget, and her father, when she occasionally complained to him about her job. They would just say, well that's what happens when you take this sort of job, you'll just have to learn how to live with it.

Part of her just wanted to take off her nice shoes, spread out on a few more pillows, and keep talking to Bianca about how it was so difficult to see jaundiced, gaunt, often impoverished people on an almost daily basis, or how much work and study it took to understand much of the scientific research that she was supposed to promote. She wanted to tell her how it was painful to be chastised by doctors for not being sensitive enough to the patients, or for being too involved with the patients, or to be screamed at for not knowing enough science or being thought of as wildly impertinent for thinking she did. Then there were the battles with Laurence and others as to whether she let too many reporters in or not enough, that she didn't do enough to control what they reported or that she was overstepping her jurisdiction by trying to overly influence their reports.

Jenn was sure she had a "please rescue me" look on her face that she hated to display, especially at work. She also knew that if she didn't get out of the room in the next five minutes she not only wasn't going to be able to call Channel 12 for Mark but that she'd be going beyond what she and the hospital considered proper patient-staff relations. And she certainly was not ready to become a patient's patient. Not today, and not with Bianca Fiona.

"Well, I'd better go, I have to take care of that affiliate business for Mark and Nadine," Jenn said wearily, finding it tough to get off of the pillow and back on her feet.

"That's fine, Jenn," Bianca said gently. "We will talk again at another time. But do me just one favor. Try to find just one nice thing to do for yourself today."

Jenn managed to stand up and nodded a weak assent to Bianca.

As she walked off the station at a pace slower than that of some knee replacement patients, she tried to think of something nice to say to herself, but all she could think of was how hungry she was. She wondered if a real lunch in a real restaurant (rather than something from the downstairs cafeteria) would count as a "nice thing."

Station 89 omnipresent Laurence turned away from his computer as Jenn strolled past his desk. He gave Jenn an almost paternal, quizzical look, as if to ask if everything was okay.

"Yes, Laurence, everything is fine," she said in a duller voice than she'd ever used with him. "Not too much has gone wrong yet today."

Chapter Four

Tony had already passed on the suggestion made by the incredibly hot waitress that he try the house-made Icelandic hot dog (made with lamb as it were and, Tony thought, probably some cute little puffin too). He looked down at the young scientist's almost untouched beer, drumming fingers and fast-blinking eyes and knew he was probably going to have to try a little harder to get the kid to relax. As esteemed as Tony Fionarello had become in the fairly small volcanologist community (the size of which made him think his alleged fame all too bizarre), he still saw himself as just another short Italian guy from San Francisco who liked to see things blow up and at one time also was very good with a slide rule. He actually disliked it when his celebrity got in the way of his work, especially since he knew all too well that a spewing volcano could sear the skin off of so-called rock star volcanologists just as fast as it could kill everyday people.

As much as he knew he needed to focus on the work he was here in Iceland to do without getting killed he had a difficult time not thinking about Bianca. Would she still be around by the time he got back to the U.S.? Would Yuki be able to do his part in pulling this caper off? He thought about whether he and Bianca would ever witness a full return of the closeness they experienced from the time they used to wander around as small children in their then quite middle class San Francisco neighborhood looking for soda bottles (not always to cash in for a deposit, but to use as containers for voluble substances for the experiments they liked to perform in their back yard for other kids) until Bianca's drinking got to the unacceptably, irretrievably nasty level at several points between several husbands. He remembered that he was the one more interested in making things erupt but that even as a child, Bianca already could discern when their explosions would get them in trouble with their parents and when they would only draw admiring remarks. Tony knew he wanted to be a volcanologist from the time he was around eight or nine. He now wondered just how old Bianca was when she realized she really did have psychic gifts. She always said she didn't really know until she was an adult. Tony wasn't so sure.

It was true that Bianca's illness had partially restored some of their old ease. Some. They went to the old hippie pizza place in Berkeley before she left for Minneapolis, although this time, they drank no beer, no wine, and the place no longer allowed smoking so there were no cigarettes either. He had been angry that she had not been willing to accept more responsibility for all of her many actions that led her to liver transplant candidacy but realized it was now fruitless to have those sorts of arguments anymore. And at first, he had not been at all in favor of the idea of involving Yuki in getting Bianca to Minnesota, but Bianca was able to convince him (in the utterly irresistible manner she often had used when they were younger, a manner her three husbands also had found irresistible, at least for a while) that Yuki was the only doctor they could enlist in their cause. As such, Tony agreed to have many late night telephone conversations with Yuki, some of them more than testy, to convince Yuki that Bianca needed to receive any possible transplant at the University of Minnesota. Did he do the right thing to make Yuki do as much? For some four decades, he and Yuki had been as close as brothers who actually got along most of the time. He would sooner jump into searing lava than jeopardize his friendship with Yuki. But then he knew the last thing he needed to do was to look distracted and worried. Calm. Patience. He was doing the right thing. He was doing the right thing.

"Come on now, Erik, we are going to be working like dogs over the next couple weeks, and you're going to be just worn out and pissed at me for pushing you so hard," he said in his best drinking buddy way to Dr. Erik Bjarnason, an esteemed member of the University of Iceland faculty and a rising star on the Young Volcano Turk circuit. "Try to take advantage of this fine drinking establishment," Tony said, trying to push down large swallows of beer while he was talking. "It's certainly swanker than most of the Irish pubs I've ever been in."

Erik broke a very small smile but he did not stop the finger drumming. Like his sister Bianca, Tony was a great reader of people's moods and demeanor, although he did so in a very different way. He knew he was going to have to say even more to Erik, which he really didn't want to have to do, because being sensitive and using the gift that he always denied having had always been hard for Tony, especially when he was drinking. Or preoccupied with other thoughts.

"Listen, I'd think you'd try to take advantage of the fact that you are in much better shape than me, and you're tall, also kind of dark, and a hell of a lot younger," Tony said while almost, but not quite, wishing he had a cigarette. "If the mountain blows particularly badly, you are more likely than me to be able to run away and become a hero to the local women."

Erik stopped drumming on the polished emerald green granite for a few seconds and laughed somewhat hesitantly at Dr. Fionarello's typically American humor. As it was, Erik had been born in the United States while his father was at school; his own undergraduate degree in geology was from the University of Washington. He did have to say that he included himself among the foreigners who would admit they admired the self-deprecating and often dark way many Americans dealt with awkward situations.

Still, this was no wasted dormitory roommate from Bend, Oregon sitting across from him with a beer in his hand. This was Tony Fionarello, subject of numerous television documentaries and scientific conferences and the world's most published volcanologist still actively working in the field. Even though he could see that Dr. Fionarello was trying to be informal, he thought it best that he not drop all professional guard just yet, at least not until he was certain that Tony had gotten more anesthetized from the Icelandic beer that was much stronger than any American brew Erik had ever tasted. As an Icelander, Erik almost always called people by their first names, but he also knew that beneath many "hey, I'm just an ordinary guy" proclamations of American modesty was the ego of an insecure academic determined to not have the world forget he had earned a real doctorate and held tenure at a major university.

"Yes, Dr. Fionarello, perhaps you are right. Perhaps I had better consider all of those local women who will be looking for a real Icelandic hero to idolize, plus all of the women around the world who might see me on television," he said while hoisting his pint and then putting it down again before he could take a sip. "But sir, you must realize that all of us here are quite honored that you have decided to come to Iceland to help us monitor Mount Hekla's latest temper tantrum."

Tony was trying to listen to Erik's earnest praise but he didn't catch all of it because he had been distracted by the entrance into the bar of an extremely attractive young woman who had to be at least six feet tall. Tony tried not to stare. She had large breasts covered just a little bit by a tight pink bandage (or maybe it was a sweater) and had hair so filamentous and shimmery blonde that Tony wasn't sure it was real.

He recovered quickly. "Erik, if you don't stop calling me Dr. Fionarello and just call me Tony, I am going to leave you with this whole bill, and I think I know what you make and I believe I can more easily afford 1,100 krónur per beer than you," he said with a wide, white smile that he knew the tall blonde would never notice. "Second, I'm glad all of you boys are honored, you know, when you get to be the old man you become a target for all sorts of honors, but it's about time I got here for one of your major blows. I'm still so mad I had to miss the whole big Vatnajökull spurt a while back, not to mention Eyjafjallajökull, the volcano every transatlantic air traveler loves to hate. Hell, that nasty bit of volcano cost me a trip to Portugal." Tony suddenly realized he was already on his way to getting drunk. "But it's true, I have waited a hell of a long time to see an eruption of the type that made those saga authors of yours write about so much madness and utter destruction."

"Well, we're still glad you made it here, sir," Erik said while now believing it safe to drink his beer but still thinking he should try to sound like a real scientist. "You know, it's really too bad you weren't here for Vatnajökull, because the glacial flood, you know, the *jökulhlaup*, was really and truly a nightmare. And, of course, it was not over right away, as we know we will experience flooding and other consequences in that area for more than a decade yet to come. Fortunately, the area is not inhabited and so any human suffering can be kept to a minimum."

Tony tried to focus on both Erik and the blonde who had arrived. "No, not like the human suffering we are likely to see in this bar tonight," Tony said while noticing the blonde was now standing at the bar holding a martini glass filled with a liquid the color of lake algae. She was wedged somewhat closely between two very blonde men, one short and one tall, although Tony wagered to himself that only the tall one might have a real chance to leave with her that night. Damn, he thought, this is the story no matter where you go in the world, you can have the intelligence of a maggot but if you are tall and very decent looking, and look as if you have any kind of money, you can build it and a whole lot of women will come.

"Ah yes, this is just one bar in a Reykjavik full of places of potential misery," Erik replied quietly. "But you know, all of this street fashion and high prices for ordinary beer and foreign men looking at, but not obtaining, tall, blonde Icelandic women are scenes of quite recent origin."

This caused Tony to rightly refocus on Erik. "Oh, I'm sorry," said

Tony, smiling wryly at his momentary attention deficit.

Erik continued: "My mother told me that in the early 1950s, my grandmother was still washing clothes in huge iron cauldrons set over open fires. Serving coffee and cake to visitors was then, and still is for older people, a very, very important part of being polite in Icelandic society. But sometimes my grandmother and her friends didn't have enough money to have a different kind of cake available to serve every time a visitor came over. Much less a really fancy cake. She and her neighbors just got used to serving and eating very thin slices of cake. No one said anything. It isn't our way. I ate fish just about every day as a child because most beef was very expensive, it had to be imported, and I'm about the only Icelander alive who doesn't like lamb, not even in a hot dog. So I don't know. I think that sometimes we as a nation have trouble reconciling our supposedly stylish present life with our simpler past."

This eloquent summary of Icelandic society made Tony take even more pause from his blonde reflections. This young man was not just a fine scientist but obviously a fairly careful thinker. Tony realized how hard he was going to have to work; clearly this was no innocent babe in the volcanic woods.

"It's interesting that you should talk about reconciling the past with the present," Tony said thoughtfully, his eyes now locking with Erik's and his mind momentarily empty of the pub's distractions. "Even though I've wanted to come to Iceland for as long as I have been studying volcanoes, which is some 40 years now, I wasn't sure I should come this time because my sister, my only sibling, is quite ill back at home. She's at the University of Minnesota waiting for an organ donor so she can have a liver transplant. I'm the big brother, and I've always had to look after Bianca, or at least I've always thought I've had to look after Bianca, and I wasn't sure I should be away just now. I'm still not completely sure I should be away."

Erik sensed that Tony probably wanted to talk seriously about his sister. He also was familiar enough with the curious American willingness to talk about intimate issues with almost anyone, even relatively new acquaintances, but he wasn't sure he was going to be able handle things in the way Tony might expect or want. Given this predicament, he decided it might be best to just sit and listen and let the famous Dr. Fionarello talk and hope that they could get down to discussing volcanoes and television crews before they ordered another beer.

"Well, perhaps your sister feels it is best that you are here to do your work, you know, you must trust your own sense of justice," he said in a way that he hoped conveyed his unease but still sounded respectful. "And you know, if something does happen, you can easily get to Minneapolis from here nonstop on Icelandair in not many hours."

Tony took a big quaff of beer and saw from the corner of his eye that the tall blonde and the tall nice jacket were indeed leaving the pub together. So soon, Tony thought, and after so little apparent expenditure of cash or charisma.

"Oh yeah, I know I can get back quickly enough if I must, and I should say that Bianca insisted that I come, she was adamant. She's a much better debater than I am," Tony said with some determination. "She told me my scientific mission was as important to her survival as her liver transplant and so, you know, I'm here, I'm here to do my work. I can only hope and pray that everything goes well for her and that I'll see her soon enough."

"Well then, you are doing what she wants," Erik said with a bit of relief when he figured he wasn't going to have to get into a deep and intense personal conversation with such an esteemed person. Not when there also was a lot of work yet to do back in his lab at the university. God knows what those hooligans masking as his graduate students were up to when they were left without supervision. There would be hell to pay if they made him look bad in front of the famous Tony Fionarello. "Besides, those television guys might drive us crazy enough if things don't blow according to their schedule and you may just want to leave sooner than you expected."

Tony smiled at Erik's insightful attempts at humor and thought that yes, he probably was doing the right thing by being in Iceland right now.

"I don't know whether you have any siblings, Erik, but when you do, and when you are as close as I am to my sister … I don't know … now I'm afraid I will sound like Bianca, who happens to be a pretty famous psychic in San Francisco," he said, already feeling some of the soothe of the Icelandic beer but fully aware that it might be best if he and Erik did start talking again soon about hot spots and TV requirements. "But the connection between siblings doesn't leave you. My life would be a lot emptier if Bianca were not in it. Do you know what I'm talking about? Do you have any siblings?"

"No, I'm an only child," Erik said softly. "I was adopted and my parents stopped with me. Actually, I was born in the United States myself. My parents adopted me while my father was in graduate school in Los Angeles. But I think I know what you mean, I have friends who are quite close to their brothers and sisters, and I see how they act together."

"Oh, so you didn't have to share any toys while you were growing up," Tony said while spotting another tall blonde enter the bar, this one not quite so beauteous but not too lacking in eye candy quotient either, despite the overuse of midnight blue eye shadow. "Well, having a sibling, or more than one sister or brother, can be a real pain in the ass or a real gift. Bianca has been both for me, believe me, I've been ready to throw her out the window at times. But you know," he said with some return of his normal professionalism and the grit that helped make him famous, "talking about her and her psychic musings probably won't help us with our measurements, so maybe we had better get to work and plan a good show for those television boys so we can keep getting funding for our work. So, what do you say, do you need another beer as much as I do?"

"Sounds good," Erik said happily, as he really was pretty thirsty by this time and thinking that having another beer would buy social capital with Dr. Fionarello, who plainly appeared to be displaying some effects from the hops. "But maybe you should call your sister while you are here and put your mind at ease before we get down to work. You know, we in Iceland live quite closely with our elves and spirits. I wouldn't discount her work altogether. Maybe some of it could be useful."

"Okay, sure," Tony said while finishing his beer with audible satisfaction. "But you know, she has never once been able to give me a precise hour and minute reading on when a volcano is going to blow, just that it might definitely blow. I think she's a lot better at telling people they are going to get divorced soon or that they will not become millionaires in the next year."

"Yes, well, maybe once she has a new liver her psychic sense will be improved and our work will be much easier," Erik said lightly. "I'll admit it, and I hope you won't hold it against me, but I am one scientist who is always looking for different ways to find answers."

"Looking for answers is a good idea, a very good idea," Tony said in an almost whisper. "And we do indeed have a lot of answers to find. I personally want to know how that blonde over there with dark blue eye shadow all over her face thought she might look pretty coming out like that tonight."

Erik did not want to tell Dr. Fionarello that he knew the blonde, although perhaps due to the beer he could not remember her name. No one could ever affix the geek-scientist-who-did-not know-his-way-around-the-world-of-women label on Erik Bjarnason. Not ever. And if he were lucky, soon a whole lot of women around the world who might like watching television shows about volcanoes blowing up would realize the full extent of his charm and smarts. That would be good. Although Erik had truly been busy pursuing his career and the success it brought, he did like pursuing and obtaining beautiful women just about as much. He knew he wanted a wife and maybe two kids. Some day. But that day had not yet arrived. Focusing back on his career aspirations, he knew it also would be good if some university geology department chairs in the U.S. or Canada saw the show as well.

"I have no idea either how she thought she'd look fetching while painted in such a way," Erik said while trying to muffle a laugh that would have been considered quite overdone for an Icelander if it had been released in any place besides a bar. "When we are finished with this next beer, I hope we can go over to my lab. I'd like you to meet my graduate students who'll be working with us and just familiarize you with a lot more than I can show you here."

Tony just nodded his assent. "Erik, I think even Blue Eyeshadow Face has gotten lucky tonight," he said as he lifted his beer and looked about the bar. If one of these women would talk to him, maybe he and Erik could skip the lab duty for tonight. Maybe.

Chapter Five

Olaf tried to keep a relaxed hold on the computer's mouse as he moved it around to show Marco the design for the main auditorium of a Jesuit university headed by a president who wanted as much beauty and grandeur as his foundation funds would allow.

"That's really, really quite impressive," Marco said, while intently peering at the screen so he could follow Olaf's many moves and still listen to his careful explanations for this and that and whatever. Even though Marco's peak as an architect had come at a time well before three-year-olds could use computers, he was hugely proud that his former student could create such wonderful things within these small electronic boxes.

"Thanks, Marco," Olaf said a little hesitantly. "I wasn't sure about some of these changes in space allowances. Of course, this whole project is quite a bit of a departure for me, you know, this is a big city Jesuit university we are dealing with here and not just another Lutheran concrete-and-glass pillar in the middle of a corn field. But I'm working on the assumption that the Jesuits need plenty of room to orate their brilliance."

Marco laughed loudly at what he knew was just a small sample of the humor his protégé and good friend seldom unleashed. To those who knew him only slightly, and there were many such people in that camp, Olaf Bergquist came off as a very talented but very tightly wound man who disliked even the slightest hint of disorder or unnec-

essary augmentation. He certainly knew that Jenn, Olaf's somewhat more outgoing only child, thought as much. To Marco Leonardo, as his former teacher and former boss, Olaf was someone who not only had the ability to design wonderful buildings that might appear sacrilegious to many Lutherans as well as Catholics, but also harbored the desire to do so.

"Well, Olaf, you know, the Jesuits haven't been in trouble with popes throughout the centuries because they are so fond of hairshirts and moldy bread," he said while still laughing. "I think you are doing the right thing with this building; those boys certainly like to think they are worldly and sophisticated. And I've even met a few who are. I do very much like the way you are blending some … shall I say, more savage elements with your customary Nordic restraint. I think my people back in Milan might even applaud what you are doing this time around."

Olaf smiled at the latest in the string of gentle jibes Marco used to remind Olaf that even though he was now 60 years of age, Marco Leonardo was still very much his teacher, and a teacher without peer when it came to defining elegance. And he was all too happy to let Marco revel in the role. Olaf's father had been dead for decades and Marco was the proverbial father figure for him, as is so often the case with mentors and their protégés. Although, as is also true in many such situations, Marco was nothing at all like Olaf's father and definitely not much like Olaf himself. For years, Marco had encouraged Olaf to support Italian carmakers and buy a Ferrari or an Alfa Romeo, or take every opportunity possible to turn his discerning eyes to any and all beautiful women they might encounter in public places.

Olaf sometimes wondered why Marco hadn't returned to Italy once the austerity and poverty left by World War II had been replaced by real prosperity and massive sex appeal. He had asked Marco once, when he was still a graduate student, and received one of the stoniest and most incomplete responses possible, even by Olaf's own reserved standards. He knew better than to ask again. He knew Marco's father, a wealthy corporate titan, had suffered greatly at the hands of Mussolini's Fascists. Marco's graduate education in architecture had been abruptly halted by the war and he had been forced to serve in Mussolini's army. Olaf knew that Italy was Marco's real and spiritual home, and that it was a home he could never live in again without feeling crowded by ghosts.

"Well, Master Teacher, I am glad to do what I can to impress the Milanese," Olaf said. "God knows they still run your world."

Olaf was now gripping the mouse with as much strength as he might need to lift 300 pounds. He looked just slightly flushed. Marco knew Olaf well enough to know that something must be wrong. It just couldn't be the work, as Olaf had been as excited as Marco had ever seen him when the firm won the commission to design a new student commons for the big Jesuit university.

"My friend, if you grip that mouse any tighter, you will indeed make it blind," Marco said quietly. "Is anything wrong?"

Olaf kept his grip on the mouse but slowly turned away from the screen and looked directly into Marco's eyes. He wasn't sure what to say to his trusted mentor.

"Jenn and I had a most interesting dinner last week," he said guardedly while starting to flush just a little brighter in the face. "We should have invited you over. She made pasta with a great deal of garlic and we drank a lot of wine, believe it or not. Anyway, we had a short conversation about a patient who's at the hospital."

"I see," Marco said, now more than a little perplexed by Olaf's reddening face as well as the fact that Olaf admitted to drinking a lot of wine. "There's no chance that the patient is that little ferret from Chicago who tried to steal our commission on that children's hospital, what was it, 20 years ago? Because I always thought that such an unsavory person would become physically ill soon enough."

"No, no ferrets," Olaf said while grinning just a bit. "No ferrets. Just one Bianca Fiona, who you may remember as Bianca Fionarello."

Marco's customary grin drained quickly from his face. He sat straight back in his Danish Modern chair and put his hand on top of Olaf's now slightly sweating hand. He knew Olaf had done more than his stoic Nordic best to put California behind, far, far behind, locked in the recesses of time and youth and bad decisions often made in the course of unknowing youth. God knows it had not been easy for Marco to deal with what happened there either. His late wife never really understood the reasons for such secrecy either but she too kept her silence through the years.

"What, how can that be … I don't understand," he said in a suddenly hushed and very aged tone, a voice that sounded more like the kind one would expect of a 92-year-old. "Tell me what happened."

Olaf slowly pulled his hand out from under Marco's.

"Well, there was a television crew in from San Francisco. The photographer, by the way, is supposedly very cute and well dressed. Jenn ended up going out with him. We can only hope this one is not a roving cavalier."

Marco started to laugh, but Olaf was obviously not trying to be funny, so he stopped. Olaf was often hard to read, even after so many years.

"Anyway, they were here to interview Bianca," Olaf said. "Apparently, she's become a quite famous psychic. And she's in for a liver transplant; Yuki Atagari accepted her on the list. Because she also became an alcoholic over the years, although she's now dry, you know, you can't get on the liver list if you are still drinking, but Jenn said she's everything you'd expect in a psychic, makeup that looks as if it had been applied with an industrial air compressor, very bejeweled, the falsetto voice, all of it."

Marco went over to the nearby teak cabinet where Olaf maintained a neatly arranged supply of Canadian whisky, already decanted into crystal flasks and available for Marco when he made his frequent visits. It was softer than single malt Scotch for him to down now that he was a bit older and had a sensitive stomach. And no one would say it was a tragedy to mix many Canadian whiskies with ginger ale.

"Olaf, I think today is a day for you to have some of this with me," he said as he far too swiftly collected glasses and went over to the freezer built into the wall (so as to be as unobtrusive as possible) for ice. "Maybe we should drink a shot or two and while I'm preparing our fortifications, I want to hear the whole story."

"Kind of interesting to talk about drinking while we are discussing an alcoholic, but I can't say that a drink wouldn't go down well right now," Olaf said quietly, his face starting to resume a little more of its normal paleness. "Maybe it will help me think of some way to deal with this situation so things don't get out of hand."

Marco almost dropped the ice-filled glasses. "What do you mean?" Marco asked almost angrily as he carefully filled the glasses with more whisky than Olaf would have normally thought proper at two in the afternoon. "There is no way. I know you don't want to hear this, but obviously, it's beyond the time to finally face the truth. It's been so many years. My God, I think the statute of limitations on heinous war crimes is shorter. There's really no grievous, irreparable harm to be done to anyone. And aren't you tired of carrying this burden, which didn't have to become such a burden at all, all by yourself?"

Olaf winced as he drank some of the whisky, wishing he had even more ginger ale to mix with it, while he looked directly at Marco's beseeching eyes.

"Really, Olaf, my boy, you can be sure that Jenn is in all probability going to hear it all and quite soon enough," Marco said in a slightly quavering voice. "Bianca almost certainly will tell her if she is still the same impulsive person she was back then. I really don't think you want her to learn about things this way. Because she will tell her, you can be sure of that much. Sick and dying people love to spill their guts if they are able, and please pardon my choice of words given her illness, but I know you know what I mean."

Olaf steadied himself with a sip. All the years of secrecy started to well up in his throat. He looked at the sleek row of bookcases that held his life as he knew it, how he defined it, and how he had lived it. None of the art on the walls hinted at anything but a life lived in, and for, order and a love of Nordic landscapes and sternly lovely buildings. "I don't know what to think anymore," Olaf whispered. He then finished the whisky in steady gulps, his white-knuckle grip transferred in whole from the mouse to the glass. "This happened so many years ago and you know what I promised Christina before she died. I told you what I told her before she had that last operation, I promised her I would never let Jenn know. I'm just so angry … so … that this has surfaced after all this time."

Marco looked hard at his shaken but still resolute former student. Olaf was such a fine man, protégé, artist, scholar and friend. He truly admired Olaf's resolve to always do the right and honorable thing, even the rigid sense of honor that was displayed when Olaf faced the most difficult of life's situations, such as when Christina died and Olaf said it would not do for he and Jenn to mourn too openly, or to suggest in any way that he and Christina did not have a most acceptable marriage. But he knew Olaf was wrong this time and Marco felt a compulsion to make him see another sort of reason.

"Olaf, I know you made your promises to Christina," he said. "But we all know there are times and situations when promises should be broken, maybe especially when the promises should not have been made in the first place. I'm an old man now, believe me, and I know a little bit more than I'd like about promises and life's letdowns. And I know you don't believe for one minute that Bianca Fionarello, Bianca Fiona, whatever her name is now, won't tell Jenn. You know she will and then you will have to decide whether keeping a promise to your quite dead wife is more important than retaining the love and trust of your still very much alive daughter." Marco, who was beginning to feel as if he was at the classroom helm with an important diatribe, was glad he could get the words out as fluently as he did. While remaining quiet for a couple of seconds from the lecture high, Marco suddenly felt he needed more whisky to keep at bay the tears that seemed to come about much more frequently now that he was in his 90s. That would have never happened in the classroom.

"Oh, I don't know. Maybe you're right. I'm not sure, but maybe you are right," Olaf said while looking at the ceiling so as to not notice Marco's wet eyes. "But I do not know where to start, where to begin to tell Jenn everything. It's been so many years... Damn."

"Olaf, listen to me," Marco said. He grabbed both of Olaf's hands and forced him to look him directly in his still teary eyes. "Bianca did not come to Minnesota for the weather. You and I both know she came here with a purpose in mind. I am certain she knew exactly what she was doing when she made her plans. They do have transplant surgeons in California, after all. So, my friend, we can make this into an awful situation or we can treat it just like in the movies. You have a glass of wine to loosen up, and then you start at the beginning and you tell it all until you are finished. Jenn either hugs you or she runs off with this television photographer who may or may not be gay. Maybe that Caroline could help you, you've adored the woman for years now. You know it would make me ready to die quite happy to see you in the arms of such a sensuous woman with such good taste in furniture and shoes."

"You always have the jokes and the lectures, don't you, old man," Olaf said testily as he pulled away. "Let's leave Caroline out of this, okay? God knows what Jenn would think of me if I went after her on top of all of this mess. You know, you don't have to tell my daughter, I do, and I don't have your gift for stories, I can't make this into a made-for-television saga where everyone skips off into the sunshine at the end."

Marco turned from the window. "No, you don't have my talent for making beautiful tales, that much is true," Marco said in more of his customary lighthearted voice. "But this may be a time when the plain old, colorless Olaf Bergquist truth might just work. I might wish otherwise, but my boy, I don't think you have any other choice this time. Sometimes you just don't have much control, whether it be of your bladder, once you reach my age, or your past."

"You know what you are saying, don't you? You...you... realize what could happen if I tell Jenn the whole story?" Olaf said while staring at the floor and wondering if it needed a new coat of finish or just a mopping with wood soap. He was thankful for such mindless distractions. "This could change a whole lot of things, to put it mildly."

"Yes, yes it could change a lot of things," Marco said firmly. "And as I said to you before, sometimes you just don't have control all the time. Sometimes things have to change. I know you don't like change but I just don't think you are going to have a choice this time. So if you insist on having a plan, I would suggest you get to work on it. And soon. And you know I'll be here to help you do it, as long as you continue to supply me with Canadian whisky when I visit."

Olaf barely nodded his head. He decided that a thorough mopping with wood soap would be just fine for the floor.

Chapter Six

For reasons she could not reasonably attribute to any sort of logic, Jenn read, during the course of only one night, the entire book Bianca had given her. It was called *Living That Love You Make*. Jenn still couldn't believe she had been so entranced by the thing that she kept whipping through it, all 530 pages, including the index and the glossary, even though it was way past two in the morning. As much as she hated to admit it, she had been almost hypnotized by a book with a very weird blue cover that had been written by a whacko who used to drink too much.

Now she was at work, barely, and feeling like pure hell and looking little better despite her best efforts with the new light-radiating concealer she had been talked into buying. She was gulping down a second can of diet soda, reminding herself that she was trying to cut back on how much soda she drank.

It was good that no patients were dying this morning and no nurses or doctors were yelling at her because she just wanted to lie back on Caroline's fake mink beanbag chair with cold soda cans on her eyes and talk about the book. And fortunately for Jenn, Caroline was not slaving away either, barely glancing over some numbers but more concerned about the dark roots showing in her champagne blonde hair and wondering whether she needed to get them done tomorrow or if she could risk another week of roots. Thank God their boss seldom checked to see what they might, or might not, be doing.

"So, you read this book all night long and now you're here, sprawled out like I don't know what on my nice, new beanbag, God, watch those legs in case Dr. Lindahl comes in, you know he would like nothing better than to screw you while you are wearing black tights," Caroline said while putting her makeup mirror up to her scalp.

She next turned the mirror to inspect the lines on her face. "And now you think that maybe, just maybe it's possible you have lived before? Listen to me, and listen to me good! You have just got to start getting some, from someone mildly decent, I'm not talking about any master of the universe but someone who does not work here, someone with no Norwegian blood in his system. I don't know what the hell is going on when you, the alleged princess of reality, starts believing in stuff you used to call crap. Because I don't have the energy to be worried about you, I have trouble enough trying to make these numbers add up and keep my hair reasonably blonde without going broke."

Jenn shifted in the bean bag and turned to Caroline. "Hey, give me a break, I did almost get some with that photographer from San Francisco, that Mark guy."

Caroline started to mark up her numbers sheet with thick red lines. "Even if you did it with him, your reputation would be just fine," Caroline said blankly. "I don't know, he was kind of cute, not my type, of course, but he probably would be okay for you."

"No big deal, I doubt I'll ever see him again," Jenn said rather listlessly. "I've got his number in Iceland, because he got that job doing the volcano documentary. But I don't know if I want to spend my international minutes just to ask him if his girlfriend is still angry with him for being gone. Do you know what I am saying? He seems kind of neurotic to me, not fashionably neurotic like you and I, but the other type that is less desirable."

Caroline made some furious marks on the spreadsheet. "I didn't know we were fashionably neurotic," she said softly while staring at the paper. "Although, you know, you come to think of it, I suppose we should be as nuts as your friend Ms. Fiona after working here for as long as we have."

Jenn moved the soda onto her neck, which seemed to ache more than her head. "First, she is not my friend, she is a patient who I am starting to find a little bit interesting, and this doesn't happen often with patients because, as you know, most of them are too sick to be interesting to anyone beyond their family, and it doesn't mean that I still don't think she's on the barely functioning side of lunacy," Jenn said. "Second, all I am saying is that maybe some of this stuff she's talking about in the book is worth a look, an observation, some consideration. That's all I'm saying. When have I ever said I don't believe in any of this stuff? I mean, I let you do my astrological chart last year."

Caroline put her folder aside. "I'm just wondering where this sudden burst of tolerance for new philosophies came from," she said while looking Jenn directly in the eye. "I'm glad to see it, don't get me wrong, but I'm just wondering what brought it on."

Jenn looked at the refrigerator and wondered if there were any more cold diet sodas. "I don't know either," Jenn said. "All I know is that I looked pretty nice, no, I have to say I looked really great, I wore those really low-rise indigo jeans my father hates, just to go for sushi once again with some too-handsome guy who lives thousands of miles away who is allegedly involved with another woman. I came home and I was like, oh, I keep telling myself I'm so intelligent, so why do I keep doing stupid things, you know? If gay people have 'gay-dar,' well, why can't I have a similar early warning system about guys who are, what, I don't know, in transition?"

Caroline pulled one of her other velvet chairs over to use as an ottoman and put up her feet. "In transition is a kind way to put it, although I'd just say screwed up, because to say they are afraid of a commitment with anyone is way too nice and just too therapy-talk," she said. "But this does not explain why you come home, your tight jeans are still securely affixed to your body, and you decide to spend the next night reading some big mystical book."

Jenn yawned so hard the cans fell to the floor. "I don't know either, I really don't. I got home, I washed my face, I realized I don't like octopus all that much, I saw the book sitting there on my nightstand and I thought I might as well see what sort of stuff she could write that would sell so many copies and make her so famous," Jenn said. "But I had bad stomach cramps from that sushi so I said I'd read the book later, later happened to be last night, and I started reading it. Don't tell me you haven't ever been a little curious about something. I don't think there's any spiritual idea or herbal medication you haven't tried at least once, even that stuff you are only supposed to take to induce labor and not to quell hot flashes."

"I have, but I'm just surprised as hell to see you have the same sort of curiosities, although I think it's a good thing," Caroline said while polishing the tips of her five-inch red patent leather pumps with some paper towels. "It's about time you opened your mind up to some other things. I meant to ask you, were you wearing those jeans you bought downtown with me a couple weeks ago? Maybe your dad doesn't like them on you …but I think he'd really, really like them on me."

"You think yourself such a comedienne," Jenn said, sitting up as straight as one could on a fake mink beanbag while fighting a headache. "You keep thinking that my father has a thing for you. I'm telling you, I am not saying he doesn't think you are pretty, for your age, which is very close to his I might add. But I know Olaf, and if you think he's going to take you out and then bring you home to bed you on his crisply ironed and starched Egyptian cotton sheets, you'd be better off staying home and ordering a pizza."

Caroline laughed and struck a stiff middle finger at Jenn as she took her feet off her ottoman-chair and swiveled around to pick up her phone.

"Get out of here now, your line is ringing too," she said. "Maybe it's your dad, maybe he's receiving the vibes of this conversation and wants to tell you to stop picking on me after I let you sweat out your psychic hangover in my presence."

Jenn got up to get her phone. "This just goes to show how little you know my father, okay," Jenn said, adjusting her skirt to a decent level. "My father would not call me at work unless someone died. Anyway, he's going out to New York again this week on that university project he's got, he doesn't have time to bug me."

Jenn got to her office in time to see that the call had gone to her voice mail. She sat down and waited another minute or so to let the person finish the message. She was praying it wasn't anything requiring her instant attention; she was still too tired to deal gracefully with upset people.

When she finally picked up the phone and started listening to the message, she recognized Bianca Fiona's voice, although it was not the purr to which she was becoming somewhat accustomed. It was a raspier, completely exhausted stammer that was as quiet as a baby's yawn.

"Jenn, I hope you aren't real busy, but I was wondering if you could come over here this morning, the sooner the better," she said. "I'm not feeling very well today and I need to talk to you."

She hung up the phone and swung her head down between her legs as she tried to massage her temples and forehead in the hope that doing so would make her feel a little better. She had sworn how many times, in front of Caroline, their boss, her father, that she was going to stop getting personally involved with patients, that she just couldn't take it any longer, and now she had not only gotten to know this patient enough to recognize variations in her voice but had foregone sleep in order to read her book. She felt terrible.

She sat up, pulled her brush and compact out of her handbag and started to fix her hair and see how much the cans had smudged her makeup. She knew that she had to go and see Ms. Fiona. She put some of the new lipstick on, the shade was not too girlie-frost-pink and she hoped it contained good moisturizers so she wouldn't have flaky lips on top of concealed dark circles.

Jenn stuck her head in Caroline's office on her way out, only to see that she was talking on the phone with her hairdresser about a new shade of blonde.

It wasn't too cold outside, but Jenn was in no shape for running even if it had been cold. She walked fairly slowly over to the hospital, waved to the volunteer at the desk, staying far enough away so any floral scents wouldn't give her multiple chemical sensitivity, and got an elevator right away to station 89. No one was in it and Jenn thanked God for granting her a few more moments of quiet.

There were almost no people around the station desk when she got there, no Laurence, no Laurence yeomen, and so she thought that all she had to do was make it over to the hand sanitizer dispenser without being detected and she could probably handle the rest without difficulty.

She knocked softly on Bianca's door, heard no answer, rapped a little harder this time, still no answer, so she opened the door just a sliver and saw that no lights were on and all the blinds were drawn. Maybe she's sleeping, she thought, maybe I should have called first, but then if she were sleeping and the phone rang, well, that would be way worse than waking her up this way.

She saw that Bianca probably was sleeping, as she was on her back with her eyes shut and her hands folded on her chest, IV lines protruding from arms that looked very much like lacquered chopsticks in the making. Oh no, she thought for a second, what if she's dead, but then she guessed that Bianca might not have been physically or mentally able to arrange her hands in the death pose if she really were planning on dying within the next few minutes.

"Ms. Fiona," she called as softly as she could while still making some sound as she stepped lightly into the room. "It's Jenn Bergquist, you called and asked me to come up and see you."

It was hard for her to completely tell in the dark but she thought Bianca's eyes were fluttering and that her hands were unfolding. She was worried that maybe Bianca was going to want to tell her something intensely, insanely personal, maybe that one of her three husbands was an investment banker with Communist sympathies, something like that, as she just didn't know enough about this woman's thought process to know why she wanted to see her on such short notice when she was so sick. She couldn't believe that she would have wanted just to see whether or not Jenn liked her book.

Bianca pushed her hands to her mattress and used all the strength they could produce to pull up into a sitting position. She noisily strained to turn on the tiny table lamp which produced just enough light so Jenn could see that her hair had not been washed for days; it had been in a bad bun and the elastic band marks were still clearly visible.

Jenn stepped closer to the bed and suddenly felt the deep muscle chill she was sure she often felt when a patient was not long for this world. She never told anyone about this chill, not even Caroline, because she thought no one would believe her, they'd think she was just really scared or that the patient's room was unusually cold or that she'd seen too many previews for teenage slasher films. But she was certain that she had felt this chill before and had attributed it more to a combination of truly icy rooms and of being sickened by the patient's deteriorated condition than to any sense of precognition. But she definitely was feeling the ice now, and it was worse than the other kind of cold she'd experienced as this one ran an unusually prickly course from her toes all the way to her forehead.

"I'm sorry I dozed off after I called you," Bianca said in the same whisper Jenn heard on her voice mail. "I should have known that you'd get up here fast."

"Yes, I do move pretty fast, Dr. Atagari can tell you that much for certain," Jenn said in the voice she worked hard to keep calm whenever she felt a cold dread. "You said you weren't feeling well so I thought I'd better get a move on."

"Yes, the last few days have been kind of tough," Bianca said as she looked hard at Jenn with eyes that were absent of any makeup. In fact, there were no cosmetics of any kind to be seen anywhere on her now moderately sallow face, and not one ounce of jewelry to be heard.

"I had a little giggle when I saw the report Nadine prepared on me, although I have to say that the photographer, what was his name, um, Mark, well Mark made me look pretty human," Bianca said with a touch more of her usual verve. "Now you went out with him, didn't you? You need to tell me how things went."

Jenn noticed there were no pillows nearby to sit on and thought it best anyway that she sit on a chair today. So she pulled the room's only chair up to the foot of the bed and as it was, it was a badly broken chair that squeaked like a cricket whenever she made the slightest move. "Gee, now I would think that since you thought our auras were in such nice harmony, you'd already know how our evening went," she said in an attempt at humor that she hoped Bianca would understand.

Bianca did smile broadly, a smile that made her seem less ethereal and more like any other seriously ill person. Jenn couldn't say that she didn't welcome the humbling effect; she was hoping that she wasn't going to have to joust with Bianca this morning.

"Oh, yes, but just because your auras connected well, which they do, doesn't mean that I thought you two would immediately fall in love," Bianca said as she further straightened herself against only one pillow. "As you know, the best relationships take time to take shape, lots of it. I learned that one only after many, many screwups, but you know all that already."

Jenn tried to sit still in the chair so it would stop squeaking. "Well, that's probably true about the time factor," Jenn said. "As a matter of fact, and stop me if you already know this, but Mark has a girlfriend back in San Francisco, at least he said he had a girlfriend, and although it doesn't sound like a fun relationship, he still claims to have somebody."

Bianca laughed a bit and Jenn was glad that she was able to parry to this woman's satisfaction.

"Ah yes, girlfriends, relationships, fights, so many of us have so many monstrous happenings to endure in our present moments," Bianca said as she tried to pour herself a glass of water. Jenn saw that she didn't seem able to reach the pitcher so she made a really big squeak and got up and poured her some. "Your correspondence with Mark is not over, because I think you are going to find that he's going to help you find some of your future. Don't close the lines of communication with him. I think you are going to see that he's meant to become a very great friend of yours. And you know, not all girlfriends are forever because they are not right. Believe me, not even all wives or husbands are forever, which is as it should be given the state of some marriages."

Jenn laughed just a little bit at this last comment. As much as she hated to admit it, she was not having a bad time talking with Bianca, but she also saw that Bianca was not doing well at all and that she probably should, as always, just do her job and find out what she wanted before the woman talked herself into a state of dangerous exhaustion.

"So, what did you want to talk to me about, besides the fact that I shouldn't toss Mark overboard just yet?" she asked quietly. "Is there something you need for me to do for you, do you want me to keep Nadine from calling, anything like that?"

Bianca sipped her water cautiously, as if she thought she'd drop the glass at any moment, while fixing her large eyes right at Jenn. "Don't worry about Nadine—she's not a problem," Bianca said, carefully putting the glass back on the table. "I need to talk to you about something else, something not really related to my illness but it's something I need to do all the same while I can still do it, because I don't know when I'm going to be able to have this transplant, maybe I won't even be able to have it, and I need to get this done."

Jenn paused so as to not let the sound of worry creep into her voice. "Well, just tell me, you know, I can probably take care of things. Just don't ask for anything too outlandish, you know, I can't have the hospital cancel your bill or anything," Jenn said lightly. She was starting to realize that the more worried or agitated she sounded, the more mental power she might be handing over to Bianca.

"Oh no, no, don't worry about my bill. I'm surely not worried about my bill," Bianca said as she gently laid back into her pillow. "Jenn, I just wanted to ask you if you would ever consider doing some other type of work, maybe just for a little while. It would still be in the science world, but it's not here in Minnesota. You must have wanted to do something else at least once in this life?"

What in the hell is up with this woman, Jenn thought. Why is my career happiness or unhappiness so important that she feels she has to keep probing me on her probable deathbed?

"Well, yes, of course I'd like to do something else someday," Jenn said in an abrupt, almost discourteous fashion, although she thought at the same time that maybe she was being a little paranoid. What major trouble could this sickly woman who happened to be a friend of the hospital's chief of surgery really cause from her bed?

"I worked for a public relations agency in Los Angeles for a little while after I was done with school out there because I thought public relations would pay a lot more than starting out as a city hall reporter for a small daily newspaper, which it did, and then I worked for a chemical trade group for a longer time," she said in a voice that probably was just a bit too hesitant, even if it was more courteous. "Then I came back here when my father told me this job was open as I did miss home a bit, the cost of living in Los Angeles as well as not being blonde was really getting to me, and I had started to think when I was working with chemists that working in medicine might be a lot more fulfilling and interesting. And now I've been here for seven years, so yes, I might be interested in doing something else. When I really think of it, I know I don't want to spend the rest of my life dealing with serious illness. It would be different if I were a doctor or a nurse." Jenn paused for a few seconds, thinking it strange that she had been allowed to speak for so long without interruption or having had a hand or gold pen flicked her way. "It depends on what sort of job, I guess. Are you're looking for someone to publicize your next book? Although I'm not sure everyone would call what you do science."

"No, no, although that's not a bad idea," Bianca said while laughing a genuine laugh, not the sexpot giggle Jenn found so grinding. "If you can make Yuki Atagari love you and then forcibly tame someone like Nadine and still get a decent story out of the deal, one can only imagine what you could do with one of my books. But no. What I did want to talk to you about was whether you'd be interested in doing some work for my brother, Tony, the volcanologist your friend Mark is now helping make even more famous than he was before."

Jenn tried to contain a mixed sense of great astonishment and utter excitement that she felt at hearing about such a preposterous and unlikely prospect. "What do you mean, work with your brother?" Jenn asked as carefully as she could manage. "What could I do for your brother? I mean, I believe he's affiliated with a university, they must have their own public affairs people who can work with him … why would he need someone like me around? I barely know medicine, much less mountains and lava. And you barely know me."

Bianca suddenly looked almost as pale as she did on the day she and Jenn first met. "Well yes, I guess some people would say I barely know you and yes, Tony does work with people at his university, that's true, but he told me the other day that this deal in Iceland is turning out to be more of a media headache than he would like, and Tony hates headaches of all sorts, including those brought on by women he can't have," she said a little smugly. "Sooo, Tony and I and even Yuki decided to get all intelligent and we thought about you, because this project Tony's doing is mostly independent of his university. Besides, Mark told Tony all about me, and he lied splendidly about my condition just as I had told him to do. He also told him about the marvelous public relations woman who was taking care of his sister. Now don't tell me you wouldn't love to get out of here and go off to Iceland and see some volcanoes spit up while you carry Mark's duct tape?"

Jenn chose her words carefully, trying to contain her excitement.

"Yes, you're right, Ms. Fiona. I guess I don't spend much time think-ing I am marvelous, but yes, I would love to go to Iceland and work with your brother. Of course, I don't think I'm nuts," she said firmly. "If Dr. Atagari is in on this deal, then I am guessing it won't be a problem for me to get a leave of absence from this job. So, if you are not having me on, tell me what I have to do … do I have to talk to your brother or what, send him my résumé, anything like that?"

Bianca slumped in her bed as if she were suddenly exhausted after a long battle finally won. "I'm glad you are being smart and not letting your really quite entrenched cynicism get in the way of what might be a very exciting opportunity for you," Bianca said. "Because you'd be a really stupid girl and not a marvelous one if you turned this chance down. I'll have Tony call you right away. He's what … six hours ahead, so I'll try to reach him and maybe you can finally do some work that doesn't cause you to be upset and nervous so much of the time, and that will make you feel exhilaration for at least once in your life," Bianca said with a dramatic uptick in her voice. "My God, you are 36 years old and it sounds as if you have done little else but try to make a bunch of bastards happy and worry about how fat you are at any one moment."

Jenn was smarting at the idea that Bianca thought she was both boring and maybe a little stupid. "Thank you. It's kind of you to do this for me. I have no idea why but I guess it is useless to ask someone like you about the wiles of fate I wouldn't understand," Jenn said with just a touch of welcome resignation. "So tell me," she said as sardoni-cally as she could get away with and not be considered stupid, "is your brother as interesting as you seem to be?"

"Oh yes, Tony's very, very interesting," Bianca said in full cat purr. "He's probably more like the people you are used to working with than you might think. He's a real scientist, although he doesn't really full out yell all that much and he has never passed up any chance to have some fun, although he never did any serious drugs or anything like that. A little pot, of course, but no creative person would ever call marijuana a serious drug. Besides, you just never know what may come of this job, you could end up finding out all sorts of things about the world, your life, your destiny, you don't know. No one knows a damn thing until he or she gets out of his or her little miserable cave and does some real exploring."

"Whatever you say, it sounds great," Jenn laughed. Her mind was whirling with all she'd have to do before going off to Iceland for a few weeks, if this turned out to be a real thing and not just something Bianca had dreamed up in some psychic storm. But she could not help feeling about as excited as she had ever felt in her life, and that was saying a very great deal. "Still, don't you want to give me some predictions before I go, wouldn't that make you feel a little better, maybe you could tell me when some of the volcanoes are going to erupt so I can stay out of the way?"

Bianca smiled a wan smile. "I've predicted all I will about you and I try to leave the volcanoes to my brother. You just talk to Tony and listen to what he has to say. Give him some of the benefit of the doubt. I know, it might kill you, but try it, and even someone like you might be quite surprised."

Jenn nodded her consent and made an enormous squeak on the chair as she got up to leave.

Bianca looked as if a nerve had been pinched in her neck. "And please get rid of that damn chair now. Christ, for what I am paying for this room you'd think that Nurse Laurence could get some decent furniture," she nearly screamed. Jenn suddenly bolted up back, grabbed the chair and rushed to the door, clumsily dragging it behind her with one hand, while Bianca shouted, "I DO NOT want any more squeaks around me right now!"

Chapter Seven

Tony was glad he had gone a little crazy shopping and let the young, leggy salesgirl talk him into a better and (what he considered) massively expensive 66 Degrees North made-in-Iceland parka and another pair of really good super-Polarized sunglasses. The combination of mental and physical fatigue, biting cold, and sunlight that seemed more blistering white than any he was sure he'd ever encountered was proving to be more than miserable. Especially as he was trying to sit still in the helicopter as it whirled around the volcano's vicinity like an owl on speed.

Erik didn't seem to be having any problems with the situation, shouting over the noise to describe what they were attempting to see just below. Tony tried harder to look alive as he definitely didn't want to be the old man who couldn't handle early morning work in the field anymore, much less a simple helicopter ride. They'd already examined the three main craters of the mountain's southern end and he was hoping that this latest pass would be their last, at least until he had gotten a bit more sleep.

Even though Tony had wanted to visit Iceland for as long as he had been interested in volcanology, he wished he felt more awake and alive. Unlike the verdant Hawaiian and equally lush Caribbean landscapes he was used to working around, he had trouble staying focused in the face of so much blinding snow and a countryside that really was an All Lava, all the time construction. No trees. More sun than most people would have thought possible this far north. Several of the geothermal geysers everyone who knew anything about Iceland knew existed. Lots of steam puffing out from those geysers. But, still, it was fascinating. Tony hated it when people said things were "hauntingly beautiful" but those were the very words he would have chosen to describe what he was seeing. He vowed he would find some other way to describe Mount Hekla's vicinity.

"So there is the famous Mount Hekla, the source of all of our trouble and fascination," Erik yelled almost directly into Tony's eardrum over the din of the helicopter. "It's rather beautiful right now, with all of the bright snow cover and bits of wind, don't you agree?"

"Yes, it's beautiful all right," Tony screamed back. "I'm just happy we are flying so low over it now, before it erupts. I know the steam columns this baby can puff are pretty high and hot."

The helicopter started to veer away from the mountain. "The columns have gone as high as 15 kilometers or so when there is an eruption, what is that in American measurements, we'll have to keep that in mind when we talk with the television people, so that's about 45,000 feet," Erik said in a lower tone of voice as they headed back to the west. "Then you mix in the thunder and lightning that sometimes happens with an eruption, plus the tremors and the ash, not to mention the necessary fire, and you can have a very great challenge before you."

Tony adjusted his cap to cover his now sore ears. "I'm just very happy I was able to budget the extra money to take a flight overhead before it decides to show off, if it does so, and without any of those reporters around asking us questions we don't have answers for at the moment," Tony said. "It helps to have a little bit in the way of financial resources around to make all of this go a little easier, doesn't it? And oh yeah, speaking of splashing cash, I think I told you about this communications person I'm bringing in from the states. Don't worry, I've got my own private money to accommodate her expenses. She comes highly recommended from my sister and her doctor. Her name is Jenn Bergquist, and she sounded absolutely great during the few minutes I spoke with her on the phone. I just hope she can take care of these media guys so we can concentrate on the volcano."

Erik chuckled. "If she's worked for seven years at a university medical center she ought to know how to deal with scientists such as ourselves. I like the fact that her surname is Bergquist. She might be a nice Norwegian-American girl."

Tony noted that it probably wasn't necessary to again question whether Erik would remember names, licked his badly chapped lips, and stared out at the glacier in the distance as the helicopter picked up speed and moved altogether away from Hekla's mountain range. He had long heard other scientists go on and on and on about the wildness of Iceland's geographical offerings, although all he seemed to remember most of them saying was that the country was heavily cratered like the moon and that you couldn't buy a tree to save your life. Still, not everyone knew that Iceland, about the size of the state of Kentucky, also contained enormous swaths of dark green moss and grass, huge rocky waterfalls, hot and bubbly geothermal springs as well as geysers, and lakes and rivers that looked like gilded heaps and flows of very finely chopped raw emeralds and sapphires. Now that he was seeing a little bit of it for himself, he wished he was not so tired because he knew he wasn't able to appreciate all of it and he worried that he might nod off and really give Erik reason to think him past his prime.

"Yeah, I suppose with a name like that she would be of some sort of Scandinavian origin, but whether she's what you define as nice or not, well, that remains to be seen," Tony said definitively as he slowly turned away from the window to get a better look at Erik, who appeared to be about 6'2", with not overly chiseled features, and with smooth dark hair and big brown eyes that looked like big scoops of double fudge pudding.

Pudding? Pudding? When Tony was tired, he often thought of food. Especially sweets. He also thought other Icelanders probably figured Erik looked a lot like one of the Celtic monks who brought their religion and their ale to the country centuries ago. He'd heard of Erik's growing reputation for a few years now, and knew that if anyone was capable of becoming the next deserving star of all things volcano, it would be Erik Bjarnason. He also had heard from some colleagues at the University of Washington that Erik had not been very pleased about returning to Iceland to start his academic career. Actually, Tony had heard that Erik went back to Iceland with a reluctance that smacked more of duty than of excitement in taking a decent research position at one of the world's preeminent centers for volcano research.

Erik had done his graduate work at the University of British Columbia. He had a brilliant career there, perhaps too brilliant, as he was publishing more papers in the big scientific journals than might have been considered seemly for a mere foreign graduate student. He also had fallen in love the year before he finished his dissertation with a French-Canadian medical student from Ottawa, Veronique Vadeboncoeur. He and Veronique had reveled in all that life in Vancouver could afford, including a lot of sea kayaking, bike rides around the Stanley Park seawall, and sushi in Kitsilano. Erik even learned to speak a C+ level French. But there were no faculty positions open at the university after he finished his doctorate. Erik was convinced that more than a few faculty members who envied his brains, his looks, his ambition, and his Veronique, had made certain that no positions would be available. And then Veronique decided she wanted to move to Nova Scotia to practice medicine in the type of remote village Erik didn't even like to visit on holiday. She ended up marrying another French-Canadian physician who wanted to live in a town with only two bars, no real restaurant, and no department store. He wished her well in his most stoic Icelandic way and did not date anyone else for a very long time. He packed his things and his bruised (but reasonably well concealed) heart and went to Corvallis, Oregon to do his postdoctoral work at Oregon State University. He could have stayed there, the department chair was fascinated with what many of his colleagues there considered his manic quest to get a better handle on magma chamber activity (he just thought he had a good work ethic) but the money wasn't great and Corvallis was not Vancouver. Or even Reykjavik. So he went home. That made his parents happy. He wasn't happy, but it made him happy to see them so happy to have him back in Iceland.

"So about this Jenn Bergquist, yes, my sister, who doesn't ordinarily like public relations people or most anyone who works at what she considers an ordinary job, likes her very much," Tony said, consciously trying to put some verve and pep into his voice. "That chief photographer we'll be working with, the one with the fancy leather jacket and the Rolex, Mark, he said she was good, but then again, who knows what he really means when he says she's good. I can only hope he's a journalist with honor. And then my great friend, Yuki Atagari, who happens to be my sister's physician and the chief of surgery at the medical center where Ms. Bergquist works, well, he thinks she's about the best publicity person in the world. He says she has dealt well with reporters from all over, so you know, that's good enough for me for now."

Tony then turned to the pilot and asked if they were indeed stopping in Hella before continuing to head west and back to Reykjavik, where there actually were a fair number of trees in the few areas Tony had seen since arriving in the country. Nice ones.

Erik decided he had better say something good about Ms. Bergquist. "Yes, it was fortunate that you were able to get someone with such recommendations and that sort of a background to come out here on such very short notice, even though it doesn't sound as if she has worked in volcanology before," he said with more than a trace of the bluntness Tony had heard Icelanders regularly employed. "Having someone around to attend to the needs of journalists and photographers is a luxury I've not been lucky enough to partake of in my career."

"Well, I suppose it's sort of a luxury," Tony said as he privately thought these Icelanders must be ascetics, to think that having some-one around to mind the needs of a crew from the world's premiere science news organization an indulgence. "But it is my first trip to Iceland, and, seeing that we'll have these witnesses to our work, well, I just wanted to make sure everything would go smoothly. Take it from me, when you have television people around, especially big deal television people, you need someone to mind them, if only for liability purposes. I've done other documentaries before but this will be a big one; you'll be glad you are part of it."

Despite Tony's best efforts to look awake, Erik could clearly see that the esteemed American looked far more tired than he might want to admit. He reached for the thermos of the best espresso the helicop-ter company could provide and quickly poured Tony a large cup.

Erik now rued his desire to appear so professional and work-focused, and realized there probably was no real need to whisk Tony right from the airport after his long flight to the pub. He should have seen that two beers were quite enough to tranquilize anyone who had just flown many thousands of miles. But no, he then rushed him straight to the university for a late night session so his graduate students could fully brief the great man on the increase in the earth-quake activity they had detected during the previous two weeks. And show him that they really did have outstanding equipment in places outside of the United States.

"Here, take this espresso, I went to some difficulty to get it for you," Erik said with a smile, remembering that Americans often liked to mask the giving of help in the form of humor so as to not make the recipient feel all too needy. "If you want more, there are plenty of good coffee places back in Reykjavik, some with fine female scenery too."

Tony laughed as he carefully took the cup

"I'll just be glad to get back to town and go back to seismograph duty," Tony said as he cautiously sipped the not-so-terrible coffee.

"This mountain's earthquake activity is most interesting to me, very different from what I've seen in a lot of other places. Although I guess I shouldn't be surprised given how active this volcano is in comparison to a lot of others."

The helicopter came down at the barren landing spot just about as abruptly as it had flown all along. Tony could not remember when he had been on a less smooth helicopter. This one was bumpier than the one he had on that bad day over Mount Vesuvius when one of the other scientists actually got sick in Tony's lap. Today, Tony found that he had to grip his cup hard so as to not get burned, which was the last thing he wanted, to be both worn out as well as burned by coffee. The drive back to Reykjavik wasn't going to be that long and he hoped he could keep his eyes open long enough to finish reading some of the reports Erik had prepared for his briefings. He knew it would be more lunar landscape. No trees. Tony didn't know why he was so fixated on trees, because he knew by now that what he would see would be a road and a gray, spare, spooky, rocky, and utterly mesmerizing land. Surrounded by a fierce, cold ocean.

"Erik, these data sheets look really excellent. You went to a hell of lot of trouble just for me," he said as he walked ahead to the truck. "You keep this up and I'll have to rescue you from this place and take you back to my lab in Hawaii with me. Although don't worry, you'd be an employee with a little more freedom given your record of accomplishment. I am sure I would let you go out and chase women once in a while."

Erik hopped in the truck and started the engine. "And if you keep this up, I may have to take you up on that offer," Erik said just as slyly. Tony just grinned as he got in the passenger seat, fixed his cap once again, and then finished his coffee. As they started off on the road, Erik realized he was going to have to find the time over the next few days to watch more satellite television in order to refresh his command of American vernacular. Despite his best resolve to stay awake, Tony did not read all of Erik's magnificent reports. Instead, he woke up in the parking lot of the hotel with his cheek firmly attached to the truck's still cold window. He could think of no fashionable or athletic excuse for having passed out and having his face look as if he had purposely glued it to the window. He thought he would say as little as possible, say good night gracefully, go get some needed sleep, and then blow them away later on with his descriptions of work in Montserrat and other places where truck windows would never be so frozen.

Erik apparently read his mind. "Tony, it might be a good idea for you to sleep for a little bit, you probably still have some jet lag and it's my fault, I shouldn't have taken you out drinking right after your flight to meet the others in the lab," Erik said with all of the earnest humility he had first displayed in the pub. "I can meet you again when you like … we really can't do all that much now, especially with the TV crew, until it looks as if Hekla is going to really make a serious blow."

Tony nearly half-stumbled out of the truck and wished the sun would sink at that very moment. He looked around beyond the hotel and thought he might still be dreaming. He felt as if he had landed in a sunny children's playground, with all of the houses constructed from chalk-white building blocks and yet as colorful as if the kids had melted down all of their crayons in order to make the paint for the roofs. What a place, he thought. He found it hard to believe that such an innocent-looking city had such a reputation for wanton sex, large-scale drinking and other debauchery.

"Yeah, Erik, it's what I told you, I'm an old man, give me two beers and you may as well be ready to wheel me into surgery, the anesthetic effect is that good," he said with emphasis on the word "good." "Don't worry, I just need a little nap and I'll be fine."

Erik carried Tony's overloaded briefcase. Tony made no objection to his doing so. As they walked into a too hip-looking, lavender glass-sheathed hotel, they ran into Mark, who was stretched out on one of the lobby's massive gray suede sofas and wearing yet another supple black leather jacket. Tony wondered not so much as to whether the photographer was a part-time gigolo or not but how much the guy was actually making to be able to have a different designer coat for each day of the week.

Despite appearing asleep, Mark saw them and jumped up with the enthusiasm of someone who, to Tony's mind, clearly had not yet had his day's quota of agitated helicopter rides. "Dr. Fionarello, good to run into you! We were just going to go with some of Dr. Bjarnason's people on our own reconnaissance mission of Hekla," he said with enthusiasm bordering on authenticity. "We want to get up there and back before the sun goes down and then get back here to watch you monitor some more. I don't know, do you think it's really going to erupt soon enough?"

Erik could see that Tony was too tired to try to launch into his "volcanology for dummies" lecture, so he knew he would have to deal with this guy, who he thought was too well dressed and with too much product in his hair and on his face to possibly be straight.

Erik readied his broadly polite, yet blunt way of addressing someone that was very common among many Icelanders. "Yes, when you said your crew wanted to come out here to include Iceland in your program on the world's most, how did you put it, 'fiercely volcanic places,' we told you that although Iceland is the world's most volcanic island, and Hekla is Iceland's most active volcano, we could only tell you that the seismic activity had picked up some," he said crisply. "The repose period since the last eruption has only been five years, which doesn't mean it won't erupt, even though the activity we are measuring thus far is indicating we likely could have an eruption, but you know, volcanoes are not totally influenced by television ratings."

Tony was beat and ready for bed, but he still noticed that Mark seemed to understand he had been put down, and with just a few whacks. He guessed that the guy probably was reasonably intelligent, which was good, as it always was easier to work with smart journalists and not just empty cans of hairspray. He also realized he was going to have to play the role of the "life's a big party American" again in order to make sure things didn't get messy, as he was not keen to see these two guys start sniping at each other when he was worried about Bianca and trying to supervise an expensively televised volcanic eruption at the same time.

Tony stepped up. "Well, Mark, don't worry, we aren't in the volcanology business just to sit in labs all day and watch instrument readings. So if we can arrange a nice eruption for you, you can be certain Dr Bjarnason and I will do just that," he said, reaching over to pat Mark's shoulder, partially to see if the jacket appeared to be the soft and high quality lambskin it looked to be from a distance. "From what we saw today, I think it won't be too much longer. And Jenn Bergquist will be here soon, so that ought to make the waiting and watching a little easier for you."

The rather beautiful public relations girl in Minneapolis? She was nice, Mark thought to himself. Didn't seem to like octopus. Also seemed to be much more perceptive and capable of irony and sardonic humor than he figured anyone at that hospital gave her credit for at any time. Well dressed. Looking for a boyfriend while trying to look like she didn't care if she had a boyfriend. He admired that type of woman. Somewhat.

Mark smiled an almost imperceptible smile, careful not to nod too enthusiastically. He was sure Dr. Fionarello had talked to Ms. Fiona and probably thought all sorts of interesting things had gone on when he took Jenn out. Yeah. But he was happy Dr. Fionarello was around, as he seemed to understand the requirements of the television documentary business a little more than these idealistic, badly dressed Icelandic scientists who were in the unfortunate position of having to receive all of their relatively meager salaries from the government.

Erik looked at his watch and realized that the quicker Tony got to his nap and he got himself back to his lab to work, the better things would be for everyone. Despite his feeling that the television people were not as serious as he might like, he knew enough about baseball to know that he was currently batting about .200. That was not going to be enough to get him in the All-Star Game or much of anywhere else on this project. At times like this he sometimes wished he were just a bit more American. Or at least a bit more sophisticated. Erik realized it was imperative that he appear friendlier, at the very least. "Well, Mark, I had better get back and get that eruption going for you and your crew, but we'll be courteous, we'll try not to do anything until you get back from your flight," he said, even though he was not sure it was going to be worth it to him or anyone else to expend so much effort to be more affable. "It takes a lot of earthquakes to make that happen."

"Yes, you just do that, Erik," Tony said as he took his briefcase and hoped he remembered his room number as he headed for the elevator. "Have a good look around, Mark. Oh, and one more thing, I wouldn't eat anything spicy before you go up, although I don't know if you can find anything terribly spicy in this country anyway."

Mark resumed his sofa reclining as he checked his own watch and wondered what was delaying the others. His mind wandered to thoughts of Tony, who must be older than he seemed and was so unlike his sister, the renowned psychic. Then he thought back to his colleagues on the shoot. He hated it when he was late to appointments and such because others who outranked him didn't think being on time was important, as he felt it just gave average people even more reason to think that television journalists were a bunch overly paid imbeciles. He knew from hard experience that many producers and correspondents were indeed brats and worse.

Erik stood there for a moment while Mark appeared to be engrossed in thought. Fascinating, as Spock might say. Erik thought he had better keep trying to be a nice guy so he gave Mark a fast wave as he walked out to the truck. As he ran to the door to get out of the wind he thought about all he wanted to get done when he got back to his lab and that he hoped Dr. Fionarello would not be too angry with him for the jam-packed schedule. But he also pondered for a few seconds the idea of how things could possibly be nicer when Ms. Bergquist did arrive in town. He had always liked American women and their independent, sometimes brash ways, including the fact that so many of them seemed to engage in amorous action quite soon. However, he had decided that he probably was not going to take her to any bars as soon as she got to town. At least not the first night. After all, he did not know what she looked like just yet, because who knows if the photos people put online are real ones, or even current. Or if she was as smart and clever as advertised. Or if she would even want to, simply put, put out.

Chapter Eight

Jenn was like a tornado, holding up clothes, folding ones she'd chosen and running from dresser to drawer and closet to suitcase. "Marco, which parka should I take?," Jenn called out to her father's friend from her bedroom doorway to the kitchen, where Marco was spooning out some of the famous, massively spicy *puttanesca*, translated from Italian as "whore's pasta" that he sometimes he made for Jenn, but never for Olaf.

"I think you had better take the warmer one plus the wind jacket," Marco said loudly as he studiously grated a small dishful of Parmesan, the good Reggiano, not the cheap supermarket sand (as he called it). "You spent enough on both, though 66 Degrees North does make good quality clothing. So take them both. Listen to me, you can finish packing a little later, come in now and eat. *Mangia!*"

Jenn hauled the one fairly large, expedition-quality suitcase into the foyer, taking care not to scrape the hardwood floor or the walls. "Okay, you're probably right, I guess they don't call it Iceland for no reason," she said to Marco. "No, wait, don't correct me. Iceland is really not so icy. Greenland is the really cold place—Erik the Red just called Greenland 'Greenland' to get more Icelanders to settle there."

"I see you have been reading some Icelandic history! Your father would be so proud," Marco said, placing a large bottle of very good champagne in a bucket of ice. "I just think it is marvelous that you have this chance to go out there, see a volcano in action, and just

maybe have a small fling with that photographer. You don't have to tell Olaf, but I want to know everything. I want to see you finally do something scandalous with your life."

Jenn just smirked as she sat. She tried to breathe in as much of the food's scent as possible. She was crazy about everything Marco cooked, no matter if it was Northern or Southern Italian, simple or elaborate, healthy or touching on perilous. She knew that when he insisted on making her dinner before she left for Iceland, she could not refuse, although her father said she should remember that even though Marco was so energetic, he also was now 92 years old, and so she should pay attention to the wine consumed, lest the evening wear him out and send him to a nursing home.

"Well, you know, these volcano guys are still doctors, they just have a Ph.D. instead of an M.D., so I am sure you still have to be plenty deferential," she said as she wondered how much of the heavily dressed Caesar salad she could politely eat while still leaving some for Marco, who she noticed was wearing yet another lustrous custom-made jacket from Milan. She wished she'd worn something nicer than chinos.

"I don't know about any flings with any photographers. I told you Marco, the guy said he has a girlfriend. You know how that goes—I don't need any unnecessary trouble. Besides, I am supposed to be going over there to work, I don't know any of these guys, except that photographer, and I have never been around a volcano in my life. I only talked to this Tony guy a few minutes, which was weird, but no matter what, I am going to have to pay strict attention to things so I don't get consumed by any pyroclastic flows."

Marco smiled at Jenn's quick adoption of the volcanology lexicon. Her father's daughter, she was a smart girl. Not in the same way as Olaf, but a smart girl nonetheless. "Yes, I suppose it would not be right to get killed on international television in front of the famous Tony Fionarello," Marco laughed softly as he put a little more than two forkfuls of Caesar salad on his plate and looked at Jenn as if to say, "go ahead, I know you want it, take the rest." "But this is fantastique. You are not only going to be working with someone who is probably the world's most esteemed volcanologist, but with someone who also happens to be of Italian heritage. Speaking of Italian, I have heard that there are a few acceptable Italian restaurants in Reykjavik, even one that allegedly makes decent fresh fettuccini, but I cannot imagine anything more ridiculous than thinking one is eating Italian in a country where they still happily eat putrefied shark fin."

"Don't worry, Marco, I don't think I'll have time to go to many restaurants anyway, even if they don't serve rotten shark," she said, her mind wandering as to whether she had packed a strong enough sunscreen. She was eating way too fast, this time a large slice of crusty, very tasty bread Marco had purchased at a bakery not far from his condo. She knew she was anxious about the trip, and she knew she only really started feeling stressed when she told Olaf she was going to Iceland. He was uncommonly vocal when she called him in New York and told him what was going on.

"Marco, did my dad say anything to you about this whole trip? I just want to know," she said cautiously. "I think he's not totally miserable that I'm going, but he sounded, I don't know, almost panic-stricken on the phone when I told him everything. As you know, Olaf doesn't get panicked all that often," she said.

She took half of the salad and planned to eat whatever was left soon enough. "He was totally freaked out, went on and on about getting burned by magma, how expensive everything will be, how I don't even know this Tony Fionarello and how can I think about just up and leave my job, on and on. It was very, very weird."

Marco paused as he slowly reached over the table to get the champagne, although he then hoisted it with his usual strong grip. "I do think Olaf was a little upset, mostly because the news came up so fast," he said quietly. "Your father loves you dearly; he just wants you to be safe and secure. You know this, he wouldn't be a father if he didn't worry about his only daughter, his only child, going to work near a volcano on the recommendation of a psychic that you just met, even if her brother is justly famous for his work. It's important to him, and to me too, I might add, that you stay safe."

"I suppose so," Jenn said as she looked directly at him and stopped eating for a few moments. "I can't help but think there was something he wanted to tell me. But you know, maybe it was too much for him at one time. He is going a little crazy with those Jesuit clients— I think they want things to look a little more lush and worldly than he had originally envisioned."

"That's probably the case, but he'll be fine, and the Jesuits will survive Olaf Bergquist," Marco said. "But alas, no more idle chat right now, let's have our bubbly and toast this voyage of yours. I could not be happier for you, my child, you know that. You know how much I support any sort of adventure and discovery."

Jenn could see in Marco's eyes that he was getting just a touch emotional, in the manner she'd seen before when she did something he thought especially worthwhile or bold. If Marco was her father's other father, he certainly was her other grandfather, although she was sure most grandfathers didn't give their grandchildren several packets of condoms before dates, provide concise written reviews of cocktail lounges in any almost any major world city, or explain why it was seldom a good idea to buy clothes in France.

"Thanks, Marco," she said just as quietly, holding out her glass for him to fill. "I'm happy I am able to do it too. You know, I never thought anything this, I don't know—fulfilling—would come out of meeting a liver transplant patient."

"I always had my hopes such a day would come for you. Maybe not a trip to Iceland, but something more out of the usual than what you have going for you right now," he said as he looked approvingly as Jenn, who he thought was looking much too lean of late despite her ability to consume large quantities of food. "And I do hope you have some time to get to know Dr. Fionarello. From what I have seen of him on television, he seems very kind as well as brilliant. And before we forget and just start drinking away, we must think of some sort of positively sparkling toast, and we probably ought to say something kind of, oh, perhaps fiery, don't you think?"

Jenn laughed a little as she looked at Marco across the candles, his full head of silvery hair set in precise place with gel and obviously carefully styled that very afternoon, his ever-tanned face still relatively free of jowls or deep etches. She so loved Marco and wanted to say something fairly meaningful and expressive. She'd always felt she could be more open and demonstrative with him, and not just because he was from Italy, but because that was how she had felt about Marco since she was old enough to remember feeling anything fuzzy about anybody. He had always been there for her when her parents couldn't seem to tolerate her alleged outrageousness or supposedly unacceptable teenage behavior, like when she started drinking soda for breakfast or got caught kissing David Rubin behind the garage when she was 14 and David was supposed to be leaving for Yom Kippur services (even though she still could not believe the time she caught Olaf admiring David's mother's miniskirted backside). She also knew that Marco would like it if she were more voluble, and maybe that was why he liked wine so much, as it really did allow you to be messy and mushy and get away with it.

"Well, Marco, you think of something, you're the charming one. Maybe you should say something in your own tongue," she said. "Or, what do you think of this: perhaps we should make the toast in Icelandic."

"It's a pity I don't know any Icelandic," he said with a smile as he brought his glass nearer to her own. "But I know they say 'skol' or something like it all over Scandinavia, at least they do in Denmark, the Danes always have more fun than those sad Norwegians. So let's say as much and just hope that your time in Iceland is exciting, enjoyable, and I suppose we should add educational, just to show that we are not total pagans."

"Okay, that sounds very good to me," she said as their glasses made a careful clink. "And let's also toast to your continued good health, because you know, I tell you all the time, I cannot go on without you."

Marco drank a truly big but still dignified gulp from his glass. "Now listen to me, I've always told you I was going to live to at least 100 and I have no desire to shirk on my commitment now," he said with his eyes twinkling. "You still need me, and God knows your poor father still needs me. I can't die before I know Olaf can find amore, maybe even with the lovely Caroline. One never knows."

Jenn was a little startled to hear yet another mention of Caroline and her father in just a few days. Was something going on that she missed? Was she just too wrapped up in another world, as usual, except this time with windproof jackets and hot lava on her mind? She could not say that she was truly unhappy with the idea; she did really like Caroline, as she might like an older sister who was stylish and not embarrassing. She knew there were days when she thought of Caroline as a mixture of older sister-replacement mother. She would think such thoughts, although she'd never voice such thoughts, because she didn't want to make Caroline feel uncomfortable or old. And ever since Caroline at least once admitted to being at least 55, it did not take much to make her feel either old or weird.

Jenn did have a little trouble comprehending the thought of her father, Olaf, the man who was Quite Concerned about not being thought of as the least bit wild, going out with someone like Caroline. Everyone who knew Caroline knew she was many things that Olaf would find repellent: a devotee of champagne, wine and most New Age philosophies, someone who wore clothes that didn't just suggest sexual delights, they often told the whole story, and someone who had admitted to having undergone at least two plastic surgery sessions on her eyes.

"Yeah, well, I think Caroline is very nice, you know that, she's one of my best friends. She and I are like that cartoon about the screwed up single woman, which would be me, who confides in her older, wiser friend. That said, I am not sure Caroline is always so wise," she said as she slowly drank all of her champagne. "I do know Olaf thinks she is pretty, which she is, especially for her age." She paused audibly, because she was aware that everything she said was being listened to very carefully.

"You know, she's so uncontrolled compared to Dad," she continued, looking as directly at Marco as she could while hoping he might say something. "She thinks she is some flamenco dancer in Spain with her wanting to go to dinner at midnight, and you know Olaf, he likes to go to bed as soon as the weather guy tells him at approximately 10:17 p.m. that no tornadoes are going to hit Minneapolis and mess up his lawn."

"You greatly underestimate your father. I have been around him when he did not go to bed until at least three in the morning and he was not paying attention to the next day's weather," Marco said, leaning back just a bit. "And you know that tiresome yet true saying, opposites attract. It is for the most part a very stupid saying, but, in this case.... Caroline is most certainly opposite from your father, very opposite from your father, and she could be just what he needs to stop thinking he must suffer at all times."

"I am not saying you aren't right, all I'm saying is, I'll believe it when I see it," she said, absentmindedly tearing another slice of bread from the loaf and sprinkling crumbs over much of the table. "And you know, Caroline likes to party, she likes to have fun, Olaf can't say, 'oh, this place is too loud or too expensive.' She'll just go home. I know her, she said one of the few good things about being older is that you are better at knowing within about two minutes as to whether a guy is worth your time or not."

"You know, there are things about your father that you don't know, that you couldn't know, and I think his admiration for Miss Caroline is maybe one of those things," Marco said as he poured more champagne into both of their glasses. "I think it would mean a lot to your dad to know that it would be acceptable to you if he called Caroline."

"Are you telling me that he has already talked with you about taking her out?" she asked, stuffing the bread into her mouth in large chunks, realizing it was possible that she'd actually been outsmarted by her choirboy father on this one. "Well, duh. Here I think I'm on the ball, and I guess I don't know anything at all about anything."

"They have my blessing," she said after finishing the bread. "Maybe you ought to tell him that she really wants to go to that new Brazilian restaurant downtown. That way he can take his antacids ahead of time."

Marco laughed at the way Jenn seemed to always mix sincere devotion with sarcasm when she talked about her father. Still, he was glad to hear her talking about Caroline. He could tell Olaf that the mission had been accomplished. Maybe that would ease his mind a bit regarding both the Jesuits and Jenn's trip.

Jenn was eating a bit more slowly now. She gave Marco a look that let him know she realized he'd planned this ahead of time, and that was okay with her. Yeah, she really was leaving town.

"So, Marco, can we maybe talk about what I might be doing in Iceland. I suppose I should be ready so I don't look totally stupid when I get there and have to meet these volcanologists, because that Dr. Bjarnason guy from the University of Iceland sounds like a pretty serious dude."

"Well, my darling, I have not had the privilege of being near a volcano when it was ready to erupt, but I can tell you that I think you should just keep your eyes open, your mouth shut when necessary, and listen and learn as much as you are able from these experts," he said. "This trip ought to be one of the defining moments of your life so, pardon the pun, don't blow your opportunities. And wear good boots. And maybe behaving yourself around Dr. Bjarnason is not such bad advice."

"Well, I don't know about it being the defining moment of my life, that may be a bit much." she said. "Still, this whole deal does get me out of the hospital and out of the country, and right now, that is good enough for me. But you have to promise to call me if my father does take Caroline out, okay. I want as many details as he will tell you, and I want to hear my dad's version before I talk to Caroline, because she'll probably make stuff up too."

"Oh, rest assured I will tell you as much as he tells me," Marco said, laughing his more usual hearty laugh. "You know how guarded your father is about his private life."

Jenn quickly drank more champagne and watched Marco do the same. She tried hard to not think about things like Caroline tearing her father's shirt off, working her teeth quickly down a row of perfect mother of pearl buttons before taking on his belt. And then she knew she had to stop thinking about Olaf and Caroline.

"So, um, Marco, which volcanoes have you seen before?"

Chapter Nine

"I guess you don't really think it's too cold to be out walking," Caroline said haltingly as she tried to pull the pashmina scarf she couldn't afford but bought anyway up closer around her neck. She wished she'd worn tights under her jeans. "I'm glad you wanted to go out and all, Olaf, I am, but I guess I had something else in mind, maybe someplace indoors, maybe with a little wine and some hot food, a little central heating."

Olaf looked directly at her and beamed. He had thought a quick stroll along the river in the cashmere coat Marco had ordered for him might help give him the guts he would need to get through the night. Marco had never yelled at Olaf as much he did the other day, not only to make Olaf pay him in full for the coat and stop being a cheap bastard but to finally ask Caroline out and see if he could have a real conversation with a real, flawed yet perfect woman who happened to have a most tremendous rack.

Olaf had thought himself so clever when he coded the situation "the damn eternal secret" eons ago, back when he at least thought he could keep things neatly covered up and almost completely forgotten for eternity. After several nights of ingesting sleeping pills that might as well have been butter mints, he thought he had better do what Marco ordered, if only to prevent the old man from having a stroke. But if anything, each pounding step he took just increased his anxiety. He prayed Caroline would not notice the perspiration that was

forming on his forehead.

Still, while he had been miserable ever since Jenn first mentioned Bianca Fiona's name the night of the shrimp pasta, he simply could not get over the idea that he had actually called Caroline just two days before, without getting drunk first and without Marco on hand to coach him, and now was on an actual date with the woman about whom he'd been having multitudes of explicit sexual fantasies, fantasies that to his only occasional shame started long before Christina's death. What form the fantasies took was variable. Sometimes Caroline was dressed in nothing but a small cotton candy pink feather duster and was feeding him maraschino cherries as he lay stretched out like a Persian cat on a fluffy angora chaise. Sometimes she had just a little more clothing on and was lying on the floor and looking up at him as if he were Atlas himself, her gloriously lean legs wrapped in white lace stockings and the legs then wrapped tightly around his neck. He never knew that shame could feel so comforting.

"We only have to go a little further and then you can get on the car's heated seats and we'll go someplace warm," he said wondering whether he might have sounded slightly vulgar. She didn't seem as if she was the least bit insulted, so maybe everything was fine. He considered putting his arm around her but then thought he'd better hold off on any physical contact until he had first bought her a decent dinner. "I would think that a former ballet dancer such as you might relish the thought of a little exercise in the evening," he said as he forced himself to keep his arm pointed to the ground at an angle.

"Oh, I'm all for exercise, I just didn't think you'd want to take a walk at six in the evening when it's 16 degrees Fahrenheit outside, but you know, I could be wrong, maybe it's really not so cold, the wind might be all in my head, and I'll just have a virtual cold for the next week," she said while glancing up at him with her delicately shadowed and mascaraed eyes. "But you are now going to have to spend more money than you might like on me because you made me accompany you on this nature march. I just thought I had better let you know that before we get onto those heated seats."

Olaf thought about telling her that he'd love to buy her anything she wanted to eat or drink or anything else but he dismissed the thought and slowed his step to match hers as they crossed over the path onto the soggy brown grass to reach 42nd Street. Her normally china doll pale complexion was red from the windy cold and he knew that if he wanted to have a second date with her, he had to get her into the Volvo and in front of a glass of wine before too many more minutes passed.

"Caroline, you can have anything you want tonight. I did make you walk for your supper so you deserve something nice," he said in a voice that he hoped sounded lusty without also sounding desperate, like a guy who had not had any actual sex for several years. "But I am glad you said you'd come out tonight. I really am. I have wanted to call you for some time but I don't know, I just didn't, and now I did and I'm glad."

He'd no sooner said the word "glad" than she spotted his new midnight blue Volvo parked in the block's only spotless driveway; she flashed him a quick grin and dashed off to the car. He watched her closely for a few moments as she waited at the passenger door, jumping up and down.

"Olaf Bergquist, get this car open right now or else you are going to be buying me a mink coat on top of dinner," she said, her teeth chattering. "I can't believe I went along with this, I must have been either mental or really, really happy that you finally called."

Olaf reached into his pocket for his keys. "Okay then. Stop complaining about a little cold, my God, we do live in Minnesota," he said as slyly as he could, blipping the car open with the controls. "Give me a couple minutes and I'll have these seats so warm you'll want to go to a drive-in and eat in the car."

"No, we are not going to any drive-in, Olaf," Caroline said, hopping in and checking her nose in the visor mirror. "You promised me a nice dinner. If you're still nice to me by the time summer comes around, maybe then you can take me for a little cruising in this sensible car."

Olaf laughed as he looked at her fixing her face and then looked in the rear view mirror to inspect his own nose. Her mention of cruising made him think for a minute about all of the driving around he had done as a teenager, whipping around in his father's Buick with his idiot friend Mike, who somehow managed to finish law school, become the state's attorney general and then get married to an anorexic lumber heiress. The car was so enormous that it also could have done freighter duty on the high seas, young girls in the hold (later on including Christina) who were nowhere near as alluring in adolescence as Caroline was in later middle age.

He even ran into one of the girls from the hold a few months earlier at the supermarket. One of his tennis partners told him that this particular woman had just been divorced for the second time and allegedly was hard on the prowl, which didn't faze him much —to his mind, every American city was crawling with older, divorced women on the prowl for either money or sex. But the former backseat car girl was in a hurry to get to a hair appointment so their conversation was, to Olaf's great relief, brief and haltingly polite.

"Okay, I'll try real hard to behave tonight, buy you all sorts of food, make sure you are warm, and then I'll hold you to that cruising promise," he said as he touched the seats, saw that they were quite hot enough and knew he needed to get the car moving along. "So tell me where you want to go eat. I didn't make any reservations anywhere. You said you were going to tell me where you wanted to go."

She looked at him with the widest eyes she could produce and put on some lip gloss, fully aware that he was marking her every move.

She didn't mind. She knew that Olaf Bergquist was one man who not only would call her the day after he slept with her but that he'd bring in the newspaper, serve her some tea and toast with honey, and then offer to make the bed. All she had to do tonight was not let too much of her past and all of the bad men who inhabited it come flying out at the wrong time.

"Well, I don't know, Jenn tells me all the time that you are not the biggest fan of exotic food. Maybe we should go to Le Petit Oiseau," she said as she pressed her hands deep into the cushy, hot leather. "I've been there, they're not too expensive and I know they do very lovely roast chicken, duck, all sorts of poultry."

"That sounds fine," he said as he tried as effortlessly as possible to make every green light on the way downtown and not grip the steering wheel too hard. "Marco, you know, just loves that place. He tells me they have some very beautiful young waiters there, young women, not that I would go out of my way to notice such things, but I'm sure you know that Marco remains curiously interested in all of life's many diversions."

"Well, that's okay. I just love Marco. He's still so attractive for a man his age," she said slowly and with as much deliberation as she thought he'd buy. "And what is life without diversion, hmm?"

"That's probably true," he said while realizing her very voice was making him sweat even more. "All you have to do is look at how healthy Marco is for all of his behavior and there you have your answer, I suppose."

"You're absolutely right. We all should look that good at 62, never mind 92."

Now that they were actually on their way to the restaurant that specialized in fowl, Olaf could feel the full weight of his thoughts.

Caroline had been his daughter's friend ever since Jenn started working with her but it had only been within the past year that he'd come to fully realize that he had probably fallen in love with her the year before Christina died. He was sure he could pinpoint the day it happened. He had done so many times over the past few years, even while taking extraordinary pains to constantly remind Jenn of what a tremendous wife Christina had been to him all that time.

He had gone with Marco to a Christmas party at the house of one of the few friends of Marco's who were his own age, a tiny physician who seemed to have stopped buying his suits sometime during the Eisenhower administration. Despite his age and frail body, this friend had a rather pathetic and mad crush on both Jenn and Caroline. Christina had stayed home from the party because she said she had the flu, although whether she was really sick or not didn't matter, because she often said she was flu-stricken when there was a social invitation that was optional. Jenn and Caroline were standing together at the buffet table, clearly on the way to a mild and enjoyable state of inebriation.

Many times since, instead of concentrating on his work, he would sit back and conjure the sound of Caroline's voice that day as she extended her smooth hand to him and said "so, you must be Jenn's dad. Now I can see where she gets her all of her, um, common sense." When she started dancing in a sort of whisky a-go-go style to an old Beach Boys Christmas song with Jenn and a few other women (none quite as comely as she and Jenn, he remembered that too). Marco, on the alert as always for any signs of sexual tension anywhere in any room, knew what was going on because he brought Olaf a cup of punch and told him to try to drink it all and then have another glass so the go-go would linger.

While Olaf was going through his memories, Caroline just leaned against her seat and stared out the window, occasionally looking at him as she listened to the oldies station he favored over any other, with the exception of Minnesota Public Radio. He liked the idea that she didn't seem to expect him to keep talking all the time, because he knew it would be a case of him trying to sound more brilliant but just sounding more lame with each passing second. He thought it was still pretty likely that he would blow it, Marco's patient pre-date coaching notwithstanding.

"Okay, this was a good suggestion, plenty of street parking, I like it when I don't have to go into a parking ramp," he said, looking for a spot close enough so Caroline wouldn't get cold all over again. "It must not be too crowded, which could be either a good or a bad sign."

"Well, even if it is busy, it doesn't matter, tomorrow's a slow day, I don't care how late I get home," she said as she let her fingers take one last press of the warm seats. "I know for a fact that their food is good, so don't worry, you will not be disappointed."

She was ready to open her door but Olaf motioned that he'd get it.

"This is so lovely, Olaf, I don't think a guy has opened a door for me since, well, many years ago, not everyone had cable yet, let's just say that much," she said, accepting his proffered hand. "I didn't know you were such a courtly man."

"There's probably a lot you don't know about me," he puffed out as they ran to the restaurant's door.

Once inside, he couldn't believe it. The place couldn't have been more suited to his idea of the perfect occasion with Caroline, although he would have darkened the stain on the wood beams just a shade or three.

"Nice choice, Caroline; it looks as if this place kind of caters to people our age," he said as he waited for her to sit down as the waiter showily handed them hefty menus. "I hate going to these places with Jenn where I am going to end up paying $50 for pasta that tastes more like uncooked boxed macaroni and cheese than anything out of Tuscany."

"Never mind Tuscany, what's this about people our age," she said with a girlish indignation. "Jenn told me you are 60, but I'm not there yet, not quite. Don't push me there before I'm ready to face it."

"But you are close enough, I know this from Jenn as well," he said without remorse. Scanning the menu, he was mildly thrilled to see there were many things he would be happy to pay for as well as eat. "Besides, what's wrong with admitting your age, especially when you look as stunning as you do? I actually feel better now than I did ten years ago."

"Really??" she asked, timidly peering from behind the menu. "Even after all you've been through? I'm not sure if I feel better now or not. I suppose I'm more resigned to the idea of being older now than

I was ten years ago. That's worth something. And by the way, thank you for saying such nice things to me," she added with as much sincerity as she thought he'd buy before having anything to drink. "I appreciate hearing stuff like that from a guy like you, as you are pretty handsome yourself, you know, so your words carry some power."

"Oh, I don't know about that," he said very quietly. He hoped his dinner selection would help him portray a bit more of the daring guy Marco told him he'd have to be if he were to have a chance of spending more than one evening with Caroline. "But you know, it's true. You are an astonishingly beautiful woman. I know you don't have to hear such things from someone like me. I just consider myself very fortunate to have been able to persuade you to come out with me tonight."

Olaf could tell, from the look that suddenly appeared on Caroline's face, that he had broken every single rule the men's magazines recommended for a first date, especially with a woman one very much wanted to sleep with. Truth was, he didn't really care. He was too old to worry about whether he had said too much; he just didn't want to wait any longer or to play games just to get her into his life as well as his bed.

"Well, Olaf, you know, there's no luck or persuasion involved here at all, I've told Jenn for, hell, probably three years now that I wish you would ask me out," she said, gingerly unfolding her napkin. "Glad we're finally doing it."

"Yes, at last," he said. He figured she knew exactly what she was saying and didn't care that her words implied the overture he was taking them to suggest. "So, you said you wanted some wine. Let's have some wine. I will have to let you select it; you must know from Jenn the Sommelier that I'm not only not a spice man, I'm not a wine man either."

"Oh, I don't care what we have, some sort of nice red, I suppose. It will be good for our platelets, as your daughter always says," she said as she laughed at how Jenn made people nuts with her persistent questioning of waiters and sommeliers about their wares. She had been with Jenn on many occasions when she grilled the poor waiters so much that Caroline thought they'd give them the wine for free or else smack a bottle over their heads just to get away.

Olaf let Caroline order the wine. It did not taste too much unlike what Marco drank all the time, and he wondered if she just ordered something dark and Italian so as to make Olaf feel more comfortable. If that was the case, it was yet another thing to like about this woman.

Their food came before Olaf could even attempt to make amusing banter about his Jesuit clients and the way one of them talked about Fifth Avenue shopping excursions as if they were the High Mass itself. The partridge turned out to be quite delicious, roasted to a gourmet magazine-perfect brown glaze and thankfully, not too gamey. Caroline had ordered chicken sautéed in a lot of wine and butter and he watched with awe as she almost professionally moved the silverware here and there, stripping the bones of all meat and sinew without any fuss or mess. If she was this conscientious about some chicken, she'd probably come in quite useful on some construction projects where they needed meticulous detail work. She seemed to devour food in the same style as his daughter. Olaf found himself contemplating his dinner more than he'd ever thought about any restaurant meal, letting Caroline do most of the talking and finding her opinions concerning the intelligence level of some presidential candidates to be even funnier than Marco's memories of V-E Day and all of the women he claimed to have had in that one afternoon.

As he watched her go silent so as to scarf down a huge and steaming chocolate pudding cake, he wondered how she could eat so much food and yet have such an adolescent figure. Then he thought he had better get talking and stop concentrating on knives and pudding before all of the courage wrought by one fairly small glass of dark red wine vanished into outer space. He knew he'd never get it back; he'd been in similar situations before and Marco wasn't here this time around to bail him out.

"So, Caroline, I was wondering, this patient at the hospital Jenn has been talking about, this Bianca Fiona," he said, almost lapsing into the stutter he had overcome more than 40 years earlier. "Did you get a chance to meet her?"

Caroline was carefully scraping chocolate from her plate, looking genuinely unhappy that there was nothing left of her dessert.

"No, I never met her, although I have been reading the book she gave Jenn, pretty interesting, kind of my deal, as you probably know," she said hesitantly as she put her utensils down, fully realizing that the only way she'd get more cake is if she ordered another slice. She figured she would wait for the second date. For now, she would simply drink the wine he was paying for but clearly wasn't going to drink. "I know you don't approve of that so-called New Age stuff, so I'm sure Jenn never showed the book to you."

"She didn't, no, and I suppose I would not have wanted to read it," he said as he leaned in closer to her, the way he did back when he was trying to get a girl out of a bar booth and back into the Buick. "So you didn't meet her?

"No, although I've heard plenty about her. She sounds a little nuts, but that is how anyone with such a gift is going to be—you can't live in this world and be above it at the same time without people thinking you're a nut case," she said, surprised that Olaf knew how to lean in close. "But it was nice of her to arrange for Jenn to go to Iceland and see a volcano blow up, work with all of those famous people, don't you think?"

"Yes, yes, it is a wonderful opportunity for Jenn, as long as she is careful and doesn't walk in any fresh lava or drink too much Icelandic beer, or have too much sex with that photographer Mark," Olaf said as he felt the words forming in his brain but was somehow unable to make them all of them come down to his now thoroughly parched mouth.

He took a small sip of wine and tried to breathe without making too much noise. "So, did you know that Jenn was born in California while I was in graduate school?"

Caroline picked her fork up again, thinking she should hang onto something because she could not figure out why Olaf was so interested in Bianca, or what he was really trying to get at in this turn of the conversation because she thought he hated California. She'd already had three glasses of wine but, as she was not driving and he seemed to want to talk about a psychic, she was going to keep sipping away until he started to make some sense or at least talked about going home.

"I do know that—we tease her about being real Hollywood," she said, holding her fork as if it were a fragile spring twig. "You went to grad school there, Marco was one of your instructors, Jenn was born, and when you graduated you all came with Marco back to Minneapolis to build churches."

"Well, Jenn was only a year old then, so she didn't build any churches, and her mother spent most of her time running to churches, none of which I built," he said in a voice that he hoped was not too sarcastic. "But yes, we came back. I've stayed here ever since. Jenn went away to school in California and stayed there for a while before she wised up and came back to a real civilization."

"Yeah, I know all this, Olaf," she said with the faintest tinge of exasperation. She too had hoped they would finally have sex tonight. If she wasn't going to get any more food, she may as well get drunk and then keep her hopes up about getting laid. "Is there something you want to tell me? About the psychic? I have to tell you I am not following your train of thought right about now."

Olaf was glad he'd worn a thick wool fisherman's sweater; at least the sweat did not show through. Say it, just say it, get it out, he thought. After that she could ask him question after question and maybe she'd even help him with the answers. He hadn't even said anything much yet and it was getting way too complicated. This was one of the reasons why he did not like to go on dates all that much.

"I can assure you I am more organized when I try to design buildings," he said. "Yes, I do want to tell you something, something about Jenn, something that also involves Bianca Fiona, interestingly enough. I apologize in advance if this is not the best official first date banter."

Caroline put the fork down and was immediately certain, she was sure, that Olaf was going to tell her what she had heard in a million or so different variations from many other men, even though she found it hard to fathom that fresh-faced Olaf Bergquist could also be a scum who once cheated on his wife. And now she was no longer sure she wanted to sleep with him that night, or any other night.

"Well, tell me. You brought me here and bought me dinner so I guess I have to listen to what you have to say," she said softly, while wondering if she had brought enough money with her to pay for a taxi home.

Olaf took a deep breath. He looked around the restaurant wondering how so many people could be having such a relaxing evening while he had to stash his own desires away to talk about something so terrible, so miserable, something that he wanted to keep in the attic or the basement or even a closet, anywhere but out in the open.

"Yes, well, where to start, I told you about Bianca Fiona. You know she's from California, and then you know that Jenn is from California," he said, swallowing so hard he felt his esophagus would collapse into his stomach. "Let me put it this way. Have you ever wondered why Jenn has such dark features, such atypical Norwegian looks, well, different from how most Americans think Norwegians should appear?"

If Olaf's esophagus was indeed going to collapse, it might have collapsed in Caroline's throat, because she also felt that very same way. This was worse than a bad made-for-television movie and, moreover, she was starting to get a headache from the wine. She should have ordered something nicer or maybe just not had as much.

"You don't mean to tell me that Bianca Fiona is Jenn's mother, do you?" she said, fighting to suppress scalding tears that to her massive surprise seemed to be popping out from all under her eyes. "Is that what you are saying to me?"

Olaf was a bit relieved that he'd told Caroline what he needed to tell her without really telling her, even though he sort of thought it was pretty unmanly of him to do it this way. Now all she needed to do was to start asking questions, although he could feel his throat start to close up again because he suddenly realized what Caroline had just realized.

"Yes, it is true, Bianca is Jenn's birth mother," he said as calmly as he could, breathing as deeply as possible without sounding like he needed a large paper bag. "But before you start thinking what I know you are thinking, you need to know that I am not Jenn's natural father. She carries none of my DNA, if you will. She's still mine, of course, I raised her, I love her, but she didn't sprout from me, if you want to put it that way."

"Sprout, is that what you want to say about… this child you picked up when she fell and scraped her knees, taught to ride a bike, this girl you worry about every minute of the day…your daughter for Christ's sake, this girl who is now trying to not get burned by lava as she works to protect her famous volcanologist UNCLE from journalists," she said in a moderately raised voice, aware that people might be listening. "My God, what the hell is your problem?"

"Okay, okay, it's not as bad as you think," he said while thinking about how he would tell her the rest of the story.

The truth was that Christina had wanted a baby right away. But she'd had a most unplanned hysterectomy at age 22. Bianca was a beautiful teenager in trouble. Bianca's father was all too willing to have a respectable young couple like Olaf and Christina take his daughter's trouble far away from Los Angeles and his well-ordered world. "Let me just tell you, okay, I know this was a lot to lay on you tonight. You know Jenn so well, she likes you, she trusts you, Marco told me you would be able to help me out," he said, feeling some of the steel ever so slowly return to his voice.

Caroline didn't know if it was the drink or the cold or the fact that this was a guy who seemed willing to tell the truth, no matter how rotten the truth turned out to be, but she knew she was going to have to listen to what he had to say. Half of her wanted to take her phone out of her bag and call Jenn in the middle of the night to tell her that her father wanted to talk to her now. But she pinched her thighs and thought, you have to listen, you have to listen, do not go insane this time around, this may not be another total jerk, though he certainly seems like one at this moment. Besides it was flipping cold outside and she probably only had around eight dollars in her wallet.

"Okay, Olaf, talk to me," she said, measuring her words. "Tell me the whole damn story, and I mean all of it. If I have to hear more about what I've just heard, I want to hear it all. But don't lie to me. I cannot deal with any lies, especially about poor Jenn, who is probably freezing to death in some youth hostel, sleeping on the floor, with no idea her biological mother is dying, much less, oh man, this is just too much, that she was even adopted."

"I won't lie to you, Caroline, I promise. Jenn will be in a good hotel, not a youth hostel, I looked at the website," he added. "Do you want me to start from the beginning?"

"I want to know why you never told Jenn she was adopted, much less by someone who clearly has come here to connect with her," she said, folding her now sweating hands tightly.

"You are right. Jenn does not know she's adopted, Christina never wanted her to know. I could not say no to Christina, I don't know why, I know it was wrong, I've known for years it was wrong, Marco has told me it was wrong, but I just didn't do anything about it," he said, forcing himself to stare unflinchingly into Caroline's very bright eyes. "So Jenn doesn't know anything."

What he was astounded to feel was that he was still thinking about when he and Caroline might actually have sex and what he'd have to do to get her into one of their beds.

"At this point, I really don't care, Olaf, I cannot f-ing believe you are telling me this stuff on our FIRST date," she hissed.

"Well, just to finish out the story," he said with the fluster of a kid who was already failing and still was bluffing his way through a report on a book he had not actually read. "Jenn also has a twin brother, but she's obviously never met him either."

Caroline started to count the money in her purse in her mind. Her head really was starting to hurt. She needed some water even though she wanted more wine too.

"Let me guess, because now it is all too obvious, it just has to be that this Erik Bjarnason volcanologist guy in Iceland is Jenn's brother," she said.

"Well, you've made things a little easier. Yes, Erik Bjarnason is Jenn's brother," he said quietly. "I did not know the people who adopted him. His father apparently was in the U.S. from Iceland to get a Ph.D. in physiology. He was already an established physician back home. I do know he and his wife had tried for years to have children and Bianca's father knew them from the university. And Christina and I did not even know about Dr. Bjarnason and his wife at the time, she had one of those 'dottir' surnames Icelandic women have instead of any married name. We found out about them just before Bianca's father died about ten years ago; before he died, he thought he ought to come completely clean with Marco and me. We did not even know there were two babies until that time. When Christina found this out she almost went completely and utterly insane. It was a very, very bad time, believe me. Christina refused to see any sort of psychologist or counselor, not that I would have either. And from what Bianca's father told us, Dr. Bjarnason and his wife did not know about Jenn."

Olaf stopped spouting for a moment and realized he needed to breathe.

"Anyway, yes, now Jenn and Erik will get to meet," he continued once he thought he could go on and exhale at the same time. "Given that Bianca's brother was obviously in on this whole plot to get Bianca to Minnesota to die or get transplanted, 'bond' with her biological daughter and then send her to the middle of the northern Atlantic

Ocean in the winter, I can only imagine how all of this is going to play out. And I really don't want to imagine any of it, but as you can see, matters have been forced upon me and I must imagine."

"So what are you going to do?" she said with much more understanding than he expected. "What if Jenn and this Erik, you know, what if they start to like each other, you know, in that way? That cannot happen."

Olaf thought he might have a heart attack. He knew he should have thought of this before Jenn went to Iceland. Clearly, he was as clueless as Jenn thought. But why didn't Marco say anything either? He panicked badly at the thought of his daughter rolling over the Icelandic moss in a sexual stupor with her brother.

"I think I need to call Iceland. I think I need to call Iceland soon, I don't know what I am going to say but clearly, I have been very, very wrong."

"Hold it, hold it, hold it," she said, grabbing the scurrying waiter's apron to ask for a big bottle of mineral water and two large cappuccinos. "Remember that this Tony guy, their uncle, knows the whole story. I am sure he is going to do his damndest to keep them apart in that way. Just try to calm down and then let's think. I wouldn't do this for just any guy, but I can't stand that this is happening to Jenn, the girl who thinks she will be arrested for solicitation if she wears five-inch heels and eyeliner. So let me help you try to clean this mess up as much as we can, never mind the fact that we don't have a hell of a lot of time and I'm just a little tipsy right about now and I don't know why you aren't tipsy now either."

Olaf almost wanted to leave at that moment. He knew she was right as well as tipsy, even more than a little tipsy. He knew this was one totally messed up situation and he did not really know what to do. He drank some of the mineral water as well as a few sips of coffee, which helped him to stop thinking about sex, not that he would be in any kind of reasonable condition to have sex with anyone tonight anyway.

"Okay, you have a deal," he said in a fairly measured tone as he noticed the floor tiling was really quite lovely. "So let's work on a plan. And thank you."

"Let me just think for a minute, I need to get some more water in me first," she said as she carefully massaged her temples and looked as if she might cry or vomit. "I don't know, but we ought to be able to think of something that might work. Maybe."

Chapter Ten

The sun was streaming mightily into the room. Bianca wondered why the nurses (including Laurence, the chief sadist in this punishment parlor smartened up to resemble a hospital intensive care unit) insisted on continuing to open the blinds every time they came into her room. Didn't any of them realize that it might be more comfortable to die in the dark?

Because despite Yuki Atagari's constant state of near tranquility, Bianca knew she still had enough ability to sense beyond his words. She was certain he was trying to tell her that she was not going to be alive, at least within the form of a human body, for much longer. And she didn't have to listen to Yuki give her any creatinine counts or other status reports to know that she felt as if her entire body was turning into a sort of mound of gel, littered with any manner of itchy pollutants, and stabbed upon the increasing occasion with a pain she hadn't known was possible. There were times she could have sworn she was seeing her legs and arms fall away and, feeling as if she really had been reduced to a filthy, goopy state, she had no way of setting out from her bed to retrieve the limbs and put them back into place.

But she felt a balmy sense of accomplishment that she'd had a chance to have one last talk with Jenn before she left to be with Tony in Iceland, even if it was a fairly short one. The feeling was even better than when she was able to stay off booze for a few months before she got real treatment. All the same, the girl's persistent skepticism as

to why Bianca and Yuki arranged for her to go was annoying, more than she cared to deal with, although she couldn't say she didn't fully understand some of the girl's doubts. She was pretty sure that during the course of that last conversation, Jenn thought Bianca was a lesbian as well as an alcoholic nutjob. The idea that she might be lesbian was more than amusing given Bianca's bustling and very heterosexual sexual history. But all she had to do was look at the type of work Jenn was choosing to do, and from what she knew about her parents, she could see why Jenn could not seem to accept the fact that a seeming total stranger would want to take her away from antiseptic solutions and Lord Laurence and head for a volcano. For one thing, she couldn't imagine having any sort of job where she'd have to wear structured clothing and talk to people so much of the day and then at least pretend to be nice and give a damn about what they were saying. How this child could have come from her own body was clearly more evidence that environment really mattered as much as genetics in determining human personality. Then there was the matter of Jenn's karma, but the thought of that just made her feel worse.

During the moments when her pain was just bad and not shrieking, she made a conscious effort to focus hard and concentrate on the past with an intensity she never could have managed when she was drinking a couple bottles of wine or bourbon every day. One of the nurses periodically asked her if she had a tension headache and needed any more pain medication. And once, she let the nurse give her more pills to try to numb the one part of her body, her brain, that she didn't want numbed.

When her heavy concentration worked, she would be able to clearly remember people and things, like the time she and Tony succeeded in building a campfire out of paper plates in their basement when she was eight, or the smell of her second (and favorite) husband's imported sandalwood soap that he never quite completely rinsed from his chest hair. And with a more studied effort, she even managed to conjure a picture of what Olaf Bergquist was like 36 years ago. She'd only met his wife, Christina, for a very short time while they were talking about the adoption before the babies were born. From the little bit that Yuki told her about the woman, it didn't sound as if the two of them would have managed even one amiable cup of coffee together, never mind a tarot card reading or deep conversation.

But when the picture of Olaf was fully composed, she could recall his rather naïve mien, silky smooth complexion, U.S. Marine Corps posture and clothing creases, and hair that was just too beautifully blonde to have been produced by chemicals. Of course, since she was only 19 at the time, most men over age 20 (Olaf included) seemed to have something tangy and yummy within them that appealed to Bianca's still rather immature sexual tastes.

And when she was thinking about Olaf she also couldn't help but reminisce about Marco Leonardo, her late father's faculty colleague as well as Olaf's advisor. She didn't know Marco well at all but she was very aware (thanks to her father's frequent and sometimes nasty comments) that he was one of the few people in her parents' age group who actually liked the Beatles and the Who and knew that oregano was a poor marijuana substitute. She knew that he was still alive. Although it took her a little time because of the fog that was starting to choke her senses, she calculated that he would be quite elderly by now. She wondered if he was still handsome and virile or if he had become a victim of the scourges of age, hunched up, frail, and wearing elastic high-waisted pants.

She thought too about actually being pregnant at such a young age, being ostracized by friends who didn't want to hang around with someone they either considered a slut or someone who just couldn't have fun anymore because she weighed 35 pounds more than usual and wasn't supposed to drink or smoke cigarettes. Some of those bitches came to the signing for her first really successful book and she was thrilled to see they were fat, unhappily married suburban drudges. As it was, actually giving birth to the babies was painful as hell until all of the drugs took effect but having those beings out of her was really more of a relief than anything else. She only saw them briefly after they were born. They were beautiful and tiny and looked just like her but she was glad to have them taken away soon enough. Her life was waiting and she wanted it back as soon as possible. The pangs of motherhood lost never hit her, not once, not even when she was sometimes happily married. She did think about both of the children some through the years, not a tremendous amount, but some, perhaps when there was news of a huge Minneapolis snowstorm or that a cute orca whale was swimming around Iceland. It was only when the haze of alcohol left her in full, to be replaced by the reality of being very sick, that she knew she wanted to see how Jenn and Erik had actually turned out. She wasn't really interested in being their mother. Not that much. She just wanted to know that something she had produced was a good and decent thing. She wanted them to know she was their biological mother. In some ways, she wanted to do something that would make Tony and her late parents at least somewhat proud of her and her life. One thing was certain. She never would have named them Jenn and Erik.

In the conversations Bianca had been able to have with Jenn, she could tell that Jenn was definitely more wantonly worldly than the Olaf she remembered might have wanted. But she also thought that Jenn felt a real devotion to her father and thus was absolutely sure she had told Olaf all about Bianca. She was too woozy most of the time to imagine every one of the possible scenarios that probably came into his head when he learned that Bianca was in Minneapolis, but she guessed that he was none too pleased by the intrusion, her life-threatening illness notwithstanding.

She also knew she had made a blood promise to Yuki before he let her come to Minnesota that she and Tony were going to contact Olaf and explain the whole situation; Yuki was fuming mad at her because she and Tony had not yet done so. Tony was furious with her, too, because he wanted to have the discussion with Olaf as soon as Bianca entered the hospital, especially because, as he put it, he was courting a lot more heat than he thought would be the case when he agreed to help Bianca with her mission. But she was adamant about wanting time alone with Jenn before they told anyone. And she was grateful that she was able to have that time while Jenn remained unaware of the whole story. Sometimes the universe was not completely unkind.

Because she was sure (as she was convinced that her extrasensory abilities were exceptionally strong when it came to Jenn) that Olaf hadn't told her anything about Bianca. That probably was in everyone's best interests at the moment. The nondisclosure, as it were, plus the fact that Bianca was able to talk to Jenn so much and send her semi-happily off on Tony's field trip, was proof enough to Bianca that she really was going to be in charge of at least part of the outcome of her original plan. And for once, maybe no one was going to be able to accuse her of screwing things up.

Just as she was thinking that maybe she should be feeling more weepy about all of this rather than smug (despite the admonitions in her books about pride being just a little degenerate), and ready to take one of the many naps that now marked her days, Yuki walked in the room, his white coat absorbing the sun so much she thought she'd already died and seen the tunnel of light. If she hadn't been so messed up when she was young, or so messed up even a year or two ago, she might have ended up with Yuki or someone similar. After all, this was a man who admitted to meditating when he could find the time and the solitude, and her father and brother worshipped him as if he were the Buddha himself. And he was handsome in a way she couldn't really explain, at least not while sober. Besides, how could any woman resist a man who wore such beautiful ties and could slice vegetables and people with such precision? Clearly his beautiful artist wife could not.

"Let me just close these blinds for you, Bianca," he said in that melodious voice of his that made Bianca think of quiet, cold brooks and plush green tea fields, when she bothered to listen in the way she told her fans and students to listen. "I know you don't like the sunlight but I suppose the nurses think it is too depressing to always have to come into a blackened room."

"Thanks, Yuki," she said in a markedly weary voice. "You've always been so considerate," she said as she forced herself to find the energy to half-sit up against two of her silk pillows.

"Yes, that's true, and for that, you are very lucky."

"I don't believe you came in here to talk about how lucky I am that you are still being nice to me," she said as she tried hard to look into Yuki's eyes. "I take it you have even more evil test results for me."

Yuki audibly tightened his clasp before responding. He hated giving bad news to any patient but he especially hated giving it to patients with whom he was acquainted. And, of course, Bianca was not just an acquaintance. If he had been completely and thoroughly professional, he might have told Tony and Bianca that it was not possible for Bianca to come to Minnesota and have him oversee her treatment, much less get involved in all of the rest of the drama. But he was far too fond of Tony, as well as Bianca, to send her anywhere else. He also was not sure he could fully trust some of his fellow surgeons at other medical centers. He often thought, but only to himself, that their temperamental dispositions and enormous egos should never be combined with surgical knives and anesthesia.

"Well, Bianca, I'll give it to you very straight, as you say you like it, and I'll spare you the technical details, which also is how you claim to like it, if I correctly remember your last set of dictates," he said as he hoped his face was dry and free of emotion. "Your body is in bad shape. Your test results are not encouraging, and I think you can see how you are declining. I know you are in tremendous pain. And if we don't find a donor for you soon, I don't know if we are going to have enough time. Even if we do find a donor, your condition may be such that it could be too late, although I maybe shouldn't say that because I've operated on people as sick as you and they have made pretty full recoveries. But you're right, at this very moment, it does not look good."

Bianca just smiled at Yuki's sweating face. It was a good thing she didn't fear death, and it was doubly good that she'd had some contact over the years with spirits on the other side, otherwise it would be tough for her to try to cheer Yuki up.

"Yuki, glorious outlooks depend upon how you choose to see things," she said with just a smidgen of her usual feline voice. "You know I am not afraid to die. You've known that for years. And besides, being so-called 'cured' of my liver disease by means of having a big blob of brown-green protoplasm that once belonged to someone else implanted into my body was not my primary aim in coming to Minnesota. You know that. You know I wanted to establish some sort of relationship with Jenn. You helped me do so and for that, I will forever be indebted to you. I'll still be grateful even when I pass over to the other world. I'll try to look in on you now and again, just to see if you keep your taste in ties."

"I've thought a very great deal about the ethics of this all, but, of course, the rub is that, in essence, I have not broken anything related to your confidentiality, being that you are the patient and Jenn is not," he said, knowing full well the nature of his ethical worries. "What I've done to a really very wonderful young woman and valued staff member is another thing entirely, but, I suppose in the end I can rationalize things by saying it probably was the right thing to do. If nothing else, Jenn certainly could use the break from this hospital," he continued. "But we have got to get Tony on the phone with her father and we have got to explain what is going on. We must. The one thing we have going for us, I suppose, if you want to call this a plus, is that Erik's parents are already dead."

"Tony told me. A car accident when they were on holiday in Sweden, I think it was about five years ago," Bianca said in a manner that made Yuki think she finally was realizing the extraordinary seriousness of what they were doing. "My father never got around to telling them there were twins; he only told Marco the full story because I don't think my father wanted to die without telling someone about the semi-disaster he helped broker all those years ago.

"Maybe things could have been worse, but from my chair, I think this is about as mucked up of a situation as I've ever seen in my life," Yuki said as he stared at the floor.

"It is mucked up, I know," Bianca whispered. "But, I suppose some people would think it was a lovely coincidence that Erik unwittingly followed his uncle into volcanology, but of course, I know better. Although he is Icelandic, and Iceland IS a volcano. Still, I guess we should be happy things worked as they should, because it made it a lot easier for Tony to help me know what Erik was doing once he grew up, although Tony took great pains to never meet Erik until now. It would have been too much for him."

"Tony called me just before I came down to see you. He and I talked about how we need to talk to Olaf, and he said he will call you this evening at the usual time," Yuki said, looking furtively about the room for something else to sit on that was not a silk pillow or a broken chair. "He said Jenn sounded like a very charming young woman on the telephone, eager to get out to the volcano and do her best work. He also said that his, um, how shall I say it, his colleague over there, young Dr. Erik Bjarnason, appears to be a fine scientist. Anyway, Tony seems to think he is a little repressed, but he thinks that of lots of people, although he also said the young man certainly possesses sterling professional credentials and is, as only Tony could put it, one sickeningly handsome guy who looks very much like his mother. He did say he was proud to be his uncle." When Yuki mentioned the proud uncle bit, Bianca really thought he might cry, which would have been awful.

"Tony would notice things like that," Bianca said softly as she laughed a bit and glanced toward the blinded window. "And I would not be surprised that he would be jealous of his nephew. Anyway, I'm happy that things are going well enough. The one wish that keeps me on your organ waiting list, and you know it, is the chance to get myself cleaned up enough so I can go over to Iceland myself and meet

Erik, young Dr. Bjarnason, in person. But I still don't know about Jenn. I just hate to think I produced something so riddled with fears and rigidity."

Bianca straightened her pillows and sat up about as properly as Yuki had seen her do since she arrived at the hospital. "I do know that you and Tony are right, we have to talk to Olaf, this is asking a lot of Tony to have to deal with these two kids, given all he knows and all he has on his mind," she said as she looked directly at Yuki while she took the huge amethyst ring on her right hand on and off. "Tony just hates emotional unrest, and you know that almost better than anyone, Yuki."

"Oh, Tony will be fine, he's a man of science, you know, he is like the rest of our kind. He knows how to block things out when necessary and concentrate on his work."

"Really, Yuki? Then why were you sweating just now, you hallowed man of science?"

"You saw me sweat, Bianca, because you are reaching the point in your life here on this planet where it would not be good for me, as your friend, to withhold my feelings from you," he said with a crispness that somehow was tender. "You ask for the truth and I try my best to give it to you in the way you want. I just hope we can make all of this work out without too much pain for anyone. I have never done so much lying in my life as I've done in the past few weeks. You know, Olaf Bergquist and I know a lot of the same people. I see him at parties once in a while. I don't even want to think about what he will think when he finds out what you and I and Tony have been plotting all this time."

"It'll be fine, don't worry so much," she said, exhaling with some difficulty. "Olaf Bergquist will just have to deal with things. This is his story too. And as you just said, I'm at the point in my life where it is very important that I tell the truth. Well, you know, now is as good a time as any to start. And if you have to lie a little to help me do it, risk a little cocktail party social status, well, I don't care. Tell me you don't agree with me. I know this is very hard, and I appreciate what you are doing, I do, but tell me you know I have done the right thing. Please tell me I am doing the right thing."

"What I do agree to at this time is that I want you to rest," Yuki said as he got up and made sure the blinds were as tightly closed as possible. "Let's just take this whole ordeal one moment at a time. Because as crazy as you make me, Bianca, I'd rather have you alive here in this world than making everyone miserable from the other side."

"I'm glad you realize my power, Yuki," she said as she slowly slumped off the pillows. "I plan to use it until someone mightier than me tells me to stop. But speaking of power, you have got to find a way to get me to Iceland. That's what I want more than anything. I mean it. Either I've got to get there or those two kids have got to get here. This has got to happen to make all of this suffering worthwhile."

Chapter Eleven

Jenn fought hard against fatigue and tried to look out of the smeared window at the gray rock world all around, while still trying to keep up with what Tony Fionarello was shouting to her and the two other guys in the jeep.

Sven, the jeep's alleged driver, wore a black fleece balaclava and was a volcanology graduate student from Greenland who worked in Erik Bjarnason's laboratory. He was driving fast enough to pass most terrorism-avoidance driving tests (which she thought also might explain the head gear), but she figured that when you have to get to an exploding volcano, time really was worth more than money. Sitting next to her in the back was Fridrik, another graduate student in Dr. Bjarnason's lab, although he made it clear right away that he was Icelandic and a natural blonde who had never used hair color. He was completely focused on trying to keep his computer steady whenever Sven hit rocks or potholes. When he wasn't trying to type, he was yelling in Icelandic into one of the smallest mobile phones she had ever seen in her life.

She wished she was not so jet-lagged. Even she knew this was an experience totally worth remembering but she was so tired that she thought the only thing that might wake her up was a caffeine patch or a hit of cocaine (she had never tried either, but she was imagining their usefulness right now).

Still, she was coherent enough to know that when Dr. Fionarello was shouting, he was just trying to explain something that no ordinary civilian would understand. When he was screaming, he was trying to get Sven to either drive faster or use more caution, or to have Fridrik say something else in Icelandic to whomever he was talking to on the phone.

"Dr. Bjarnason, Erik–they go by first names here. There is a surplus of democracy in this nation, you'll meet him. He's brilliant. He's been out near Hekla for the past day or so, AND he's got some of his other people there and the TV people, let's hope they have not wrecked the place for us," Tony said in a fairly moderated shout as he kept whacking Sven on his black-gloved hands every few seconds, only to have Sven say he would be happy to drive if only a certain American bastard would stop hitting him. "We've been monitoring the earthquakes out there for a while now, this is important, write this down, multiple earthquakes precede volcanic eruptions. And now the place has gone insane with quakes, this thing is going to erupt. We just have to get there to see it."

She'd been in Iceland exactly 90 minutes. Tony Fionarello met her at the airport without Sven or Fridrik, accompanied solely by the driver of a limousine who was holding a small sign bearing Jenn's plainly printed name, along with the title of "Miss." Seeing the liveried driver and the big black car and knowing what she now knew about the country's stratospheric cost of living, she figured any doubts she may have had about her expenses being covered while keeping journalists out of the way of serious scientists were exercises in foolishness. As nice as the car was, and as bland as their conversation was (Icelandair is a pretty decent airline, isn't it?) they didn't spend too much time in the limousine as they transferred to the jeep within just a few miles, never mind any hotel for sleeping or unpacking, as Dr. Fionarello kept reminding her that there was a volcano ready to explode. It would not wait for any tired people who probably should have been hired a week or two earlier.

Dr. Fionarello seemed just as rushed in person as he had on the phone when he called her to let her know she'd be going to Iceland, in a way-too-smart-for-this-world, mad-scientist way of being hurried. But he was not impolite. She noticed that he did peer into her eyes for a long time when they first met and she hoped they didn't look too bloodshot; she'd had whisky on the plane in an attempt to sleep. She also felt that he shook her hand a bit too long, and rather carefully at that, as if he did not want to crush her veins. She was impressed that he did not just nod at her as many physicians would, as if to say, yes, here is your prescription, call the nurse for your next appointment. She tried hard to push an idea out of her head: he reminded her of the drawings on the paper old-time pizza parlors wrapped their pizzas in, the exuberant chef, all flaring mustache and wild dark, curly hair, artfully draped chef's toque and neckerchief, fingers circled in the OK, and that's a mighty good pizza signal. Because if she thought about it too hard, it would have been just too funny, and laughing at the guy probably would not be the best thing to do right now. She was still trying to figure out why she agreed to come to this place to do a type of work she had never done before.

Jenn pulled a notebook and pen out from her bag. She thought she'd better try to take some notes of the screams and shouts. Writing things down had become almost as natural to her as talking or breathing. Or feeling out of sorts. Which she felt at this moment, as well as a bit nauseous.

"Good, you just might be smart enough for us, and you probably look good on camera too," Dr. Fionarello said to her when he saw her furiously scribbling, obviously without realizing his condescension, as the jeep stopped hitting boulders. They suddenly arrived at an open area of huge craters, with one flat surface containing a battered helicopter.

"Move it folks, we have got to be there soon, soon, soon, this all started charging up on us a hell of a lot faster than I thought possible, how can a volcano start up in minutes without my permission," Dr. Fionarello yelled in a voice that Jenn thought was more Brooklyn baseball fanatic than San Francisco-raised academic. He jumped out of the car and started to run toward the helicopter, shouting to everyone that they had to get going.

God, is he always this wired, Jenn thought, scrambling to get her stuff out of the jeep and into the helicopter. She wondered what would make someone like Dr. Fionarello or Dr. Bjarnason choose people like Sven and Fridrik as assistants as she watched the two of them fling expensive equipment into the helicopter, seemingly without care for price or damage as they told her to hurry or scurry, she could not tell which word they actually meant to use.

She got into the helicopter and wondered whether they might already be too late, that maybe the volcano had already started to blow. She looked into the distance as she was crawling under the door and swore she saw a plume of fire spouting from the earth, even though she knew it was probably not possible for a fire to shoot up from a stretch of rock. But she also knew better than to say anything stupid to Dr. Fionarello

As the helicopter took off with a violent series of shakes, he did think to herself that it would be a very good thing if Mark got his pictures without risking death or injury. She felt certain she was in a Purgatory full of fire and screaming lunatics who could not drive very well, even if one was a natural blonde.

They were chopping along in the bluster for just a few minutes when Fridrik started screaming even louder than usual in Icelandic before he punched the phone off and let out a loud whoop.

"The mountain has blown, the mountain has blown," he screamed in English. "The whole place is going to hell! It's absolutely massive, there's thunder, there's lightning, they say it looks like lava is flowing like mad from the three craters near the southern end of the fissure, it's absolutely nuts."

Tony Fionarello smiled and slapped his hand hard on his thigh.

"Great, good and bloody great," he muttered loudly while Sven and Fridrik jabbered in very cacophonous Icelandic. "Fridrik, get back

on the phone with them NOW, this time I want you to humble yourself and speak entirely in English. Let's stay on top of this situation,
see if you can pick up anything useful from them on that computer.
I just hope those television people are getting their pictures without
getting anyone killed. I just can't believe the mountain blew before we
got there, this is so damned... DISAPPOINTING!"

Even though she kind of wanted to be there when the mountain
first blew, Jenn was glad to hear the volcano had finally erupted and
she hoped everyone would be safe, because to tell the truth, she was
more than a little afraid to get so very close to fire and earth tremors
and hot lava. But as she listened to the men emote around her, she did
wonder if she really did see fire spouting from the rock while she was
getting in the helicopter. Probably not, she thought. She was just way
too tired. And everyone was yelling too much.

Chapter Twelve

"Are you sure you don't want me to drive?" Caroline said anxiously as Olaf was quickly, but very carefully, stepping over an errant piece of ice to get to his car. "I'm happy to do it, really, and I won't wreck the Volvo."

"I'll be fine, it's a very short distance," he murmured as he opened the driver's door and then remembered that he needed to open her door as well.

"You're going to be okay, Olaf, everything will be fine in the end. Yuki said Bianca and her brother had a long talk about things. It sounds as if everyone is ready to finally set matters straight," she said, patting him lightly on the shoulder while he held the door open for her to get in.

"I feel a lot better about things than I did a few days ago, thanks to you and all you've done to make this happen today," he said, wishing the ride to the hospital had taken a bit more time. It was bad enough that he insisted Caroline stay in the room while he called Jenn the day after his first date with Caroline so he could see how things were going. Thank God Caroline insisted that she needed to stay in the room so she could help ensure he would not ask anything more. It was soothing to hear that Jenn was loving the whole adventure. She had told Olaf she thought Tony Fionarello was at least partially insane; young Dr. Bjarnason appeared to be much too busy with his volcano work to pay any attention to Jenn or to any journalists who might want to make him famous. He did not even care that Jenn prattled on like a schoolgirl for a minute or two about how well dressed this Mark guy was and how talented he was (with the camera, she didn't mention any other talents), although at this point, he didn't really care what his daughter did, as long as she stayed safe and happy.

As it was, Olaf could not remember ever hearing Jenn sounding so buoyant. Maybe all of this was the release Marco and so many others said she needed. Just how much anger and hatred she would release upon him once she heard the whole story was another matter. As much as he had unintentionally stifled Jenn throughout her childhood, she did manage somehow to develop a much more colorful personality than he or Christina ever could have imagined. It frightened him to think that maybe all of this needed to happen to free his child from so many of her fears and worries. Hours of endless talk and philosophizing with Caroline made him admit that he had not been the very best father all these years, and certainly not since Christina's death, but he was going to have to deal with that demon at another time.

"I'll be fine, don't worry," he said again, hoping he would not start blubbering in front of Yuki and Bianca and her brother. "I just didn't expect we'd have to deal with anything like Bianca being on death's door when I finally dealt with this issue. I had thought that Christina would have been along to help explain things to Jenn. I did not think that there would be this tremendous sense of urgency and danger, with Jenn going out to watch volcanoes with her unknown twin brother."

"If Bianca had not come to the hospital and met Jenn, who knows when you would have approached the situation," Caroline said. "I just hope no one goes nuts today. We all need to realize that no one will win if any of us gets too upset."

Olaf laughed a bit as he gave her a big smile. "Well, perhaps some of my ways are already rubbing off on you, hmm."

"I think you already rubbed some of yourself onto me last night, sir," she said quietly.

"Yes, that's true," he said after a small pause. He still could not believe that he had seen Caroline for four days in a row, and that he'd had sex with her at least that many times. She was not one of those women who wanted to talk while they were doing the deed, and she didn't seem to want to dissect any "relationship" they might or might not have at the moment. Maybe she was a free spirit, or maybe she had just become very, very good at keeping her cards close to her quite lovely chest. Of course, he wanted to say he loved her almost more than anything.

But he'd never been so tired in his life as he had been after having sexual relations with the lovely Caroline Smithson, who, amazingly enough, was as beautiful in person as she was in his mind. And her legs. How could anyone stretch their legs so far? Even at seven in the morning and without makeup, she was as close to a Playboy fantasy as he ever could have imagined possible. All of the tennis he played had not prepared him for these sorts of athletics. Maybe he was going to have to listen to Caroline and get into yoga and Pilates if he was going to need to be so flexible so often in the future. Thank God for ibuprofen and the freedom to take a day or two off from work.

"And speaking of, um, rubbing, I am glad you agree that we need to get through all of this first before we tell Jenn about you and me. This is going to be more than enough for her to handle without her having to think about you and I, what is the term they use now, hooking up, I don't know."

Caroline suppressed a very small laugh. She knew he was trying to sound upbeat but realized all too well that he was in a pretty terrible mood. The thought had crossed her mind more than once that Jenn may not want to speak with her again, that it was okay to be friends but that her father was off limits. She'd only had one fairly short email from Jenn, which was okay. She knew she was busy, and she was relieved that all seemed to be going well with the volcano work.

She saw the hospital and suddenly got very scared about having to face Yuki and Bianca in this very new and still rather uncomfortable role as Olaf's partner and accomplice of sorts. She had never had to function as a mediator. "I really don't think Jenn will be as upset as you think, if you do this right and don't lie any more than you've already done," she said with forced optimism. "But the poor kid is going to have more than enough on her plate for the foreseeable future," she said. "Don't take this the wrong way, but I really and truly hope that if Bianca is meant to die, that she does not do it too soon. We need some time for everyone to vent and fume and then find some sort of peace."

"I may think this Bianca to be a complete societal disgrace, but she did give birth to my daughter and she gave me the chance to be her father and I cannot discount the fact that Jenn may have some feelings about her once she knows the truth. It's just very hard to have to stomach all of this after not saying anything all of these years. But I know I have to take it."

"It will be okay," she said as they got to the ramp. "I'm just glad Yuki is in on things. He will do a lot to make sure things stay reasonable, he won't permit any screaming and shouting, not that getting upset is going to make matters any better."

They slowly walked hand-in-hand to the hospital. He looked at Caroline and thought he'd never seen anyone look more alluring in a black fox fur hat than she did at that moment, even though he had a fleeting thought that Christina was looking down on him from the other world and telling one of her angel supervisors that her husband had completely abandoned his Christian strength and fallen for a real trollop, one who wasn't even of Scandinavian descent or Lutheran.

Caroline looked at Olaf and realized he was having yet another love-struck moment. While she really liked seeing them, as this was probably the 105th such moment of his she had witnessed since the dinner at Le Petit Oiseau, even she knew this was the absolutely wrong time for such ideas. Even though she had waited a long time to finally meet a man who found her absolutely beguiling. And vice versa.

"By the way, I called Marco and he agreed to meet us there. I figured since he knows the whole story already," she said, hoping yet trusting that he would not explode. "I just think it is easier for everyone to have their say today and get it all done."

"It's fine, I figured someone would have called him," Olaf said dryly as they reached the hospital's lobby desk. "This whole nightmare is just full of people not telling anyone anything. Everyone knows a little bit, but absolutely no one really knows what to do. And everyone will still be talking after it is all said and done. I have started to get used to the idea that I am not going to be in charge of everything from now on, which is killing me, but I am getting used to it. So let's just get up there and get this over with, and as fast as possible, please."

Caroline gave his hand a very firm squeeze and said nothing. She felt a lot like the little woman standing by her politician man after he got in trouble—smiling pretty at the news conference.

"So, Bianca, I hope you are ready. We need to get this done," Tony said, his voice coming in much too loudly on the scratchy speaker phone. Yuki rushed in to turn down the volume. "Yuki, are you still okay with doing this today?"

Bianca motioned for Yuki to stay quiet as she pushed her freshly washed, conditioned, colored and styled hair back, making sure she did not get even one stray hair caught in the peridot drop earrings she picked to wear today. "Tony, it's fine, everyone is already on their way over and I know, you've told me this now about five million times that we need to get this done while you've got Jenn and Erik settling down to their assigned homework," she said sadly, looking vacantly at one of her pillows. "I'm as ready as I am ever going to be. I just want this over, and as fast as possible."

It was hard for her to admit to herself that she had let things get out of hand just so she could, as always, do things her way. Tony was pissed at her and she knew it; she hated the feeling. Her brother may have set a new record for use of the "f" word on the phone the other day. If she did not know beforehand that Tony was angry with her about how she handled things once she got to Minnesota, she certainly knew it now. She knew he was angry that his work was involved as well, even though he also said he knew it was useless to still be angry with her about everything. The same was probably true for Yuki, although Yuki did not engage in emotional nuclear reactions like Tony. He had just taken to wearing a look of sad disappointment much of the time.

"It's kind of interesting that Olaf had this co-worker of Jenn's do all of the arranging of this conference," she said, throwing a few of the pillows into a corner. "But today is as good a day as any to die."

"So we are agreed that we'll let Yuki get everything going, he's the one who talked with Caroline. He'll talk about how awkward this must be for everyone, all of that crap, and then you just go into how you wanted to get to know Jenn while she was still an innocent with regard to her being your natural child, right," Tony said, in the way he talked whenever he had to maintain composure in front of other people. "Let's just do it the way Yuki and I want to do it, just this one time, let's not get any more emotional and bent out of shape than we have to because this is already one hell of a bloody mess."

Yuki stood in the corner with his arms folded, nodding silently in agreement, while Bianca stared at the ceiling.

"Tony, we're all set. We'll just have to do our best," Yuki said with more than a touch of resignation, not looking up from the floor. "Now we just need everyone to get over here."

Tony asked Yuki to turn the television in the meantime to a cable channel so he could hear if there was any more news about either the volcano or the president's latest sex scandal, as the Icelandic news media did not seem to think it was worth getting too upset about something like extramarital American presidential sex and thus did not provide very much coverage of the story. Laurence, always eager to see a real show, especially one where screaming might be involved, knocked loudly at the door just when the three of them had become rather engrossed in an unwittingly amusing exclusive interview with the woman linked to the president. She was claiming she had been hired to do nothing but research on the president's election opponent: how was she supposed to know the president would find her so attractive, or that she would not be able to resist him. One could not say no to one's commander-in-chief.

"Thank you, Laurence. You can tell everyone to come in," Yuki said while suppressing an uncustomary big laugh, thinking the president could do much better. "We're all here."

Chapter Thirteen

"Actually, Hekla is the Icelandic word for 'short, hooded cloak,' and we can sort of understand why the volcano was named that, given that it is frequently shrouded, or you might say hooded, by cloud cover," Erik said as charmingly as he could to the British wire service journalist. He was pleasant enough, and he spoke in a very posh manner, very Queen's English, but since he had difficulty grasping the difference between magma and tephra, never mind volcanic ash, Erik thought further attempts at explanation would be futile so maybe he could at least make himself look learned in Icelandic lore and language. He hoped the reporter would stop asking questions and perhaps go off for some tea.

Charming was not exactly on Erik Bjarnason's to-do list for the day, but he knew charm helped when you wanted to get on with your work, which included trying to find some time for a nap. Nor was heeding Jenn Bergquist's admonition (friendly enough, but still a firm admonition) to put on a nice sport coat and a pressed and starched shirt and let her put some powder foundation on his face to cut the shine so he could sit in his sunny, well-equipped laboratory (clean enough despite the presence of Sven and Fridrik and the leftover pizza and hyper-caffeine drink containers they were constantly leaving behind) and give interviews about the wonders of this latest volcanic eruption to a bunch of journalists. At least Jenn did not make him put on a suit and tie, though she did watch him conduct the interview with the British journalist with pursed lips, and he wasn't sure if she was concerned about the journalist's lack of comprehension or if she thought Erik's English was not posh enough for use in the United Kingdom. Even though Erik very much liked the two suits he had custom-made, they were not right for these interviews given the fact that most serious scientists (and especially volcanologists) were supposed to look sort of char-broiled and grungy.

And charming took some doing. He'd just put in too many days that required saint-like patience and a great many hyper-caffeine drinks to get through the work of dealing with the television crew (including that Mark guy, who seemed to be checking Erik out a little too much for the specific needs of television and did not seem at all romantically interested in Miss Bergquist), being the proper Icelandic volcano specialist while still showing due respect to the chummy enough but loud and kind of obnoxious Dr. Tony Fionarello, not being abrupt with the well-meaning, very attractive, intelligent in an unexpectedly flinty way but clearly Not-Ready-for-Real-Life-Volcanic-Eruptions Jenn Bergquist, and handling everything else involved with managing and studying the mountain's latest big blow. Including keeping Sven and Fridrik and the rest of his group at work and in line with no breaks for any alcoholic beverages or herbal substances of any type. On top of it all, he was panicked the whole time that the curious volcano watchers, who traveled the world in search of sprays of beautiful hot lava but did not seem to fully understand that volcanoes are not just spectacular, they can burn or suffocate or cut you dead, would try to come too close to the site, even though it was now known that Hekla was capable of producing very dangerous pyroclastic flows.

But this time around, there were no pyroclastic flows. He was very glad he had taken pains to put on his diplomat hat and give as much of a thorough briefing as possible on the situation to the government (including the prime minister, who was more interested than Erik had thought possible for a politician). Maybe he could help him get some additional government funding for the lab.

Because no one died or was hurt following the eruption, he was able to look like a real national scientific hero when he did the interview with the new state television anchor, coincidentally one of his primary school classmates. She reminded him that he used to tell her she was a very pretty girl and that he liked her mother's Christmas cake. He really did remember how good the cake was, very lemony.

"Well, Dr. Bjarnason, thank you very, very much for your time, I am sure you still have a great deal of monitoring work to do in the aftermath of this latest event that really does prove Iceland is, well, I really must say it, the 'Land of Fire and Ice,'" the journalist said in a state of near ecstasy as he capped his Mont Blanc pen with a flourish Erik thought more suited to an Edwardian comedic actor than to a journalist.

"The pleasure is all mine," Erik said in as unhurried a tone as he could manage, thrilled the interviews were reaching an end. "Feel free to contact me. Jenn Bergquist over there has the information, if you have any questions whatsoever," he lied in as non-slimy a way as plausible as he watched the guy stop on his way out to shake hands with Jenn several seconds longer than was probably necessary and tell her how wonderful it was that she could arrange this interview given "her" busy schedule.

Jenn's worried look was replaced with one of bemusement as she watched Erik yank off his sport coat and then carefully brush it with a lint roller and button it before hanging it on a wooden hanger in the little hut within the lab that he called his office.

"Well, that wasn't so terrible was it? No one extracted your hernia or anything, did they? You lost no blood today," Jenn said. "I'd actually be upset with you for rushing these interviews—we did tell them they'd have 15 to 20 minutes with you, and not 14 minutes and 50 seconds, but you did a pretty good job, all things considered."

"What do you mean?" he said listlessly, sitting at one of the lab's computers and motioning for her to sit down as well.

"You're very droll for a guy who doesn't do seem to do very much besides drink beer, mostly successfully chase women, monitor volcanoes, and then watch them blow up while trying not to get killed at the same time," she said as she looked at the chair to see if it was dirty, which it was not, it was low-bid Scandinavian metal office design but it was clean. "I just meant that you probably have never gone through formal media training, you likely were not senior enough within the faculty here at the university to be the lead man on the interviews the last time Hekla exploded, and you know all of these reporters will talk to Dr. Fionarello too, and you know how well he does. He knows how to massage reporters."

"I don't know if an ability to be droll, as you say, and a keen scientific intellect and work ethic are incompatible," he said as he swiveled away from the computer and looked right at her, head against the very forest green wall and hands folded behind his head. "Might I ask a question, as long as you seem to want to make comments? Are you this, what's the right word in English, insouciant, with the scientists and physicians you work with at home? Or is it just the fact that you want to stand up to this foreign guy who wasn't crazy about having you come out. I meant no offense then and I mean no offense now, but you have no background in volcanology. I don't even know if you are into hiking mountains. So are you this assertive all the time?"

Jenn smiled a tiny smile. She knew what he said was not an insult, but rather an invitation to joust. Which could be kind of fun, since he did not think her stupid in every manner. But he was right, she might not have been quite insouciant these last several days, but she was sort of surprised to hear herself tell both Sven and Fridrik at different times to shut the hell up and to please speak in English in her presence and to not throw notebooks or anything else at her anymore, no matter how bumpy the road. When they had gotten a safe distance away from the volcano—which was kind of too bad, it really was awesome to see and hear, the aural nature of volcanoes was underestimated—she told Dr. Fionarello to calm down a bit so the *National*

Geographic people could do an interview befitting his status and get some good pictures of him in the spare clean jacket she knew to pull out of his bag. He actually laughed, told her okay, and seemed more touchingly amused than angry or upset, and he did settle down. But the idea of being insouciant reminded her of some little French schoolgirl in a beribboned beret who had just found a fresh red rose in the snow to show her daddy. She might be feeling more relaxed here in Iceland but she did not think she was insouciant.

"I apologize if you think I am giving you too much grief," she said confidently and even somewhat flirtatiously, which struck her as weird. She thought Erik was sort of priggish as well as a showoff, and she was supposed to go out with Mark tonight as he was returning to the U.S. the next afternoon. "You're right, I know you don't think I belong here and you know what? I don't even think I belong here. But I'm here at least for a few more days, and I am going to stick up for myself, I'm probably never going to see you again, and while you may be the successor to Tony Fionarello in the vaunted world of volcanoes, you won't get to the top of that mountain just by hiking and being good with seismographs. You're going to have to rely some on people like me, even if you don't think we know what we are doing."

"A very good defense, Miss Bergquist," he said with a very toothy near smirk as he moved quickly back before the computer screen. "For your sake as well as my own, let's hope you are right about my ascent and, in the name of international friendship, let's also hope you are wrong, let's hope I do see you again at some point. But for now, let me show you what I'm trying to do here before Dr. Tony comes back to scream about something else. He has been on that phone call with his sister for a long time now. I hope everything is okay. Although, to be honest, I personally don't think he has much reason to scream at either of us, this was about as picture-perfect and trouble-free of an eruption as anyone could hope for or schedule."

"I'll agree with you on that. You ran a good show out there, Dr. Bjarnason. And speaking of your volcanic prowess, I want to ask you about something, because I've been doing some reading."

"What do you want to know?"

"I confess I was reading about volcanology in general before I got here and saw that the volcano at Yellowstone has a caldera. I don't know why I'm interested, I guess the thought that an eruption can cause such a collapse in the land is kind of fascinating, don't ask me why. Was the eruption at Hekla big enough to cause one there too?"

"Well, no, Hekla doesn't have one, but it's a good question you pose," Erik said, mildly impressed that Jenn even knew to ask such a question in the first place. "A caldera is, as you said, a collapse of land that occurs following a volcanic eruption. They are triggered by the emptying of a volcano's magma chamber. The reason Hekla does not have a caldera is because its magma chamber is quite deep—probably 11 kilometers or about seven miles below the surface."

"Oh, okay."

"But no, it was a good question, especially as a lot of people who might watch the program do know a lot about Yellowstone and perhaps not much about a volcano such as Hekla. By the way, 'caldera' comes from the Spanish and Latin words that mean 'cooking pot.'"

"That makes a lot of sense, I suppose."

"So listen, can I change the subject for a little while?"

"Sure."

"Um, this is a bit awkward, so forgive me, but I really feel I need to tell you why I think you are walking up the wrong street when it comes to that Mark photographer guy."

She gave him a look that said it was none of his business.

"Go ahead, I know you are going to tell me anyway."

Chapter Fourteen

"Well, Olaf, you really have surprised me. I never would have thought 36 years ago that you had this much fight in you. You were such a tame little gerbil in those days," Bianca said in a purr that was nothing less than sarcastic while trying not to look too much at Caroline, who clearly was Olaf's girlfriend or at least his friend with bedroom benefits. She wondered how she maintained such a stunning shape and thick head of very blonde hair given that she had to be about the same age as Bianca. Maybe she was even older. She guessed that Caroline probably had had some plastic work done around the eyes and forehead, didn't drink much booze and never ate anything. She must be one of those who allowed herself only one low-fat chocolate chip cookie every month.

"You know, I'll admit it for all to hear that it is my fault that I am here in this hospital. But it is not my fault that I wanted to get to know the children I gave birth to, knowing that I may not come out of this place in anything but a cardboard box or perhaps a ceramic urn," Bianca continued in a voice that she hoped sounded humble. "You cannot blame me for this. I kept my end of the bargain all these years. I never breathed a word. Their sperm donor, the now 'famous' basketball star and former cocaine addict never even knew what happened to them or where they went. I never tried to contact you or your dear, late wife, and I never bothered Erik's parents either. So.... not now."

"Yes, I can see why you wanted to get to know Jenn and Erik at

this time, I can. Let's establish that once and for all so we can try to move on here," Olaf sputtered, noticing that Caroline had not stopped looking completely mortified almost from the moment Yuki Atagari tried, in his gracious and calm way, to welcome everyone into the room. It looked like someone tripping on LSD had decorated it. "All I am saying is that I wish you had contacted me first, before you decided to come here and get to know my daughter. That's all. And maybe it would have been nice for someone to try to say something to Erik, although it would have been more difficult given that his parents have been dead for the past five years."

"Listen everyone, I think we all know that maybe none of this was done the right way, okay," Tony shouted too loudly over the speakerphone, even though Yuki and Marco both tried to dial down the phone's volume. "Olaf should have told Jenn she was adopted, even if he told her nothing else. Bianca probably should have called Olaf before she decided to come to Minnesota for her treatment. Bianca should never have become an alcoholic. Yuki should have been a bastard for once in his life and insisted that Bianca either go somewhere else for her transplant or at the least, call Olaf. But you know, in a way, we are very lucky that Erik is in the same field as I am. That has made it a lot easier for me to be involved, which, for the record, I never really wanted to be anyway. But someone around here needed to exercise some reason so these kids don't get hurt any more than they have to, because let's admit it, we're getting all hot and bothered here because we care about Jenn and Erik. No matter what sort of plan we cook up, they are going to be hurt. And some of us here also care about what happens to Bianca."

"Thank you, Tony, but you know that Erik is not a volcanologist due to pure luck," Bianca said, her sparkly shadowed eyes fixed firmly on the ceiling. She tried not to look at Caroline.

"Well, that's all well and brilliant, fine, we'll all accept your spiritual thought process and then let's let me be the monster in all of this, fine. At this point, I almost don't care what any of you think," Olaf said, his posture at its Marine best. "But can we stop throwing bombs at one another and decide what we are going to do? How are we going to tell Jenn and Erik? I came here to try to find a halfway civilized way out of this mess."

"Speaking of Jenn and Erik, how are they getting along, are they getting, how shall I say it, are they getting on a bit too well for everyone's level of comfort?" Marco added softly, all the while wishing he had a large glass of whisky and one of Bianca's large silk pillows to use as a seat cushion on the creaky chair Yuki had offered him. "I know some of us here were worried about that. Maybe Dr. Fionarello can say something, maybe a tad more gently this time? We seem to have trouble adjusting your volume on this end, Doctor."

"Please call me Tony. I have just had a crazy last few days and as it is, Jenn has been sitting with Erik while he did some interviews that I made him do. The kid is a near genius, but he does not seem to understand that publicity drives grant and government money," Tony said. "And as for the other matter, I would have to say that from what I've seen we have no problem there at all. My view is that he thinks she's a lightweight, and she seems to think he is a bit full of himself. She's had dinner at least once with that photographer guy Mark, who, in the interest of lightening things up here a bit, seems as gay to me as they get. Who brings a different designer leather coat for every day of the week when he travels overseas to a volcano zone?"

"That's a lot of luggage. I don't know if I even endorse that level of vanity," Marco said as Caroline and Yuki finally broke fairly wide smiles.

"Do you really think he's gay, Tony? I can't say I picked that up on him at all," Bianca said, sitting up a bit straighter against a new royal blue silk pillow.

"You've been very sick, Bianca, your cosmic antennae are off, but I am telling you, that guy is not heterosexual," Tony said in a manner that sounded as if he could not believe anyone's radar could be that off kilter.

"Well, yes, whatever. That is a bit of good news about Jenn and Dr. Bjarnason, although I suppose it would be nice if they could find a way to get along in the future," Yuki said, looking brightly at Caroline, who returned his hopeful look, and then glanced at his watch, wishing these negotiations would end soon enough so he could go up to his office, shut the door, pull the shades, and put a cool towel on his forehead and then wonder why he got pulled into this disaster.

"I apologize in advance if anyone thinks me impertinent, but I think I have come up with a plan that might just work," Tony said after no one else spoke. "My work here in Iceland is done. I want to see you, Bianca, and I'd like to see you alive rather than dead, so I am going to hurry home. I have gone ahead and spent more of my own personal money and am paying for a very big deal colleague from the U.S. Geological Survey to come to Minneapolis to meet me. He wanted to talk to Erik anyway, so I also will pay for Erik to come along with me. Everyone following me so far?"

"Yes, Tony, and I know you are paying for things and you know that I have the money. It will be your money if I don't make it out of this hospital alive anyway, so I don't really need to hear anything else about that part of it," Bianca said, looking squarely at Olaf's stony face. "So what's the rest of your marvelous plan?"

"Okay, so that's it. Erik and Jenn come back with me, he meets with the USGS guy, and then I figured Olaf and Marco, maybe Caroline too, I don't know, can talk to Jenn and I will talk to Erik," Tony said almost too brightly. "Maybe Yuki can help me out on the Erik end, although you don't have to tell me, you are already involved more than you wanted."

"I actually think that is a pretty good plan, considering," said Caroline. "I think the main thing is that we do this as quickly as possible."

Olaf looked around the room for an acknowledgement of sympathy that only Marco and maybe Caroline and Yuki were willing to offer. Bianca just continued to stare at him, although he did notice that she was wearing pretty good-sized peridots on her ears.

"Yes, the main thing is that we do this fast. This sounds like as good of a plan as any," Olaf finally said. "There is no other way, I suppose."

"Excellent," Tony said. "Listen, Olaf, I think this just might work. I also think that no one here wants to persecute you, at least I don't. I just think we want to get this over with and in the end, it might be a good thing. You can look at it this way if you like, both Jenn and Erik grew up as only children and now they might be able to have each other. They certainly bicker like siblings forced to share the same toys, I'll tell you that much."

"That's lovely, Tony," Olaf said without as much bitterness as Marco and Caroline might have expected. "I guess they have a right to know they are twins."

"They do have a right," Bianca said quietly while looking directly at Olaf's startlingly blue eyes that clearly were going to shed tears as soon as he left the hospital. "We all need to give them that right."

"Well, good, I think we can break this meeting up now, and we'll leave it to Tony to get Erik and Jenn back here to Minneapolis," said an obviously relieved Yuki. "In the meantime, maybe we all should think about how we will handle things once Jenn and Erik know the truth. What I mean to say is that we have to think about how they will meet Bianca. My logical side tells me that they need to meet her as soon as possible after we tell them, maybe give them a day or so to decompress and let the news settle and then they come in here, alone, and they have a chance to talk to her. But we put no pressure on them. If they don't really want to meet her, we don't force them too much, and we don't insist they stay in the room any longer than they want. And while we all do some thinking about my idea, I am going to insist again that Bianca get some rest. I need to remind you that I am trying to do my best to make certain Bianca leaves this hospital alive, well and pink with a new liver."

"That's very sweet, Yuki. Quite possibly unrealistic, but sweet,"

Bianca said, her ordinary purr in place once again.

"Very sweet indeed," said Olaf, who quickly grabbed Caroline's hand as well as Marco's as he went to follow Yuki out the door. "I think Tony's and Dr. Atagari's ideas are probably the best any of us can conjure. I don't see any other way. Let's just hope everything works out." He made a half-turn that startled Caroline and Marco and stared directly at Bianca, all of her heavily teased hair and jewelry not completely disguising her jaundice and sickness. It suddenly dawned on him that no matter what he had been thinking these past few weeks, Bianca did deserve some sympathy. She probably was not going to return to San Francisco alive. "And Bianca, let me just say it was good to see you again, despite what we said here today," he said. He hoped it did not come off as too patronizing, as he only cared that she would not upset Jenn any more than necessary when they had their grand summit. "Thank you for giving me my daughter."

"Thank you very much, Olaf. I do appreciate it," Bianca said almost cautiously as she twirled some of her hair in her fingers that then got tangled in one of her earrings. "And goodbye to you, Marco darling. I am so, so happy to have seen you once again. And goodbye to you too, Caroline. Don't be shy about coming up here."

Caroline forced a smile. There had been times when she had been a slut in her life but this was, well, this was the proverbial something else.

Chapter Fifteen

Erik concluded that being around Tony Fionarello was not always rough duty, especially when the famous one insisted on taking him and Jenn to the best restaurant in Reykjavik, arguably one of the world's finest places for seafood. It was true that Erik would have preferred to go out with the two of them tomorrow night, or the night after. He was still so wiped out from the past several weeks. It was always exciting for a volcanologist to work an eruption. But the work involved in an eruption, especially one featuring a major television crew and someone like Tony Fionarello, required a lot more exertion and muscle power than what people saw when they sat down to watch the program with a cold one in their hand. Still, he had wanted to try the restaurant from the time it opened but had always stayed away because of the cost.

But now he was sitting here in the bar waiting for Tony and Jenn to arrive, paying as much for a fairly ordinary Danish beer as he would shell out in New York or Washington, D.C. for a fine Oregon Pinot Noir. He was dressed up yet again but that was actually okay. The custom-made English suit and Italian tie needed to get out and get some fresh air once in a while. Maybe even the insouciant, no, actually kind of snarky, Jenn Bergquist would be impressed, though he knew he was no match in the fashion department with Mark, who was now safely on his way back to the U.S.

Erik didn't think Jenn was completely thrilled about going out tonight either, even if she did seem to get on with Tony in a twisted sort of way. He was reminded of the once-popular Catholic wife and Jewish husband comedy team when he saw them together, the way he would get completely flustered and hyperactive about almost anything and she would stop him in his tracks with one fairly dry, but powerfully effective, verbal slap or a quizzical look. He envied Jenn's seemingly effortless ease at throwing disdain in Tony's direction while remaining well within the sphere of respectability. What made him feel worse is that it was Jenn, and not Erik (who was supposed to be in charge: this was his turf, Hekla was his mountain), who not only handled the reporters in what he thought was a professional and commendable way, but also sort of functioned like the chief operating officer of the Hekla Eruption Operation. She even got Sven and Fridrik to agree to eat their pizza in the area set aside for breaks and to excavate and disinfect their respective office cubbyholes.

He looked at his watch and saw that they were now about ten minutes late, but he figured getting upset would not do him any good. He knew Tony likely thought him to be not much more than a really bright scientist with a great future due to his intelligence and skills (and his looks, which Tony took wicked pleasure in pointing out all the time, especially in front of that Mark) but still a wet blanket who tried to make the great Dr. Fionarello stay on schedule and do things according to the proper protocol and with some regard for efficient use of financial resources.

He also knew he had to be grateful to Tony for the whole experience, being in a big-time international television documentary, and, for that matter, getting to be the star of the show. He even knew that it was useful to have Jenn around to construct the "talking points" she and Tony insisted on preparing before they did the reporter interviews as well as to have her teach him how to do a better job of conveying complex information in a way that did not betray his science but also did not lose or talk down to readers and viewers. He still was not sure everyone seeing him on a video clip would understand, but that was not really his problem.

As he tried to sip his beer slowly so as to not have to order a second right after their arrival, he thought about how this whole saga was probably going to be very good in the near future for his lab budget, all of the people in it (even Sven and Fridrik and their trash, which likely would multiply, despite Jenn's efforts, especially if they had more money to spend on pizza and drinks) and, above all, his own career. Maybe he would not have to stay in Iceland forever after all. Maybe now he'd have a shot at a really big job, not some instructor or assistant professor deal at some third or fourth-rate school that specialized in semi-precious stone mining, but a fully tenured position at one of the great North American universities. Maybe even his alma mater, the University of Washington. It would be outstanding to be back in Seattle now that the grunge era was over and it would be a bonus to earn a decent salary. Plus, if he were on faculty at a top-notch school, he could really deliver a very firm kick to the ass of that twerp former classmate of his who thought himself so special but now was lucky to be at the University of Far Northeastern Nowhere teaching freshman geology, all thanks to the twerp's fraudulent use of hundreds of thousands of dollars of National Science Foundation money.

"Sorry we're late," Tony nearly shouted, obviously indifferent to the room's moderately decadent yet monkishly hushed atmosphere. He and Jenn were almost sprinting to the bar, characteristic of another particularly American trait Erik could not stomach. If you were already late, why run and make even more of a spectacle out of yourself? Why not just walk at a normal pace and then make your apologies in a civilized tone?

"Sorry Erik, it's my fault. This blouse needed ironing, and, I didn't want you to think we could not clean up properly," Jenn said, looking with arched eyebrows at Tony's smudged shoes. She hopped onto the chair next to Erik motioning in what Erik thought was a very expert, almost manly way, to grab the bartender's attention.

"It's quite all right. This is probably the first time I've really been able to sit still since we had to get going on the Hekla activity," Erik said as he pulled his chair a bit further away from Jenn's to make room for her massive handbag.

"Yeah, well that is ALL done with for now," Tony said in a slightly quieter voice. He saw that Jenn was already facing a tall Crown Royal and ginger ale. The girl did have promise after all—she clearly had consistently good taste in alcohol. "Time to celebrate. I wanted to come here because I wanted to treat both of you for all of your great work, and especially you, Dr. Bjarnason, for running such an efficient eruption. I had heard that this is the place for cod, especially that salted cod that apparently does not taste like dried and salted particle board."

"You're talking about bacalao, or, as we might say it more properly in Icelandic, *saltfiskur*," Erik said, appraising the scuffed orange-brown comfort shoes, worn khaki pants and frayed dress shirt Tony had chosen to wear. Why Tony was puzzled as to why he had such difficulty attracting beautiful women in bars was beyond him.

"That's it! I saw the chef preparing it on some travel program," Jenn said, taking what Erik thought were rather large gulps of her drink while surveying the room for anything more interesting to look at than Tony or Erik. "When is our reservation anyway? I'm starving, but didn't you say you made the reservation for seven, right? Although I know we got here a little late so we won't have as much schmooze time, sorry."

"It's quite okay," Erik said, thinking about how many times he was going to have continue to be gracious and concede to Tony's and Jenn's quirks before they would finally go back to the U.S. "Although Jenn says she is starving, I don't think any of us will be in any imminent danger of starvation."

"No, I guess not. I'm fine with my drink for now," Jenn murmured with a look on her face that clearly said to Erik, *God, what a pissy little creep you are.*

"Well, you're fine now, Miss Bergquist, but I think I'd like to see how you are with a few more in you. You've been so busy supervising me that it will be great to see you kick back a bit," Tony said with a sort of cockeyed wink as he finally grasped the drink it seemed he ordered hours ago.

"So you mean to tell me that you need me to return to Minneapolis with you, and with Jenn, so I can talk to the U.S. Geological Survey bigwig in person about doing some work with them in the U.S.?" Erik said with more incredulity than he had probably voiced in years. He was no longer paying much attention to his now cooling molten lava Belgian chocolate dessert, one that he thought was just too trite given his profession but actually had been excited to eat. "And we are leaving tomorrow afternoon? And you've already talked to my department chair, who has not talked to me, small detail, and he's already taken the liberty of talking to my people to tell them I'll be in America for the next week?"

"Yes, Erik, all of it," Tony said. He saw that Jenn, although happy to have heard that she would be going home in no less than Icelandair business class, was uncomfortable with all of these other revelations. She was probably going to need several more Crown Royals to wash down the cake she had devoured. "I do apologize for not bringing you in on all of these negotiations but, come on, you were busy with the work, you were doing what Jenn tells me was a fantastic job on the interviews, and you don't ever want to turn down a chance to talk to these USGS poobahs. Besides, you're an Icelandic citizen. Minneapolis is sort of the epicenter of Scandinavian life in the United States, so you should see where so many of your people went to avoid having to hunt whales and live off of turnips and dried cod for most of the year."

"Yes, well, I guess some of, as you put it, 'my people' did want out of Iceland years ago, although I think more Icelanders went to Manitoba in Canada than to Minnesota," Erik said. "I am not ungrateful for the opportunity to talk to Dr. Big Deal USGS, and I am not ungrateful for all you've done for me these past several weeks. I just wish you had talked to me first. I do have responsibilities."

"Erik, I'm sorry if I was too hasty, but I cannot emphasize enough that time is of the essence," Tony said while imitating Jenn's technique to have another drink quickly brought to the table. "The guy won't be in Minneapolis long, I have got to see my sister, our work here is mostly done, Sven and Fridrik and the rest of your crew can handle things for a week, I think they ingest enough caffeine in one hour to get the job done, and Miss Bergquist here needs to get home to keep handling my sister's media relations. So let's enjoy the rest of our dinner. Then you get some rest tonight and tomorrow we head out for another cold city. Okay?"

"That sounds just fine to me," Jenn said softly. "You know, Erik, you might just like Minneapolis. Don't be so upset, you might have some fun. You know, my dad and his former partner at his firm, that wonderful old Italian man I told you both about, they want to have me over for a big breakfast as soon as I get back. You both could come along if you want some amusement, and if Marco makes his famous blueberry-raspberry muffins, you will not regret it."

"Erik and I have our meeting with the USGS guy the morning after we get to town but for sure, we'll hang out with your father and your surrogate grandfather another day while we are there. This Marco guy sounds like what I aspire to be should I live that long," Tony said while looking at Erik as if to say, come on boy, look a little bit lively. "But I am just wondering how your Norwegian proper father, at least from what you've told me about him, became so close to such a man of the world."

"I've been wondering that since I was old enough to think complex thoughts," Jenn said with a bit of a laugh while hoping Erik would snap out of it soon, if they were going to have to be together for at least a few more days. She prayed she would not have to sit next to either of them on the plane. She wanted to get some sleep on the flight so she would be in decent form when she had to face Olaf and Marco. Because she was going to have to tell them that not only had Mark admitted to her in confidence that he was mostly gay but just a bit bisexual (and she would tell them that, so she could end the Mark discussion she knew they both would want to have quickly, and then she'd also have to make sure to tell them she did not sleep with the guy) but that Tony and some of the others told her she had done a very good job while she was in Iceland.

"Well, it seems as if I am leaving tomorrow, for fun or not," Erik said abruptly but with much less volume as he gave both Jenn and Tony a smile that could have been painted on a puppet. He took a small forkful of cake and realized that Tony was right—it needed warming if it was to be fully enjoyed. He was not finished with these two yet, even though he secretly wanted to tell them that for some time now he had wanted to get out of Iceland for something besides scientific conferences in poverty-stricken places like Manila or Jakarta. But he was not going to tell them a thing. He would let Tony and Jenn keep ordering cocktails. If anyone was going to be shit-faced tonight, he was not going to be among that crowd.

Chapter Sixteen

The feeling of having a clear and calm head after enough sleep was so wonderful Jenn resolved she would probably never again drink alcohol on international flights lasting six hours or less. It was nice to come back home to brilliant sunshine and see the snow gone from the sidewalk below her apartment, even if it was still much colder than it had been in Iceland.

And she was thrilled that she hadn't been forced to sit next to either Erik or Tony on the plane. If she had sat next to Erik, she would have felt forced to try to find something to talk about that didn't make him treat her like a bright high school sophomore or require him to snap out some sort of Viking retort. Tony's presence would have forced her to put thick swabs of cotton in her ears to withstand his manic jabbering. She had planned ahead and hoped to take an anti-histamine so she could fall asleep as quickly as the capsules kicked in. It was pure luck that her seatmate was an elderly tourist who was out for the count for the whole of the flight, nodding off to dreamland even before the fairly tasty dinner of langoustines in garlic butter. She had to admit that it was decent of Tony to upgrade them to business class, and was relieved when he told them he used his own money and not any grant funds to do so.

In fairness, Erik had perked up some on the way to the airport at Keflavik, actually laughing a few times in a genuine way about normal human things that had nothing to do with geology, and he had been visibly impressed with the Minneapolis skyline when they were approaching downtown in the cab. It was kind of cute to see his happiness when they arrived at the hotel she'd recommended for him and Tony to stay at for the week. Tony didn't say anything, but she knew he was used to staying at pretty posh hotels when he was not working in the field. She wondered if he thought this place would be too pedestrian. It did have four stars. She thought Erik was probably a little embarrassed to have been so enthused about the hotel in front of Tony, and she actually felt kind of sorry for him. It wasn't his fault he was accustomed to relatively modest travel budgets.

She looked in the mirror as she stroked on her mascara and clearly was pleased that she actually saw smoother and somewhat brighter skin. Maybe all of that talk about the Icelandic geothermal springs was true, as she did feel damn near great after days of nearly daily swims in hot gurgling water full of minerals. She had not wanted to try the pasty white silica mud masks so many raved about but the gentle yet curiously alien-like staff at the spa she managed to get into just before leaving town convinced her of their value, even if it did cost almost $200 U.S. She'd have to make sure she told Caroline all about the place and the women's very weird sing-songy voices. It was all so "Twilight Zone," minus Rod Serling's intonations.

She felt good even though she was on her way to Olaf's for one of the all-carbohydrate breakfast feasts he was so proud of making about twice a year, and she was looking forward to eating a few of Marco's muffins. Of course, when didn't she look forward to food? She had to admit that her father did make good pancakes, even though it was tough for him to tell everyone that they were from a Swedish recipe.

As for Caroline, Olaf had not mentioned anything about her when Jenn spoke with him the few times she did call from Iceland, or in the handful of short emails she sent to let him know she was alive and not indulging too much (really, not at all) in Reykjavik's fleshpots. And Caroline had not said anything either, so maybe nothing had happened on that front as Jenn would have bet a year's salary that Caroline would not have been able to keep something like that a secret from anyone, especially not herself. So maybe Olaf just really wanted to see her. Or maybe he was going to tell her he was finally going to ask Caroline out. But at this moment, Jenn almost did not care anymore. She did wish she had time to watch more on television about the president's affair but she did not want to be late for Olaf, no need to get into any tiff about the importance of punctuality when she was feeling so, well, nearly fantastic.

If she were to tell the truth, she had not thought all that much about Olaf, or Caroline, or her job, or anyone at work while she was in Iceland. It sort of amazed her when she took time to think as to how thoroughly she had immersed herself in her work once she got closer to Hekla. When she was near enough to the volcano, she knew that there would be no time for messing up, there would be no real driver education, even for someone hampered by jet lag with no professional background in volcanology or mountain sports, and not much of a clue as to what she was doing there in the first place.

Actually, she was kind of depressed to leave Reykjavik. She liked giving grief to Sven and Fridrik about their garbage house working quarters and she liked it when they gave it back to her but set about picking up stuff and figuring out how to use sponges and bleach. She could not believe two men with such questionable hygiene had bought her an incredibly beautiful Icelandic wool sweater as a parting gift, even if Sven kissed her a little too much on the mouth when they said goodbye. She still thought Tony was nuts, but she had never worked for anyone so famous who also was kind of humble, willing to take advice, and willing to understand when something was not possible at that very second but could very likely be accomplished within the next few minutes. He was this way even though she was well aware that he knew quite a bit more about effective scientific communications than he was letting on. Even Erik, although he was kind of a puke much of the time, was clearly incredibly intelligent, a serious scientist, and he did know how to behave in a decent fashion when push came to shove and he was panicked in front of a camera and needed her to tell him what to say and how to say it. She loved the hotel with the massive eiderdown duvets and the view of Mount Esja, loved eating the renowned Reykjavik lamb hot dogs everyone said were so fabulous (as they were), loved wearing jeans and hiking boots to work nearly every day and still being teased by everyone for looking too red carpet, loved almost everything about working with people who certainly had egos but knew they could not use their ego to fully tame the planet, much less a violently sputtering mountain. They knew it and while they wanted to learn what made volcanoes do what they do and why, they really wanted to know everything possible at that moment in time, they also were sincerely concerned about the safety and sanity of everyone affected.

Of course, Mark's confession was not a whole lot of fun to hear, even after a few glasses of wine in that rather eerie bar full of people who were almost too stylish for Jupiter, much less Earth, but somehow she had known all along that he was not really straight. He was looking at Erik way too much and she remembered that he also had been checking out men in the restaurant when she went out with him in Minneapolis. She snickered at the thought of Nadine, the Mackerel-Mouthed Reporter. Would she ever make it to a network? It actually was kind of funny to see Mark staring at Erik when he should have been focused on his viewfinder, as they did somewhat resemble each other, although Erik had hair more in need of smoothing conditioner and wore less expensive expedition clothing. But what was it some behavioral scientists say, people are attracted to people who resemble themselves when they can find such people. She could have gone to bed with Mark, he offered and he said he'd be very careful, but as a rule she did not have sex with people who could not commit to one partner at a time, no matter how lovely their hair or how great they looked in leather. And after going out with him the few times she did, she realized he was leaning much more toward the boy team anyway. It would have been one thing if a place like Studio 54 were still around and if she had been rich enough and famous enough to go into the disco. But this too did not really bother her very much, as she really didn't care anymore. She knew she would likely get some questions about him from Tony and Erik, as she had promised both of them that she would take them out and show them the bright lights of Minneapolis, despite Tony's questions as to whether the city's citizens spent their spare time churning butter.

Her biggest concern at the moment was whether there would not be any ice or slippery slush on the way to her father's house and whether she could watch this last segment on the president's scorned and now sobbing mistress. She wondered how many people were going to write to this woman and tell her false eyelashes were never a good idea when crying on camera. Maybe Nadine could help her out.

"Come in, come in, let's take a look at the volcano expert," Marco said enthusiastically as he had her wrapped in his cashmere-swathed arms almost before she could get through the front door. He looked very happy to see her. "Your father and I are nearly finished preparing breakfast so get your shoes off and come in and sit down."

Olaf was still in the fancy apron he won at a food and wine festival one of his dates made him take her to some years before. Like Marco, he also seemed very glad to see her, giving her one of the biggest smiles she'd ever seen on him while setting down a massive platter full of pancakes that were still giving off vents of steam.

"So, get in here and sit down, but give me a hug first, I am so thrilled you are home in one piece," Olaf said while flinging his arms open. She was happy to see Olaf was happy, true, but she couldn't help but think that maybe something was already going on with Caroline as the table contained not only the fresh-squeezed orange juice Marco insisted on when he had breakfast with Olaf but also a carafe of what looked like cherry or cranberry juice as well as one of red grapefruit juice. She knew Caroline liked to drink cranberry juice in the morning, claiming it was outstanding for her kidneys as well as her complexion. And she said red grapefruit juice was lower in sugar than orange juice and richer in potassium too.

"Great to see you too, Dad, why wouldn't you think I'd come home in one piece, you know, the eruption was not as severe as some of Hekla's have been in the past and Tony and Erik did seem to know what they were doing," she said as Olaf embraced her awfully tightly, so much so that she could detect a new fragrance on his neck, not his usual soap or shave cream.

"Glad to hear you are on a first-name basis with these men, although I guess that is the Icelandic way," he said as he released her and rather gallantly helped her into her chair. "We knew you were in good hands, didn't we, Marco? But you know, a father still worries."

"You know your father, nothing escapes his attention or worry," Marco said in his usual courtly way as he heaped about three Frisbee-sized pancakes onto her plate. "I hope you are hungry. We worried you did not get regular meals out there in the field. I do not count hot dogs, even legendary ones made from lamb, to constitute a part of any regular meal."

Jenn just laughed a little and reached for the good maple syrup Olaf ordered a few times a year from some small farm in Quebec because he didn't think the syrup from Minnesota was quite flavorful enough. "Don't worry, Marco, I did not starve. I actually did eat a fair amount of fish. You were totally right, you have not eaten salmon or cod in your life until you have eaten the Icelandic variety. But not so much with the vegetables, they are pretty expensive there and so we didn't have many, save a few $15 side salads. I guess I had better drink a lot of juice this morning."

"Well, so you feel okay, I mean, you look fabulous, you don't look tired at all," Olaf said more quietly as he very carefully poured some espresso for himself and Marco. "Maybe this trip was a good idea for you after all."

She did want to talk with Olaf, but she wanted to finish her pancakes so she could have one of the muffins that were on the table, too. It was important that she think hard before she spoke because Olaf was being so unusually complimentary and nice (what was with him telling her she looked "fabulous"?) and she did not want to say the wrong thing and get into any arguments. Because she did want to tell them all about her trip, all about the things she did. The trip was so out of her normal experience that she had to tell someone. And maybe she was completely off, maybe Marco had a word with her father, it could be that there was nothing at all going on with Caroline. Marco had been on Olaf's case for decades to diversify and expand his life some; it could be he was just starting with safe things like cologne and different types of juice before he went crazy and did something like actually ask Caroline out for a real date.

"So it sounds like you and Dr. Fionarello got on pretty well, even if he has an untreated adult case of hyperactive disorder," Marco asked as he looked at her with some amusement while she stuffed pieces of syrup-soaked pancakes into her mouth. "And you worked well enough with Dr. Bjarnason?"

"No, everything was fine, Dr. Fionarello is actually quite informal. He insisted we call him Tony," she said as she realized she probably would be full enough if she managed to chow down three enormous pancakes and that she should probably just take a bunch of Marco's muffins home with her to have for lunch. "He's mental, I mean, you both would not be able to stay in a room with him for more than half an hour before your ears would be ringing. All the same, he's really very nice, he's very generous, he's got a whacked sense of humor, he likes to go out and party a little bit, but he does work hard. It was great to see that he's not one of those who won't do what he asks his team to do. It's kind of funny but after a while, I mean, if you get enough breaks from him, if you have enough quiet time in a geothermal spring soak, I actually found myself liking him and I really enjoyed working with him the whole time. I'd do it again in a minute.

I absolutely LOVED being in Iceland. It was so excellent, I cannot tell you!"

"Would you really, would you go back and do volcano duty again?" Olaf asked as he somewhat absentmindedly cut his own pancakes into very tiny squares. "I hand it to you, I don't know if I would want to be that close to something that could kill me that swiftly. I admire such courage."

"I don't know if it was so much courage. You do have to be careful and I guess it helps if you are someone who is not afraid of heights or too terrified of helicopters," she said as she wondered how small Olaf would dice his pancakes. "But it's nice of you to say. It was just fantastic. I don't know if I've ever had so much fun in my life. And I was working at the same time, you don't expect to have so much fun at work."

"I watched the BBC coverage of the eruption and that seemed to go quite well," Marco said as he too was watching Olaf, who was putting tiny forkfuls of food into his mouth in a very dainty way. "So when will the big documentary photographed by Mark from San Francisco air?"

Jenn took a small sip of what actually turned out to be cranberry-pomegranate juice and thought that maybe she could have just one muffin, just to please Marco. "Oh, the program will probably air in about three months, you know, the show is about several different volcanoes, not just Hekla, although I imagine Hekla and Tony and Erik will be prominently featured because of the timing of the eruption in relation to the air date," she said, happy to have the chance to talk more about the trip. "What is really interesting about Hekla is that it erupts fairly frequently. I don't know if you knew that it is the most active volcano in Iceland. But Erik's group and the government did a good job of warning people, you know, they knew the big blow was coming on for some time, so they make sure that people are forewarned, as skiers and hikers like Hekla a lot."

"Olaf, you and I have never been to Iceland," Marco said, pouring some grapefruit juice. Maybe that should be one of the trips you and I do before I decide to leave the world. I think we'd have a marvelous time. And you said you went to that restaurant that is on television so much, the place with the famous chef that does the salted cod?"

"Yes, we did," Jenn said, wondering why Olaf seemed to be focused so intently on his food and drink. "I think you and Dad would have a good time there. You cannot believe the women, you'd go out of your mind, Marco, just like you've heard, very blonde, very stacked, very gorgeous, very friendly in an indifferent sort of way. They all acted like high-end cosmetics sales clerks. I felt like a little brown bird or the little match girl when we were out at night in Reykjavik."

"You are not a little match girl, you are a beautiful, beautiful girl," Marco said with what appeared to be just a touch of moisture in his eyes. "I am sure the native Icelanders were quite taken with you."

"Yes, you are a very beautiful woman," Olaf said as he finally looked up from his plate. "I suppose I should tell you that more often."

Okay, guys, okay, I think I know what is going on and it won't make me angry, just tell me that Dad is going to do something about Caroline, Jenn thought as she planned to keep silent for the next few moments to see if either one of them would say something to that effect. Her father had actually called her beautiful!

"I guess Dr. Fionarello talked a fair amount about his sister while you were there," Marco said, somehow sensing she knew something was up on the Caroline front and that he was going to make Olaf do the talking but that he was gently nudging him toward the conversation.

"Oh yeah, he talked with her on the phone quite a lot, at least from what I know. I was not with him 24 hours a day," she replied. "I know he talked with Dr. Atagari too, you know. You know Tony and Dr. Atagari were roommates when they were undergraduates, and they are still very tight. He told me a few times that she seemed to be hanging in there as best as she could but that she was not really doing all that well and that her condition was continuing to deteriorate. Which

I expected, and I didn't know this before and I guess I shouldn't have been surprised, but Tony is Ms. Fiona's only sibling. You'd think he would have been a candidate to be her adult living liver donor. But for some reason he can't, he said something about a surgery he had some years ago. I don't know, maybe it was for cancer or something, so in any case, he cannot and she continues to wait. And you know how bad the organ donor shortage is in North America."

"Yes, that is most unfortunate, that certainly is not happy news," Marco said softly. "We had heard some of this from Caroline the other day."

All right, all right, here's the reason for hot pancakes and muffins she thought, hoping her facial expression would not betray her now confirmed suspicions and amusing thoughts. Just tell me, I will not be upset, really. She'd thought about this matter a bit while she was away and had realized that it would do her father a whole lot of good to actually have a girlfriend he liked.

"I suppose you were talking to Caroline to find out how I was doing?" she asked her father as directly as she could without being accusatory. "I only had time to email her a few times. I was actually pretty busy helping everyone out and doing my work. I did not tell her too much more than I told you."

Marco looked at Olaf, who looked away, tightened his apron, and then got up quickly to go into the kitchen. He then looked at her with quite shiny eyes. "Your dad and I have been talking to Caroline a lot in the last few days, about you, and about Bianca Fiona's condition," he said rather slowly. "She's been very, very helpful."

What's this about helpful? I wasn't in any trouble in Iceland, really, Tony was very pleased with my work. I wouldn't be in jeopardy of losing my job just because I took this leave, would I? Why did Caroline always think the worst?

Olaf came back from the kitchen with a second plate of muffins, even though no one had yet touched the first platter. He gave Jenn the most heavenly look she thought she'd ever seen on a human, even better than the ones Bianca Fiona had displayed the day Nadine and Mark were in town. He placed the plate down gently and then eased himself into his chair with a model-like grace.

"We've been talking with Caroline a lot, Marco and I, because there is something I need to tell you," he said in the halting and nearly whispering way she had expected he would use once he decided to speak. "I should have done this a very long time ago."

"Dad, go ahead and tell me, it's okay," she said, hoping she did not sound too strained and hoping she really would be okay with the idea of him asking Caroline out–or more. She could deal with her father having sex with Caroline, she could.

Marco picked up his espresso and kept it at his mouth.

"Well, you know how I tease you, about how you don't look like a stereotypical Norwegian girl," he said very slowly but pretty firmly. "The truth is, well, something else."

"Dad, I don't understand," Jenn said in a perplexed way, because this is not how she thought he'd segue into the Caroline discussion.

"Well, what it is, is that you are not of Norwegian descent, at least none that I know of, none that can be traced. The truth is, well, the truth is, well, the real truth is that you were adopted."

"What are you talking about, Dad, me being adopted," she said as she instinctively looked at Marco for help. "How? I don't understand." Obviously, the pancakes and being beautiful was not about Caroline.

Olaf sat up even straighter in his chair and stared for a few moments at the ceiling. Marco had put his cup down but remained silent, hands folded, just like a monk in a winery advertisement. Jenn kept her burning eyes fixed on Marco, who did not move but looked at her straight on.

"I guess I had just better spit it out," Olaf said as he kept his eyes on the ceiling for a few seconds more. "Your mother could not have children. She had a hysterectomy when she was very young. Before you were born in fact, and not afterward as she had told you," His voice, still raspy, grew stronger. "She and I wanted a child very, very badly, even though we were still probably way too young to be parents. And you know how your mother was, very proper. She had difficulty with things like feelings and expressing too much emotion. I mean, she was even worse than you think me. And she never, ever, ever wanted you to know you were adopted. And I wanted to make her happy. I knew she felt terrible that she could not have children, so I went along with her wishes."

Jenn was looking straight down at the floor and realized she'd grabbed a muffin and was now absentmindedly crumbling it into tiny pieces. She wished the fire in her eyes would go away, but she knew it wouldn't without crying.

"I know, I know all too well now, I was wrong," Olaf continued, with the strain in his voice pure misery to hear. "Marco told me years ago we were wrong to keep this from you." Olaf paused and looked at Marco for help that he knew would not come from that source, at least not at this particular moment.

"Anyway, when I was in graduate school, I studied under Marco, as you know. Marco counted many professors at the university among his friends," he continued, the rasp still present but measurably quieter. "One of them was a Dr. Alessandro Fionarello, an esteemed professor of geology, although his specialty was not volcanoes, it was oil exploration."

Jenn kept staring at the floor. She was determined to not start bawling, if only because she knew it would not be particularly useful at this moment. It might not even be useful for some time to come. But why was the news not all that earth shattering? Shocking, yes. Enough to make her eyes feel tinged with pepper spray, yes. But not shattering. Her pulse was not racing even though her eye sockets still felt hot, not with tears but with determination.

"So," she said very slowly, as if the inside of her mouth had been coated with warm wax, "you are telling me that Bianca Fiona is my birth mother?" She paused with a very deep breath before she said more. She wanted to do this right, though she was not certain she'd really do so. One does not really plan a speech for such occasions.

"And that's why I was sent to Iceland, so I could get to know her brother? I still don't really understand. Why wouldn't she want me to stay here and be with her, hear the story from her as well as you? From what Tony told me, it doesn't sound as if she is likely to make it, with or without a transplant."

Olaf looked at her and then closed his eyes for several seconds before he started to talk again, working hard to keep his modulation steady, his hands clamped to the table's underside but occasionally pressed against his pants in order to absorb some of the sweat. "Well, there's more. First, I need to tell you that your mother and I had not been in touch with Bianca since you were born. Her coming to Minnesota was something arranged completely by Yuki and her brother. The Iceland trip for you was all set up before I ever spoke one word to Bianca or her brother. Caroline's role in all this was to help me deal with Bianca and her brother regarding the fact that Bianca wanted to have you know she is your birth mother. We had a conference call just before you got back and that was the first time Marco or I had ever spoken with Tony about this matter. Yuki and Caroline were there too."

The room was quiet. Jenn swore she could hear every thump of Olaf's rapidly beating heart. And she wondered what this was doing to Marco, who looked more unearthly than ever, although still hale enough. She didn't feel like crying anymore. She just felt a weird sense of calm, as if hers had been the only home on the block to not be totally rampaged by a hurricane.

Olaf took a small sip of juice but still managed to dribble some of it onto his chin. "There's more. Marco stayed in close touch with Bianca's father until he died, which was about 10 or 11 years ago. Before Dr. Fionarello died, he told Marco, and then he told your mother and I, some news that we did not know at the time you were born. The news, which was absolutely and completely horrible for your mother to hear, is that Bianca gave birth to twins, a boy and a girl. Two of Dr.

Fionarello's other friends, an Icelandic physician and his wife who also were students at the university, also wanted a child; they adopted the boy and shortly thereafter went back to Iceland. Why Bianca wished to split you two up, we do not know, although in all fairness, I don't know if your mother and I could have raised twins easily enough. As you know all too well, too well, we did not take to parenting like ducks take to water."

My God, Jenn thought, no wonder I was not attracted to Erik. But what if I had been? You just could not make this story up; Olaf certainly couldn't conjure such a tale.

"Anyway, we learned at the time, and you have this all figured out by now, of course, that Erik Bjarnason's parents had told him he was adopted while they were in California and that his birth mother was of Italian descent but no more," Olaf said a tad bit more calmly, knowing that the really bad stuff was already out. "He doesn't yet know Bianca is his birth mother. But Tony and Yuki should be taking care of that today, after Erik and Tony have their big meeting with the USGS official. Erik's parents cannot tell him anything as they were killed in a car accident five years ago. So, that is the reason, THAT is why you were packed off to Iceland without notice or training or a plausible reason. Bianca was desperate that her children meet each other while she was still alive. And that, as they say, is the whole story."

Olaf looked down at the table and accepted Marco's shaking hand. Jenn gave her father the strongest glare she could manage, while not wishing to telegraph any hate or disappointment. She didn't feel hate or disappointment. She wasn't even angry. Well, no, she was angry. But her anger was directed at her mother, Christina Bergquist, even though she, even at this moment, somewhat understood why her proud, sensitive, often unfeeling mother would not have wanted her to know she was adopted. She wondered if her mother's spirit was in the room now, furious that the secret had been released. And then she realized that she was Italian. At least part. And that she really was Erik Bjarnason's sister. Which explained his dark hair and features.

And the fact that the way they acted when they were together was stereotypical, clichéd sibling behavior, although she was now mad at herself in an amusing sort of way as to how she had tried to be so careful not to cross the line into disrespect whenever she spoke with Erik because he was such a big deal scientist.

"So Erik should be hearing this news from Tony today. Good thing you all are being gracious and letting him get his USGS meeting out of the way first," she said, fighting hard to tamp down the sarcasm she felt rising to the surface. "First of all, I am not mad at you, Dad, and I'm not mad at you either, Marco. It is a shock, but not completely. It sort of explains everything. I could not look or act like a real Norwegian because I am not one. Now I know why I often seemed like such a disappointment to you and to Mother. But I would like to know when I can speak with Erik again."

Olaf pulled his hand away from Marco and chugged down an entire glassful of the grapefruit juice. Marco just exhaled deeply and got up to go into the kitchen to focus on the dishwasher.

"Thank you for not being angry, Jenn," Olaf finally said as he reached across the table to take both of her hands. His hands were clammy with sweat. "I cannot tell you how badly I feel that I kept this from you and how badly I feel that I acted the way I did all these years. Can you forgive me for being a piece of crap father? Will you forgive me? I don't know how I'll go on if you cannot forgive me, although I know you may need time. So I'll shut up now."

She put her hands on top of his, one at a time, despite the sweat, and just gave him a very tiny smile, the kind a teacher gives a child who has had a successful Time Out and is sorry they ruined someone else's drawing. "It is okay, Dad. You know, I always wanted a brother, even if I did not want a smart ass Icelandic volcanologist brother. But I really would like to have a chance to speak with Erik, and with Bianca. And, as it sounds like you all made a plan, I hope you can tell me what it is. We can talk later about how I am going to be able to deal with all of this without too much psychoanalysis paid for, incidentally, by you,"

"Thank you for understanding, although I also know that you may need to scream at me later, maybe you will, and that will have to be okay too," he said, clearly relieved to have not been chopped alive or shouted at or have had juice poured over his head. Psychiatrists did charge a lot of money but if Jenn needed to see one, he could not say no at this point. "Tony is going to call me when he is done telling Erik everything, Yuki will probably be in on the talk to give Tony the courage Caroline gave me. Then you two are free to talk to each other wherever and whenever you want. And, of course, as you can imagine, and as is only right, Bianca wants to see you and Erik, alone, as soon as possible after you and Erik have a chance to, I don't know, take part in some bonding. Tony and I and Caroline, Marco and Yuki too, we'll all stay out of things from that point on, unless you want us to get involved again."

"Thanks, Dad," she said in a now rather weary voice. "Thanks a lot. I would really like to know if you know anything about my biological father, as long as today is the day of revelation."

"Marco, do you want to come back in here, the dishwasher can wait," Olaf called to the kitchen while looking almost jubilant at the idea of giving Jenn this bit of news. "Jenn has asked about her biological father. We need to tell her, this is part of what we worked out with Bianca and Tony too."

This might be really good to hear if Olaf needs Marco back in the room, Jenn thought. She just wondered who the guy was, what sort of man did Bianca go after or have chase her when she was 18 and experiencing the wild life in mid-1970s Los Angeles.

"Well, my child, I am so relieved to hear that you have taken this news so well, you don't know how many times I have argued with your father over the years to tell you," Marco said as he rapped Olaf lightly on the shoulder. "I think you may be pleased; at the least you will find the information interesting."

"Don't keep me waiting another 36 years," she said.

"Well, the big news is that the birth father of you and Erik Bjarnason is a man who, according to Bianca, Tony and Yuki, does not know what happened to the two of you," Olaf said in his normal architect-in-charge voice. "He doesn't even know Bianca gave birth to twins. And he is Steve Jamieson, the one-time NCAA and NBA all-star, three-times married and very winning NBA coach who apparently did have a cocaine problem at some point in his playing career but not when he was playing college basketball. Have you ever heard of him?"

Well, this is why they are so happy, she thought. If you are going to adopt, nice to be able to adopt the offspring of a famous athlete. She'd never played basketball a day in her life, though. She'd have to ask Erik whether he had.

"Yes, of course; you know I like basketball," she said. "This explains how Erik got to be so tall. I want to say Steve originally was from Texas, west Texas country boy who knew how to dribble. He's probably of Scotch-Irish origin given his name, plus so many Scotch-Irish settled that part of the country in the late 19th century."

"I am glad to see you know something about this country's immigration patterns," Olaf said, the composure returning to his face by the minute. "But aren't you kind of excited to know your birth father is such a star? It's no surprise you are such a good skier and skater, and why Erik is so athletic too—he is a real mountaineer from what Tony told us."

She almost felt as if she were a character in a Woody Allen film, not that such a film would ever be made in Minneapolis or Reykjavik. "What it means is that you and Mother paid for a lot of ski and skate lessons for me. What this means is that two young, unmarried, and probably selfish people who would develop tastes for alcohol and drugs and who could not raise children 36 years ago, or did not want to raise children, found a way to give us up to people who could and would raise us a hell of a lot better than they would have managed. In the best way these people knew how, even if that meant, in my case at least, being completely dishonest for nearly 40 years. That's all it means."

Olaf carefully untied his apron, pursed his lips tightly, and pushed his chair out in one screeching motion. He petted Marco's perfect hair the way one would actually pet a cute dog, got up, and walked around the table to be next to Jenn. He sat down next to her, and before anyone could say another word, he shook with a violent eruption of tears.

This was a first for Olaf Bergquist. Jenn did not even remember him crying much at her mother's funeral, or the funerals for his parents. She turned toward him, put her arms around him very carefully, and held him close. Which was another first.

Actually, it did not feel too bad. And Olaf definitely was wearing cologne.

Chapter Seventeen

"I'm not really surprised that Erik wasn't too terribly upset by the news," Bianca whispered with as much volume as she could manage, while also wishing Tony would just shut the damn blinds once and for all. She had already told him about three times to do so, never mind that she also had told him to turn the television off for at least five minutes so she wouldn't have to strain herself too much by laughing at the tales of scorn being spun by the president's former mistress. "Because he's a scientist like you, and then you add the fact that he grew up in Iceland, where I think it's the law to keep your mouth tightly shut unless someone is bleeding or has lost a limb. And you said he already knew he was adopted and he already knew his birth mother was a young American of Italian heritage, that seems so noble, doesn't it, a young woman who happened to be living in Los Angeles."

Still, she knew it was vital to talk to Tony now than to try to get any sleep, especially as she was going to owe Tony for the rest of her life and beyond for bringing together the children she had given birth to all those years ago. One good thing about dying soon might be that she would not be paying Tony much longer whatever price he dictated for all that. "The big thing I'm concerned about is that I am certain that Erik's first meeting with Jenn as her official biological brother is going to be just tense as hell," she said while Tony kept looking at the television. "Although it does sound as if they won't need to be taught

how to bicker, so they are saving some time there right off the bat. It took you years to learn that when we were kids. Now you can really savage me but good."

Tony alternated his attention (not very well, he knew that lots of people already thought he had adult attention deficit disorder) between the latest pronouncement of woe from the president's now former girlfriend and his own very sickly sister. He had not seen Bianca since she left San Francisco to come to Minnesota. Even though he'd seen a lot in his travels, as he had seen people burned and/or killed by volcanoes, he was not prepared for the very shrunken and candle wax yellow-colored being still adorned in a now greatly oversized silk caftan and slumped in the bed. He was almost glad that the television could serve as a diversion of sorts, because he was afraid that the more he looked directly at Bianca, the more he would feel like falling apart. He kept telling himself that it was all nearly over, at least the Erik and Jenn part of the story. Bianca's outcome was yet to be determined but he did not want to think about that; still, the thought entered his mind every five minutes. It had taken less than an hour to tell Erik the whole story, and then the kid still wanted to go have a few beers with Tony so he could decompress a bit. How Jenn had reacted to her father was not really his problem, and if Erik and Jenn went at each other with butter knives or worse once they had their first sibling conversation, well, that would be for them to work out as well. They were kids but they were adult kids who certainly had their acts together better than Bianca did when she was their age. He was just happy that he'd gotten both of them, and himself, out of Iceland safely.

"It was almost alien as to how calmly he accepted the news," Tony said as he carefully closed the blinds for fear of breaking them and shut the television off. "You know, he already knew about half of it, so he was more or less fine. It might have been better if his parents had been the ones to tell him everything, but you know, I don't know if the kid really gets that emotional about all that many things. It was incredible when we were at the volcano—everyone else was going nuts, myself included, but this guy just kept working and then finally said after several hours, 'oh, could I get a glass of water or something else cold to drink?'"

Bianca just stared at Tony. He wasn't sure if it was because she was unable to do much else or if it was because she was truly proud of him for going without television for a few minutes.

"Well, it doesn't matter now: Erik knows, Jenn knows, now I guess they have to talk to each other and decide how to confront me," she said struggling to sit up as straight as she could, considering the lines that tethered her to the bed. "Erik will probably want to be very professional, and Jenn will probably be afraid that she will lose her temper in a real Italian way for once in her life."

"I do think you are smart to ready yourself for the fact that both of them are likely to be at least somewhat angry with you for separating them and denying them the sibling experience they could have had as kids. And I am not sure that all of the witticisms you put in your books are going to work with these two, certainly not Erik. They are both pretty intelligent—in different ways, but both of them are sharp enough cookies. And I wouldn't underestimate Jenn's ability to cut you up with words. She took me down more than a few pegs when we were in Iceland and she didn't take any crap from Erik or those other guys either. 'Wuss' is not a word I would use to describe that girl."

"I never said she was a wuss. I just said that what I saw, and I realize it was in a different context from what you saw, was a young woman who operates within the realm of real and intense fear a lot of the time," she said. "I would actually be happy to see her get mad at me. It's not like I don't deserve it, I know. And it would do her soul a lot of good to release whatever she has bottled up inside her, stop being so damn afraid all the time."

"In your condition, they might be more inclined to take it easy with you," Tony said rather softly. "Maybe we are worrying about a lot of anguish for nothing."

"I know I am in bad shape, right now," Bianca said as she focused on her inner force field so as not to look any weaker in her brother's eyes than she knew she already did, because she knew the look of pity. And intense pity was plastered all over Tony's face. Especially in his eyes. "I know you know it too, and I hope you won't be too scared about all of this because contrary to what I know you are thinking, this is not over yet. Those kids will need you once I'm gone."

"Quit saying that you are going to be gone, you know I don't like that kind of talk, how many times do I have to tell you: I didn't do all of this so you could go ahead and die on me," he said, trying his best not to stammer.

"But you know I'd still be around…"

"Maybe that's true, but right now, I am just not in the mood to hear anything about the power of the other world. I just want to get through the mess that has been created in this world. So, can we agree to just not talk about the world of clouds this one time?"

"I'm sorry, Tony. You know all of this wasn't completely my fault. Dad wanted it all over as fast as possible and with as little shame brought to him as possible and he wanted Dr. Bjarnason and his wife to have a baby too," she said quietly, feeling the same way she felt when she first told her parents she was pregnant and her father screamed Italian curses and her mother said all the rosaries in the world would not save her from the mortal sin she had brought upon her family and herself. "And I just wanted to go back to my regular life and forget that I had disgraced the Fionarellos by getting knocked up by Steve Jamieson. Although, if you think about it, maybe I should have tried harder to get him to marry me, seeing how much money he's made in basketball. I just cannot believe all of the silver he's now shelled out to at least two ex-wives, while I had to work for a living."

Tony had to look at the blinded window. At that moment, he hated Steve for more or less throwing Bianca in a dumpster once he found out she was pregnant. He also was angry with his father for orchestrating the cloaked disposition of the babies. And he thought he was going to start bawling at any second and he still didn't think that was anything Bianca wanted to see. He surely did not want to start crying, knowing that Nurse Laurence or Yuki could come in the room at any moment. It was bad enough he cried a little on the phone with Yuki when he told Tony just before he left Iceland the news about Bianca's condition and Yuki felt compelled to tell him it was "completely acceptable" for any man to cry in such a situation. Dr. Tony Fionarello was going to let his sister maintain some of her tough mystic façade for as long as he could manage it. And for as long as she could manage it too.

"I do have to tell you that Erik was just a small bit impressed to hear he was the offspring of a famous athlete," he said while trying to inhale the bulk of his tears, hoping she'd not see that he was so on the edge of losing it. "He said he guessed that explained his height. He seemed to know a lot about him, but that's not really any big deal, Jamieson did manage to go from being poor and unknown white Texas trash to being rich and quite famous white Texas trash."

"Tony, you know that being angry at Steve is not going to do any of us any good right now, even though you are right about the white Texas trash bit," she said in a tone more like that of her regular voice, and now wishing she had not said anything at all about Steve but at least she now knew Erik was not so upset about being Steve's son. "I got over being pissed off at him years ago and maybe it's time for you to get over him as well. I don't suppose Erik said anything about wanting to meet him too, did he?"

"Not in so many words, although he did make what I took to be a rather black joke about he and Jenn turning up at some game some day in matching adult-sized toddler outfits and somehow managing to get down to the floor and saying well, hello Dad," he said, a slight smile crinkling across his wind-burned, poorly shaven face. He actually thought the idea was a pretty good one. "I think we could probably arrange such a meeting; I would not think it would be that difficult to get floor seats in places like Milwaukee or Portland."

"That would be really, really amusing," she said, smirking broadly at the thought of Steve Jamieson, standing face to face with the very attractive and accomplished products of his wild oats. "I think it would be even funnier to see the look on the face of that child wife of his."

"Well, maybe once he and Jenn have had their talk, maybe they'll decide to go and stalk Stevie, but I think it should be their decision," he said calmly, finally feeling as if he could speak without crying for at least a little while.

"Yeah, you're right. I don't want to get involved at all. I don't even really want Steve to know I am sick, although maybe he knows it if he goes to my website at all."

"Do you really think someone like him goes to YOUR website? I am not sure he even knows how to find a website."

"I don't know. He knows I was pregnant. Maybe he's still curious, you don't know."

"Curiosity about past mistakes is not a quality I would ascribe to that asshole, one I am really sick of talking about right now, and you should be too. You've had more than 30 years and three husbands to get over him."

"Yeah, well, it doesn't matter if he knows about me or not, who really cares, I've got other things on my mind."

"So, do you want to talk about what you are going to say to these kids when they do come to meet you?" he said quite slowly, knowing that it was the one discussion that still needed to be held no matter how painful it might become for him or for Bianca. "I mean, it's not really my business, but it is my business given what you've had me do and the fact that you are my sister and I am their uncle, at least their biological uncle. Have you sort of thought about what you are going to say to them? Are you going to put all of the blame on Dad for separating them, giving them up for adoption, whatever?"

She looked at him with eyes that, even in the dark of the blinded, television-free room, still radiated a bit of the light she always had before she got sick. But she still looked like she was on her way out of this world, although Tony could not figure out, New Age philosophies or not, why she did not seem more unhappy about the thought of actually dying. When he did think about her possible death and the idea that he'd have to have her cremated, he nearly always felt that he would vomit.

"Yes, I've given it some thought, no worries there," she said while knowing that while Tony wanted to know everything she planned to say to Erik and Jenn, she was not going to tell him everything. She did not want him to get upset again. "And it is not so much 'blaming' Dad, because it was all Dad's decision. I'm just hoping both of them will realize that in the end, we Fionarellos somehow did the right thing by giving them up."

"But will they realize you did the right thing by coming here now and interjecting yourself in their lives, interjecting me in their lives, turning their lives totally upside down without asking them first if you could do so?"

She always hated it when Tony was right. That was probably why he got a doctorate and went on to become famous for being smart in a way acceptable to most people.

"I don't know, Tony. All I know is that I did not want to walk into the light of the other world before I had met the two of them in this one," she snapped, although she did not really want to become testy with Tony. She was on thin enough ice with him for involving him in the whole ordeal. "It's a little late now to talk about whether what I did was right or not. All I want to do now is meet them together, tell them what I did and why I did it, and try to let them know I did it out of concern for their spirits. And mine too, if that's allowed. That's all."

"That's fine. I don't want to argue with you. I just want to make sure you realize that these kids may not have wanted to know about you, not that Jenn had any knowledge in any case, and that you accept whatever they say," he said, hoping he could turn the television on again within a few moments as a new program featuring one of the president's other mistresses was coming on at the top of the hour and he badly needed more diversion. "That's all. I just want all of this to work out as peacefully as we can manage so all of us can go back to our lives. You go back to writing books that outsell mine by a factor of thousands and I'll go back to thinking I'm still young enough to chase volcanoes."

"Good, I understand you. Let's not talk anymore about it right now" she said decidedly, collapsing back on the pillows and pulling the sheet up closer to her chin. "You can turn the TV on again. We should see what sort of advice the really old girlfriend has to give to the recently dumped presidential girl. And Tony, you know, I think you can get a razor from one of the nurses. You look almost as bad as I do. Nurse Laurence looks like he'd have lots of things around that can cut people up."

Chapter Eighteen

Jenn probably should have gone and picked Erik up from the hotel, but he insisted he could find the place easily enough, that the fact that she was his biological twin sister did not mean he could not find his way around a foreign downtown district. She was worried that it was not so nice that she was on her second cocktail while she was waiting for him, given that their alcoholic birth mother was now languishing in the hospital, waiting for a liver transplant that no one seriously thought would ever take place. But she'd just had a hell of a few days, so she felt she was more than excused from criticism. And the bartender didn't seem to think anything was wrong at all; he was paying attention to the two women at the end of the bar. Anyway, she was not going to have anything else to drink tonight. She wanted to stay as alert as possible because she was certain that this twerp who she couldn't wait to send back to Reykjavik when they arrived in Minneapolis, this twerp who now happened to be her twin brother, was going to try to take over the discussion and have his way as to how they were going to talk to Bianca Fiona, popular psychic of book and television talk show fame and of all things, their mother. She could tell just by the manner in which he talked to her on the phone when she called him the day after Olaf dropped the bomb that to him, all of this was really no different from a difficult foundation grant.

It probably was good that Dr. Atagari called Olaf shortly after he'd told her she was an adopted child. How convenient that the whole damn world knew she was what they used to call a love child, though she doubted Bianca could ever have loved Steve Jamieson, as Jenn thought he looked strange and gangly even before he started consulting plastic surgeons. It had to be the fact that he was a major jock that made her want to have sex with him at all. She was grateful that she (and Erik too, to be fair) got the bulk of their looks from Bianca. But she would have liked a bit more of Steve's height.

She was glad Dr. Atagari had magically arranged a few more days off for her from her job, as she wasn't sure what she wanted to say to Caroline. She could just tell from the way her father acted that the two of them had become one. He was actually giggling a bit after recovering from the crying jag he fell into after telling Jenn she was adopted. He had called her a few times afterward to not only learn if she had gone insane upon hearing such news but also to see if the one movie theater she liked served real butter on their popcorn. Olaf seldom went to movies, but Caroline went about as often as Jenn did, so if he wanted to know about popcorn, he was definitely planning on taking Caroline to the movies. Not to mention the fact that he was wearing fragrance. It was the scent that made the Olaf-Caroline coupling final in Jenn's mind. It was fine. It was pretty expensive fragrance that probably had been selected by Marco. It actually smelled kind of nice.

But in trying to be reasonable (which she was doing her best to be, despite a few wild but short-lived mood swings not entirely attributable to whisky) she concluded that it would have been too much for Olaf to have to tell her the Bianca story plus the Caroline romance all at once. Not that she wanted to think about it too much, but it had to be hard for Olaf to have sex so often after going, she figured, at least years without it. When she thought about the situation the other night while she was drafting the script she wanted to use when she called Erik, she actually thought the whole thing was enormously entertaining; she could never imagine her father being uninhibited enough, even if he were drunk, to satisfy all of Caroline's desires.

And she knew what they were, because Caroline liked to talk about what made her go wild. A lot. Jenn could just imagine if she were sick enough to want to do so as to what Caroline might have wanted Olaf to do to her in the bedroom, the kitchen, the bathtub, the hallway, etc. She did wonder how her father made his move in the first place.

When Erik asked her on the telephone if she was mad at Olaf about keeping such a secret for so long, she told him no, not really. At the moment, she meant it, because she really wasn't so much angry as just confounded beyond belief as to what was going on in the supposedly healthy brains of Olaf and Christina that they thought they could pull off such a caper for so many years without ever getting caught, even though they had Marco involved in the mess the whole time. In a way, she was a bit thrilled to not be biologically Norwegian, as she never really liked going to Norway and meeting stony-faced distant relatives. She didn't really care for the dry Christmas cake her mother made every year in homage to the old country she had not visited until she was 40, and hated hearing about how virtuous it was to remain stoic like the Vikings, who clearly had demonstrated great stoicism when they pillaged villages and killed monks. If she had gone absolutely mental when Olaf told her the news, she could have correctly blamed any outburst on the hot Roman blood coursing through her system.

"Sorry to keep you waiting, but I had to send a quick text back to my lab and tell them I was going to stay here a bit longer than I had originally planned," Erik said blankly as he walked quickly over to her and handed her his coat to put on the adjoining stool. "I figured I might need more time here. So, here we are. Looks like you have your drink—should I get a beer right away or should we go and sit down at the table?"

If she didn't know better she almost would have thought she was speaking with Olaf Junior, although, to be very honest, Erik was a lot better looking and slightly more interesting than Olaf. But he was so, so nonplussed. It was like he was on the phone the other night:

this was not any real problem, nothing that could not be worked out. Maybe the whisky was starting to smooth her down, but she was almost starting to believe that maybe it was not going to be a big deal. That would be fine if she and Erik could keep things calm and civilized. Find out you're adopted and that you've already talked with your biological mother, go and talk to her, maybe talk about your famous athlete biological father a little bit, and that's it, let's stay in touch, you have my email address and number and Iceland is especially beautiful in the summer.

"We can have another drink here, I know it's been a rough time for you too," Jenn said in a tone that was really quite kind.

"No, I'm fine. I already knew I was adopted, and now I know who my birth parents are but really, for me, very little else has changed except that I now have an American twin sister," Erik said as he grabbed both of their coats and proceeded to follow her find the host to bring them to their table. He was rather pleased at Jenn's choice of location, as it was difficult (as Marco had always believed) to find a really good and modern Italian restaurant in a Scandinavian country. Clearly that did not seem to be the problem in an American city peopled by many residents of Scandinavian descent. It was good to know he did not share DNA with someone with abominable taste.

"I thought it might be nice to do Italian as we now know, well, at least I now know we are part Italian, plus I know it's hard to get good Italian in Iceland," she said carefully, wondering why she suddenly felt as nervous as she might on a hot date when there was no need at all to be nervous. This was not only her brother but someone who she had already had verbal spars with in Iceland. At least she'd be seen with a decent looking guy should anyone she knew be there. "I think everything here is good. My father won't come here much because he thinks it is too expensive but I like it a lot, plus it's kind of quiet, so you can hear yourself talk."

"I think a splurge is in order for tonight," he said as he quickly decided what he wanted so they would not have to enter into interminable small talk about risotto and spaghetti. He'd noticed this sister of his not only loved food like he did but loved to talk about food, as did their uncle. "So are you really okay?"

He truly was an Icelander, no b.s., omit the pre-dinner drinks and get right to the heart of the matter. Which maybe was not so bad.

"Yeah, I'm fine, really. It was not as much of a shock to my system as you might have thought it would be," she said as she realized she had better decide what she wanted fast as Erik's menu had long been closed. "I won't say it's like I always knew, because I really didn't, but I always knew I was very different from both of my parents. Though, I guess in some ways I am more like them than I might have thought: I do try to stay reasonable, well, minus some minor outbursts when absolutely necessary. But I like to think I am a hell of a lot more exciting than my dad. I suppose you could get into a really good nature versus nurture argument, especially as we were 'separated at birth'."

"I get your point. I was probably a lot more exciting than my parents too. I insisted on going into volcanology and not medicine, which made my father very worried, and I nearly brought my mother to tears when I told her I really, really wanted to go to university in the United States. Listen, I don't want to break this train of thought, but do you know what you want to eat? I think that guy is our waiter."

"Yes, I know what I want," she said, hoping they'd have a waiter who would make minimal intrusions and not recite every detail of the evening's specials. "It's funny that we both went back to the West Coast to go to school, I was in Los Angeles while you apparently were in Seattle."

Erik ordered his meal without waiting for Jenn to go first and then asked her what she wanted for dinner. And even though she thought that this is not a 1950s dinner engagement, she told him she wanted lobster ravioli and that yes, she would have a very tiny glass of the half bottle of the actually quite decent wine that he ordered. He was a man who seemed to be able to take command of a situation, which probably was useful whether you were trying to monitor volcanoes or do something as simple as order dinner for a woman.

"Yes, I always was attracted to the Pacific Northwest," he said offhandedly, while glancing around, curious whether there were any decent looking women in this city who might be in this restaurant. "I have not ruled out moving to the U.S. or Canada someday either. Listen, I know we have a lot to talk about, but I think we really have to focus for a while as to how we are going to talk to Bianca. From what her doctor said, it sounds like she only has days to go, so we have to do this, and we have to do it fast. And as best as we can."

"So you are not going to call her Mother, which is good, as she didn't do any of the work in raising us," she said a bit abruptly. "And as I am the one who's already talked with her some, has already been inside her psychic analysis salon, I think we need to go in there acting confident and not weepy in the least about not having had her around to try and take care of us while she was exploring the world and getting drunk."

From the utterly frozen look Erik gave her following her last sentence, Jenn sheepishly realized there was no need for her to criticize Bianca's life choices right now, especially as the woman was dying. As she had admitted to Olaf, Bianca had given Erik and herself the chance to have a hell of a lot better life than she would have been able to give them.

"I agree with you on the confidence bit," he said as he moved his arms to make way for their salads, hoping the waiter would not ask if they wanted pepper or not (but he did, another so very American practice). "I also think we need to express some gratitude, let her know we don't hold anything against her for giving us up, as it also sounds like her father made all of the decisions. Tony said she actually cried a lot for months after we were born, although he said he was sure a lot of that was because our biological father dumped her for basketball and NBA groupies."

"Tony didn't tell me she cried."

"Well, I've spent more time with him, and he is the one who told me my part of the adoption story. She's his sister, he knew more about the situation, and you know how he is, once he gets talking he just cannot shut up."

"So do you wonder at all what it would be like to meet Basketball Steve?"

"A little, but to be honest, he sounds like a real jerk who happens to be good at playing and coaching basketball. Besides, he hasn't made any effort to find us. Bianca did, and she's dying, so we have to do this even if we don't really want to. I sometimes wonder what my parents would have thought of all of this if they were still alive. Although, to tell the truth, I think they would have liked you a lot."

Jenn just smiled at the thought of her brother's Icelandic and not Norwegian parents liking her a lot. She wished she could have had the chance to meet them both. "I know my mother would have gone out of her mind, absolutely nuts, if she knew Bianca had come to Minneapolis so she could meet me because, as you know, I was never to know the truth," she said. "And I know my mother would have thought Bianca a real slut."

Erik was too hungry and perhaps too used to much more liberal Scandinavian attitudes toward sex to be shocked at the thought of his biological mother being much of a slut. As much as he did want to keep talking to Jenn, although he could not figure out why he wanted to keep talking to her, it couldn't just be because she was now his sister, he started to attack his salad. Jenn saw that they had at least one thing in common, a need to eat a lot of food fast, so she followed suit. She was sort of glad that he was not a date so she could be herself and just eat without thinking the guy was taking note of her calorie count.

"So we will go to the hospital tomorrow morning, around ten," Erik said, looking back at the kitchen to see if their meals were on the way or not. They were not, but there was a beautiful blonde at the other table who happened to be sitting with a rather pudgy brunette friend. He sort of smiled at her in his best interested but disinterested way and only partially caught her attention. Maybe she and the brunette were lesbians.

Jenn saw that he was looking at the blonde and thought it a little funny that the two of them also seemed to like to take a room's temperature and geographic setting before really paying attention to anyone or anything else. They must have inherited that quality from both Bianca and Steve.

"Yeah, ten is fine," Jenn said while making a note to herself that she was going to have to call the nursing station tonight to make the appointment if she did not want to have to talk to Laurence in the morning. My God, she thought, what is Laurence going to think when he finds out the whole story. He'll despise me even more than he does now, that's what he will think. "I don't know how long we'll be able to stay; she gets pretty tired now. We should just plan to stay as long as she either stays awake or throws us out. My guess, no, I KNOW, that she will want to do most of the talking if she is up to it. When I really think about it, I don't think it is going to be all that bad as long as neither one of us lets her make us feel guilty or childish or just plain stupid. She has a way of doing that, believe me. And she also makes you sit on these enormous silk pillows."

"Well, if we keep up the confidence front, which I really don't have a problem doing, we should not be so prone to her probing or the effect of any pillows," Erik said while actually looking directly into Jenn's, and only Jenn's, eyes. "I'm actually very curious for her to tell us about her life. I mean, we know how we were conceived, in all likelihood, we know about our births, and I think we don't need to beat the dead horse about why we were put up for adoption. I really want to know about her drinking, her drug use, her husbands, our stepfathers if you will, how she became a psychic, how she managed to become so famous, all of it."

"I'm kind of curious about all of that too, although she really was more interested in psychoanalyzing me than in telling me anything about herself when I talked with her a few weeks ago. I never thought to ask her many questions about herself. I think I was too scared."

"Fine," Erik sighed. He was relieved, both that his meal had arrived and that Jenn was okay with the way he wanted to proceed with Bianca. "So I just have to ask you: Do you think your father is doing it with that colleague of yours, Caroline's her name, right? Tony told me some of the story. It seemed quite obvious to him that she is your dad's girlfriend."

Jenn just laughed a bit and gave Erik a look that said her father's sex life with this supposedly very attractive woman was much easier to talk about than deciding how to talk to a dying biological mother.

"Well, in keeping with my father's ways, he has not said anything to me about Caroline but it's painfully obvious that she has moved into his life in a pretty meaningful way. You know she set up the call they all had to discuss us, she did all the talking with Dr. Atagari, so I can figure out the rest, especially given how he's been acting since I got back."

"Are you upset?"

"No, not really," she said, hoping she could convince him and herself. "I know my father will tell me about it when he's ready. He probably figures I already know, and to be honest, I really am kind of happy. I like Caroline a lot, and someone has loosened him up since I left for Iceland, and I know it is not Marco. It's fine, really. Or it will be fine."

"Okay. Because, and I hate to sound morbid or mercenary, I don't know which word is more accurate, but Bianca is probably not going to make it. You know it. But if your dad and Caroline become a real couple, you know, get married, you will have a stepmother."

"That's true, I suppose I could."

"And since my parents are dead, and I have very little relation on either my mother's or father's side…"

"Oh, I get it, you could be the son Olaf always wanted. Even though you look Italian, you are a lot like my father. Maybe not quite as intense. And you are willing to have some cocktails. Actually, that doesn't sound like such a bad idea. I'd have the sibling I always wanted to share my care and feeding of Olaf."

"I think Caroline will take care of much of the Olaf feeding from now on, but what is this that your father doesn't drink? What kind of Scandinavian is he anyway? We all drink, sometimes copious amounts, and we are very proud to do so."

Jenn was laughing again as she saw that they both were shoveling food from their plates into their mouths. Even Erik seemed to be genuinely amused and enjoying himself.

"We shouldn't really be talking like this; we have not yet talked to Bianca. But I have a feeling Bianca would not have a problem with us calling Caroline 'Mom,'" she said, ready to crack up and spit her food out at the thought of Caroline being a willing stepmother to two 36-year-olds. "The real problem comes if you and I ever have children of our own. I don't know how Caroline would react to being a grandmother. Well, at least in being called a grandmother."

"Well, I could teach her how to make a Norwegian or Icelandic Christmas cake. That is what grandmothers do, at least in Iceland," Erik said while also laughing before quickly going somber again. "We ought to stop this now. Tomorrow could be a really shitty day, or it just could go okay—if we keep our heads together."

"You're right, tomorrow could be a lot worse day than either of us have ever bargained for in our lives. I mean, like ever. Ever."

"Right. So, are you going to eat all of your lobster ravioli?"

Chapter Nineteen

The labored breathing that was moving Bianca's sleeping caftan (as there now was much more caftan than chest) up and down like a dried-out accordion was harder for Erik to watch than he had thought possible, even in a room devoid of almost any natural or artificial light. Jenn just sat perched at the side of the bed, looking calmer than Erik also might have thought feasible for someone to look when seated near a person who clearly was on her way through death's door.

"I'm not sure we should stay in here while she sleeps," Erik whispered. "If she suddenly wakes up and sees us here, and if she for some reason doesn't remember we were coming, she could be very frightened."

"It's fine for us to stay," Jenn said in a voice softer than Erik's. "She'll remember that we were supposed to come." She looked at Erik and wanted to say, take a good look at this not-pretty sight, this is my life. I deal with this all the time, even if the patients don't happen to be our biological mother. "This way we don't have to go out there and come back in and make more of a disturbance. And leave the blinds shut—she likes the darkness." She did wonder if the vain Bianca was fully aware of just how hellish she looked at this moment, even in the dark. Not that anything could be done. No jewelry or makeup or artfully draped silk would airbrush this unpleasant scene away.

Bianca's eyes started to flicker just a bit after Jenn said "disturbance" and both she and Erik knew that ready or not, it was time.

Erik moved without thinking to Jenn's side and for reasons neither of them could deduce even weeks later, put his arm around his sister and placed his head on her slightly shuddering shoulder.

"Well, I see you two have met," Bianca croaked, not moving one inch from her recline. "And now you've at least seen me."

Erik's grip on Jenn grew tighter and she could not believe that she, and not the logical scientist, was going to have to take charge of things. Of course, this was anything but logical science. There was little that was logical about anything any of them had experienced over the past several weeks. Some people would have called it hell.

"Bianca, as you already know, this is Dr. Erik Bjarnason," Jenn said in a nearly childlike voice while trying not to stare too hard at Bianca's absolutely skeletal face. "I believe Tony told you what a great job he did running the Hekla eruption."

"I hear you both did a good job in Iceland," Bianca said, clearly having trouble getting the words to move up her diaphragm and out of her throat. "Tony was very proud of you both. I was too."

Erik loosened his hold on Jenn and tried to find one of Bianca's hands under her covers. She saw what he was trying to do and she slowly held out one of her stick-like arms. He looked at Jenn as if to ask if this was all right.

"I am glad we could both be here to talk to you, even if it would have been better if we'd been here a long time before," Erik said. If he had to look at Bianca's face much longer, he was going to scream or cry and he did not know which. "We came as soon as we both knew, you know, knew about the situation."

"I know Erik, I know," Bianca said with eyes that Jenn now saw were filled with tears. Jenn had not thought the woman was capable of crying, but she figured that approaching death, along with seeing your two long-lost children together for the first time, was more than enough reason. But she was surprised at the sympathy she felt for Bianca.

"Well, I guess what is important is that we are here now," Jenn said in the tone she used when she felt her most capable. "Guess we also ought to tell you—I hope it is okay that I'm saying this for you, Erik—neither one of us is mad at you in any way. In fact, I'd say we are both grateful for the chance you gave us to grow up with people who were ready to be parents." She could not believe she had handled that one with so much aplomb and grace. If only Olaf could see her now. Or even her mother.

"Jenn's right," Erik said in the sort of shaky voice Jenn heard all too often from family members of patients on their way out, while continuing to lightly hold Bianca's nearly nonexistent hand and keeping his other arm around his sister. "We only wish we would have known about you much sooner. And I just wish there was something either of us could do for you now."

"You've already done more for me now than you can ever know," Bianca said with just the slightest bit more verve. She looked up hard at Jenn. "It's been said before so many times but now that I've seen you two, I can see that you are not physically deformed in any way, you both are well educated, it looks as if you are capable of being together in a civilized fashion when necessary, so whatever work I needed to do is now marked 'complete'."

The strength Bianca needed to summon just to talk this much to them seemed to be waning. Erik was not ready for things to be over so very soon. Jenn looked at him and wanted to tell him it was okay to stay. Patients in this condition would often move in and out of immediate consciousness as well as energy reserves.

"We'll just stay here a while, if it's okay with you, and if you want to talk to us some more, we'll be ready," Jenn said carefully. "We did have some questions for you, both of us, but we don't want to burden you too much right now."

Bianca bolted up so suddenly that Jenn thought her IV pole would crash into the wall.

"If you cannot burden me now, well, then you two are going to have to find a way to communicate with the other world, because I am not sure just how much longer I can take your sad looks and all-so-similar eyes and hair," Bianca said with the fully operational purr Jenn had heard on the day they met. "Ask away. I'm ready."

Erik and Jenn just looked at each other, each wanting to ask the Steve Jamieson question first. Jenn knew Erik considered him more of a creep than Jenn did, as she was more or less indifferent to the guy, so she thought she'd let Erik open up the line of questioning.

"Go ahead, Erik," Jenn said while looking directly at him to telegraph the thought that now would maybe not be the best time to talk too much about what Steve was at the present time. Just focus on the past.

Bianca gave them both the sort of pitiable glare Jenn had grown accustomed to seeing her display before Jenn left for Iceland. This was not someone who was going to accept the invitation of either St. Peter or the devil or whoever with very much diplomacy.

"Well, actually, we know much of the story about our births and we know a lot about you, not that we don't want to know much more, we do, but we were, both of us, we were and are very curious about our biological father," Erik said, knowing he had to step carefully into this one because Jenn had said she was sure that Bianca still held much ill will against Steve. Even if Bianca did preach in her books and at her sessions that holding onto anger or hatred made for very nasty karma.

Bianca smiled a sort of half-smile, the kind bankers give people when they are about to tell them they are being turned down for their mortgage.

"So you want to know about Steve, well, okay, we'll talk about Steve for a while," Bianca said even more firmly while relaxing just a bit against yet another new pillow. "Well, there's not much to know, really. I imagine you know all about what he is today. I had been dating him for a few months shortly after I turned 18, much against my father's wishes, as he had no use for athletes. In those days, you could not pay a man to use a condom and I had never thought about being on the Pill, though I did think a lot about having sex with a lot of boys, including Steve."

Jenn and Erik looked at each other and knew that they were both imagining a very young Bianca. They were both a little jealous. And they both had the fleeting thought: what if Bianca was only guessing that Steve Jamieson was their father? She had mentioned a lot of boys.

"So Steve and I had a lot, a lot of sex, although he did take me out a fair bit and I have not since watched so much basketball," Bianca continued, knowing full well that Jenn and Erik were trying their best to imagine her as a young nymph and their father as a stud of the court and off. "And to tell the truth, Steve was quite handsome in those days, almost devastatingly good looking, even though he was, as my father always said, from the trashiest of white trash trailer parks. He grew up in west Texas, near Midland. His father was an unsuccessful oil wildcatter who practiced much of his wildcatting away from the family home as well as the oil fields. Anyway, one day, quite shockingly to me, I found myself pregnant. I told Steve the news, thinking he might want to marry me and take me to whichever city he was going to play NBA basketball in. Don't laugh, I was young and not yet aware. Well, as you can imagine, he did not want to marry me, he did not want children, and he was packed off by his coach to some advanced basketball training camp in Boston well before the two of you were born. My father went absolutely nuts, said there would be no Mexican abortions, and hatched his plan to subcontract you to different sets of parents on different continents. I was a wreck for months even though I really didn't want to be a mother at that time, really. I did want my old life back. Anyway, I started drinking. Smoking marijuana. Then I tried cocaine and met my first husband, a jerk, soon enough afterward. That's pretty much the story of Steve. Haven't heard word one from him since he left for that camp, though his coach did come to see me in the hospital after you were born and I got flowers from the whole damn team. Pink roses, which I hate, so ladylike. It's fine. I did have a pretty damn good life without him, overall."

Bianca's face betrayed almost none of the sort of emotion Jenn and Erik thought it might in retelling such a story. Maybe it was because it had happened so long ago that she wasn't able to get too worked up about it anymore. Or maybe she was too sick and drugged to get too upset about someone as inconsequential as Steve Jamieson when she had bigger things, like dying, on her mind. As it was, neither of them heard anything more from Bianca than they thought they might. It was all so nearly clinical, not that either of them really wanted much drama anyway. Bianca and Steve had a lot of sex, Erik and Jenn were born, Bianca was now about to die, and Steve might never know or care about Bianca or Jenn and Erik. Buying game floor seats, even in Milwaukee or Portland, would be a colossal waste of time and money.

"So, now that you know about Steve, tell me what the two of you are going to do with your lives now that you know more about your origins," Bianca said while forcing herself to remain as upright as possible. Jenn and Erik both thought her arms might crack from the strain. They both leaned in to help her up, only to have her push them away. "I just cannot believe that after all you've been through, all you are capable of doing, that you are just going to go back to being a hospital public relations girl and an underpaid volcanology assistant professor. Don't disappoint me."

"What do you mean, disappoint you?" Erik said with anger Jenn did not think he possessed, much less expected to see right then. "We have respectable lives. We haven't been divorced a bunch of times, we haven't screwed half of any city or country, we didn't abuse drugs, and if anyone should be disappointed, it isn't you. We turned out much better than you might have expected."

"Good, good to hear you defend yourself," Bianca said almost forcefully. "I never said you had empty lives or that you were failures. I just said that both of you are capable of doing a lot more. You ought to take this chance, listen to your dying biological mother for the first and maybe last time, and seize your glory. I didn't come to Minnesota and turn your worlds upside down to not say as much."

"Well, maybe we will," Jenn said as she shot a glare at Erik that indicated no further outbursts would be tolerated today. "I've definitely listened to a lot of what you've been telling me since I met you, and certainly since I was in Iceland. But as you say yourself in your book, which I did read in its entirety, the freedom to be who we are rests within us. It is not for anyone, even someone who might be disappointed in any path we choose, to say otherwise."

Erik gently gave Jenn the good work, my friend jab in the ribs.

"Well, good, it's great to see the two of you are on the same page about something," Bianca said while now slumping back down into her bed. "I just wanted to see your strength. I knew both of you had it. I just wanted to see it. I didn't come here to have any sort of 'relationship' with you as you might have feared, if only because I know my time here is limited. I just want to know you are going to try and reach more of your potential."

"Well, you saw our potential and our strength. Maybe you need to rest now; you look tired," Jenn said as she motioned for Erik to move away from the bed. "We will come back later today."

"That sounds just fine," Bianca said with obvious and sudden fatigue. "Come back around six or seven and bring your own dinner as you cannot eat what is served in this place. You might want to bring some wine too, it's too late for me to stay on any wagon. I'd love to taste a good Chardonnay or Pinot Grigio one last time. Just don't let Nurse Laurence see you."

Jenn kept motioning for Erik to start to leave but he remained rigidly in place, much as she had seen Olaf do so many times before when he felt he had something to say.

"Before we go," Erik said haltingly, and with more of an Icelandic accent than Jenn had heard him use before, "I just wanted to thank you again. Thank you for giving us to good people. I loved my parents very much and I know Jenn feels the same way about hers."

"Yes, thank you, Bianca," Jenn said hesitantly, looking at Erik's ever so slightly cracking and reddening stone face, knowing she was not all that ready to call Olaf a good man yet. "I truly am glad I met you. I may realize more of it in time to come but I am happy you came here. Even if you did make me feel a little small at times. I may understand it better later. I just wish we had met under better circumstances. This cannot have been easy for you."

Bianca stared at both of them and then gave them a little wave.

"It is I who is happy to have seen you," Bianca said in a nearly imperceptible voice, pushing the words out like so many stones in her mouth. "As you might say in science, the mission is accomplished. Come back later, and bring something chocolate, a good cake or a torte, just not any ice cream. And don't forget the wine. It might make things a bit more lively. Life is meant to be lively and to be lived."

Chapter Twenty

Jenn was stunned to see the actually modest, yet still somewhat seductive, black dress Caroline wore to the service. That Caroline and Olaf either held hands or had one of their arms around the other all the time did not bother her in the least, although she was still getting used to seeing her father dressed in an expensive and well-cut Italian suit and with longer hair that really made him look at least ten years younger. The nice sunglasses on top of his head were another thing entirely, but that could have been Marco's doing, as he was seldom seen without one pair of designer sunglasses. She was glad that Marco made the trip to San Francisco with them. Marco had told Olaf in no uncertain terms that it was imperative Jenn and Erik participate in the "hippie" rites, as Bianca had asked that they do in her will. Caroline even selected some of the incense that Jenn and Erik set alight before the highly lacquered urn. She also said the reading Jenn and Erik did from "The Prophet" was just beautiful and told Olaf that he had better agree.

Erik and Jenn had brought cake and wine to Bianca's room that evening one month earlier but, probably in keeping with the script Bianca had drafted and fully planned to execute, they were about 15 minutes too late. Tony was there and told them it had been peaceful. However, he was anything but peaceful. Strangely enough, it was Laurence who was of huge help and actually hugged Jenn before she left the station.

"So, this had to be the most different kind of funeral any of us have ever attended," Olaf said while he swished a Campari and soda around as they sat together, in an almost kind of bizarre *en famille*, at the reception in one of the smaller ballrooms at the Mark Hopkins (which was Tony's idea, as he said he just did not want to celebrate his famous sister's life at some unscrubbed temple to veganism). "I liked the incense you chose, Caroline; it was subtle yet provocative." Caroline just smiled sweetly at him and then looked at Jenn for permission to stroke Olaf's neck. Jenn wanted to tell her that such permission no longer was required. Olaf was a hell of a lot easier to be around these days, that much was certain. Marco was even more relieved at the change in Olaf.

"Well, I kind of liked it. It was so full of hope, instead of dirges and dreadful organ music," Erik said as he nodded to Marco that yes, he would get him some more of that marvelous champagne right away. "It wasn't too sad, although I think it's going to be a long time before Tony is back to his cheerfully manic ways."

Jenn knew that a lot of Bianca's friends, most of them of the same psychic or hippie persuasion, wanted to come over and meet the "children" but she sensed that perhaps they thought the situation a little too weird given the tableau the well-dressed five of them must have presented to people attired in what Marco and Olaf called "smocks." Most of them looked as if they would rather be anywhere than at the Mark Hopkins with prime rib and smoked salmon on the buffet. She thought she and Erik ought to make the rounds and greet people, as they might have at a regular funeral in Minneapolis or Reykjavik, but Erik had said that they should just wait and see if more than a handful of people would approach them first. Tony was nominally in charge of things but he seemed too busy talking with his own far-flung volcanology colleagues and with Yuki. Jenn and Erik did notice that his shoes were well polished, even if his jacket was rumpled and his pants clashed with his shirt and his jacket.

Caroline clicked her champagne glass against Marco's and

mouthed "I think now is as good of a time as any, everyone's glass is full."

"Well okay then," Marco said brightly as he raised his glass high to the ceiling. "As I am the senior member of this family, as it were, I have an announcement to make. I hope none of you will think it wrong to announce beautiful news at a funeral, but, as some say, one thing ends, something else begins. I think Bianca might have endorsed what I have to say, I do. And at my age, I don't have too much time between endings and beginnings. And we are here at this lovely hotel with all sorts of good food and drink."

Jenn and Erik looked at each other with very wide eyes, hoping Marco wasn't going to say that he was planning to return to Italy for his last years. Erik had not gone back to Iceland since Bianca's death, easily getting a leave of absence from the university with Tony's assistance. Erik hoped to God that Tony did not tell his department chair that he was psychologically traumatized by Hekla's eruption and in need of American medical attention, as he had only half-jokingly threatened to do. During his time in Minneapolis, Erik had become especially friendly with Marco and had even gone to his condo to help him with some new rugs and tables. The two of them also had gone out with Jenn a few times and Erik could not believe he could have such a good time with an American twin sister and her Italian surrogate grandfather who had to be the hippest old man he'd ever met or could have hoped to have met. This was a screwed up family, to be sure, as were many American families, but it was a family that really did have some fun. Even if having fun was a relatively new concept to them all.

"Well, don't keep us waiting, tell us your news," Jenn said as she then worried that maybe Olaf was going to retire, which would be a terrible idea, as the man had, at least in the pre-Caroline days, lived to work and keep things orderly, and not always in that order. But now that he was having sex at least daily and buying clothes and sunglasses, maybe designing churches was not so fulfilling anymore.

"Okay, the news that I am most happy to share with all of you is that my Olaf and his darling Caroline are going to be married, and only about four years later than they should have been married," Marco said while flashing the biggest smile Jenn had ever seen him produce. "I am making the announcement as the appointed patriarch of this group and am pleased to tell you the wedding will be in three months, in my beloved Milan. And yes, I am in charge of many of the arrangements. It will be black tie."

Olaf accepted Marco's effusive kiss on his cheek and then he, Olaf Bergquist, kissed Caroline for a really LONG time, in a manner that had to involve tongues, and in a way Jenn was sure she had never been kissed herself. By a boyfriend. Not Olaf. Still.

"Well, this is good news indeed," Erik said guardedly as he accepted a large hug from both Olaf and Caroline. Jenn was happy herself but still could not speak. She was still in shock, not from the news, but from the Olaf and Caroline kiss and then from the enormous embrace her father gave her as he gushed: "I hope you will be happy for me; I have never been so happy in my entire life."

She really was thrilled for Olaf and Caroline. She knew they were the loves of each other's lives and she was glad that if her father was going to be with someone, it was someone she knew, liked, and had a lot of dirt on. As it was, she had heard from Marco that the food at Olaf's had never been so good since Caroline took over the menu planning, or the selection of restaurants. She'd only been there once since Bianca's death, as she knew her head was not yet fully glued together regarding the whole hidden adoption business.

"What is this going on here? I see a lot of making out and happy people, which is probably what Bianca would have wanted to see, or that she is seeing. I have to believe in her philosophies now," Tony said as he nearly jumped right in between Jenn's and Erik's seats and almost stepped on Jenn's toes. "I take it you all have had enough to eat and drink, but drink up, the bar's open for a while yet. Bianca's will made it very clear that this was to be a real party."

"The reason for the making out is that my father and Caroline have just said they are going to be married," Jenn said, realizing she needed to be the supportive daughter, especially in front of this man who had made it clear he wanted to be a real uncle to Erik and Jenn, having almost no other family of his own. "The wedding is going to be in Milan, in three months, so if you can wangle an excuse to say you are going to check out Mount Vesuvius, you must come."

"Yes, you must come, Tony. We could not get married without you there," Caroline said, showing everyone the not-small diamond ring she had just taken out of her handbag and then had Olaf place on her finger with a fair amount of flourish. "We're all one big, mildly dysfunctional, happy family now."

Jenn was astounded at the ring's sparkle and whispered to Erik that it had to be Tiffany. He then quietly asked her how much she thought Olaf had spent. It had to be at least $30,000; it was one of the newer cuts. If she'd known that learning one was adopted meant getting an almost entirely renovated father willing to spend money, well, she might have welcomed the news years earlier. But, as Bianca would have said herself, it wasn't her karma to learn any sooner. Or Erik's. Or anyone's.

"So I think we need to have a toast to this happy couple, and to these newly united twins, and to Marco yourself, long may you chase women and wine," Tony said in a slightly drunken slur that Jenn and Erik had heard before; given the fact that this was his sister's funeral, they agreed to give him a hall pass. *A la famiglia!*"

Jenn and Erik emptied their glasses and noticed that Tony had splashed some of his champagne on Caroline's dress in his exuberance. It didn't look as if she cared; she and Olaf were making out again. They both hugged Marco, who had put on his sunglasses to hide his tears. Or to avoid looking at Olaf and Caroline, who were drawing some stares from the folk in smocks.

Chapter Twenty One

A LITTLE MORE THAN A YEAR LATER

Jenn laughed just a bit as she looked at the photo Caroline sent showing Olaf doing the tourist swimming thing at Iceland's Blue Lagoon. She wondered how they got all of the white silica mud from the lagoon out of their hair, especially as good hair seemed just as important these days to Olaf as it was to Caroline. But the trip did seem to be what they needed, as both Olaf and Caroline had small nervous breakdowns when Jenn told them at their wedding that she was moving to Toronto as well as when they fully realized that they would never be able to have a child together. Jenn understood the first breakdown somewhat but not quite the second, given their ages, although she tried very hard to put herself in their blissfully newlywed shoes. They were almost too deliriously happy. Even Marco said they drove him nuts at times, though he was always thrilled when they came to his house to do any matter of errand or chore. Caroline was fond of giving Marco neck massages and he was very fond of receiving such massages, even when Olaf teased him for openly cheating with his wife.

She looked at the time and realized she had better put her mobile away and get moving down Bloor Street, without stopping to look at any of Holt Renfrew's stylish windows or popping in at Roots to see what was on sale so she could make it to Pangaea on time to have dinner with Ken. She had never had black cod before she went to Pangaea and now she wanted to go there at least once a week. Ken usually obliged her whims, even though he said he already spent more than enough time in the Bay and Bloor area for his job.

One of the things she learned within weeks after she moved to Toronto is that Canadians, even Canadian boyfriends like Ken who were otherwise smitten with her, didn't tolerate tardiness as much as many Americans might. She still wondered how she was able to become so utterly enamored of Ken, a lawyer who was more successful than Jenn thought possible. She tried not to think too much about the fact that she had been introduced to him by Erik. As it was, Erik had acceded to Tony's reasonable pleadings that he go along with something Tony had been engineering on Erik's behalf for some time and accepted an actually big offer to join the geology faculty at the University of Toronto. Turned out Ken was a colleague of one of Erik's new best friends. All too convenient. And all what Erik had wanted for years, as long as the total compensation package was acceptable. This time it was, and Erik was so excited to leave Iceland that Jenn thought he would have gone to Toronto even if the university had told him he would have to pay them to work at the school many called Canada's Harvard.

It was even more convenient, to put it mildly, that at the same time, a great job became available at the university's medical school for Jenn. She'd been fascinated with Canada since she was a child. When she started to interview for the job, Olaf told her that when she was two, he and Christina had taken her with them on a car trip to Winnipeg in the midst of a miserable summer heat spell. At the border, Jenn apparently was a mass of tears and could not be consoled. In those more innocent days, the border agents were often quite friendly and informal. One of them, an older guard who just radiated "Mountie" peered into the car, looked Jenn directly in the eyes, and asked her if she didn't want to come to Canada. Olaf said Jenn almost immediately stopped crying. Jenn was certain she must have been absolutely terrified. But not so much that it stopped her from pestering

Olaf to bring her Canadian newspapers when he traveled to Toronto or Winnipeg for his job, as he often did when she was in high school, or go nuts and buy a real Hudson's Bay blanket for nearly $400 when she moved back to Minneapolis to take the job at the hospital.

But Ken was not terrifying. He was fairly silent, at least compared to most of the men she'd gone out with before, and a little too fond of his Scottish heritage (though she had not yet seen him in a kilt, she knew he would wear it well) he still was so much of what she said she had always wanted in a man. She had thought that never happened to anyone. Much less herself. Ken never made her feel nervous or stupid. He told her she was the most beautiful woman in the world, even in the morning. And he got along with Olaf, who Jenn now talked to on the phone more than she spoke with him in person when she was still living in Minneapolis. Revelation of the truth can either tear people apart or, given enough time for things to become better understood or at least accepted, it can bring people together. That is exactly what happened with Olaf and Jenn. Sometimes she found herself very much missing her father and Ken would always say, you know, we can go down there any time you want. She couldn't believe she had finally become somewhat of a daddy's girl at age 37. But only somewhat.

Olaf and Caroline had already visited twice. They insisted on staying in a hotel, which was great, as both Jenn and Ken did not want to listen to anyone else at night. Or in the morning. Actually, Olaf thought Ken was of much better quality than many Norwegians. Caroline thought he was eminently shaggable. It was all too incredible. But it probably wasn't going to be worth waiting for something to go wrong. The fact that their names rhymed, Jenn and Ken, was kind of stupid but she wasn't going to call him Kenneth anytime soon.

Getting the job at the U of T also was a really good thing. She no longer worked in a hospital and therefore did not have to talk to sick or dying people all the time. She was very happy to work with researchers in the university's faculty of medicine without having to tramp up to intensive care wards on a regular basis. No more Nurse

Laurence. Although she now was sort of friends with Laurence. He said he always wanted to visit Toronto and had asked Jenn that if he did so, would she show him around the Hockey Hall of Fame. She sometimes wondered why Laurence was so interested in hockey. And when those thoughts entered her head, she worked hard to dismiss them, especially when she pictured Laurence in full goalie gear. The job at the university was a lot bigger and more prestigious than what she had in Minneapolis. She actually made decisions at this place. From what she could discern after eight months, she seemed to be valued for the street smart American experience she brought to the table, as well as her trove of international media contacts. She knew some people thought (but never said as much to her face, as there appeared to be just as much Canada Nice at work as the fear-of-direct-conflict Minnesota Nice she had ingrained into her cells) that she was there just because of Erik, but her former boss in Minneapolis told her that he knew they would have recruited her strongly even without her twin brother based on what they told him during the reference checking process. She hoped it was true, but she was not going to fret about it too much. The move to another country had been stressful, enjoyably stressful, but stressful enough all the same. Although it was way easier to distinguish between fives and tens in her wallet, the subway was fantastic, and the national health care plan was nowhere near as scary as she had been warned by some of the doctors who came to her Minneapolis farewell. All she knew was that she liked what she was doing and if she ever stopped liking what she was doing, she'd find something else to do. She would. Although she had to admit that she sometimes missed some American stores, even though Ken had Olaf and Marco convinced that Harry Rosen was as good as any haute American men's clothing store and she was in Holt Renfrew as often as their sale prices would permit.

And best of all, she didn't have to see Erik any more than either of them wanted to see each other, even though they did see each other a lot. She couldn't explain that either. Caroline said it was simple: the two had become true siblings, true twins, a true brother and sister. As it was, she'd be seeing Erik the next morning.

"So show me what you got from Bianca's lawyer; I'm dying to know," Jenn said to Erik as they walked through the Saturday farmer's market in Withrow Park. She and Erik both loved the leafy, sloping park located just off the famous Danforth Avenue (which they both had been instructed to call "The Danforth" if they did not wish to sound like tourists) and the farmer's market, even though Erik thought some of the market's musical acts were a little too folksy for his taste. Jenn said it was way better than any of the markets she'd been to in the United States and the people were, as Canadian stereotypes would have it, all so friendly.

Erik was particularly concerned about finding out if kids were playing ball hockey in the park today, although he waited patiently and without making any sound while Jenn bought the same strawberry jam she seemed to buy every time they came to the market. He was just crazy about ball hockey. They both especially liked the park's urban upscale, just a little bit hippie Riverdale neighborhood (or neighbourhood, as Jenn was learning to spell. Erik already had his Canadian English spellings down pat.). Jenn was surprised that she liked the area so much, as it did have many residents who reminded her of Bianca, caftans and mounds of clanging jewelry sometimes included, but as it was, the reminders were for some reason more welcome than unwanted. Both she and Erik (and Ken) had become regulars at Rooster Coffee House, with its spectacular views of downtown Toronto and where Erik especially liked to see the different sorts of animals the baristas could create in his cappuccino and Jenn was addicted to the cinnamon rolls.

She and Erik even went to a psychic on The Danforth who had been friends with Bianca's second husband and had attended Bianca's memorial, wearing a black dress and gold serpent bracelets that might have belonged to Cleopatra. Erik said the experience with the psychic was amusing but useless, although Jenn was a bit unnerved as time passed when some of the woman's predictions came true, though she would never tell Erik what she was told. Jenn, Ken, Erik, and Erik's newish girlfriend Amanda (who, as it were, was not only beautiful in a Norwegian way, but also quite fond of patchouli oil) spent a lot of time hanging out in any number of the tons of bars and restaurants that lined The Danforth. Ken and Erik had become especially tight, tight enough that Ken thought they should both try to learn to speak Icelandic. Jenn said she'd think about it.

"Okay, let's find a place to sit down first," Erik said as he started to open the large envelope's heavily taped seal. "But first, don't get bent out of shape, I think the reason this stuff was sent to me is because Tony is the one who gave the lawyer an address and Tony cannot remember anyone's address but he was able to tell the guy that I worked in geology at the University of Toronto."

"I don't care that you got the package and I did not," she said while wondering what if anything, they were bequeathed by Bianca. It was always hard to find a bench in Withrow Park on market Saturdays, but they lucked out when some kids near the ball hockey area saw them and got up, as if to acknowledge that Jenn and Erik were indeed older and in need of a comfortable seat.

Ken was certain she had left them things like furniture, or wishes for serenity, or more ambition, something of that nature. He was sure that it could not be anything else, although even he conceded that she could have been worth millions just from her book sales. Just one of her books from the late 1990s sold more than two million hard cover copies in the United States alone. So it was entirely possible that she could have been worth millions, if she did not squander the money. And she might have been friends with one of the astrologers that even Olaf acknowledged were employed by investment banks as analysts or special project managers. If that were true, she really could have been worth a lot. "Although I am kind of surprised it took more than a year to sort this out but from what we knew of Bianca, I cannot imagine that an organized last will and testament were among her top priorities in life," she said. "Ken said messy estates can take a long time to figure out, especially in California."

"Yes, well, here's the cover letter," Erik said as he brushed the bench free of muffin crumbs with one hand before sitting down, keeping a firm grip with his other hand on the envelope so as to not lose any of its contents. The letter as very short and very much to the point, the point being that Bianca's financial estate was divided into three equal parts, one for Tony, one for Jenn and one for Erik. There was no mention of furniture or serenity, or even happiness. But clearly Bianca had been friends with an investment bank astrologer as her post-tax and attorney fee estate was valued in the range of $15 million U.S.

Erik shouted. "Can you believe she was worth this sort of money? Five million dollars each? This is absolutely incredible. I cannot believe you didn't like the woman at first."

"Let me see this again. I don't believe it," she said while thinking that Olaf would likely go crazy with both joy and advice upon hearing that his daughter was now a real millionaire. She grabbed the letter printed on the expensive heavy paper common to law firms and read it again and thought, yes, this really happened. You CAN get rich through manipulating the energy of the universe.

"I cannot believe it," she said while Erik downed the blueberry ice tea he had bought earlier so quickly she thought he would choke and spit tea all over the letter. "It is too unreal. It's like a soap opera, or some sappy movie. Something will go wrong soon enough, things have been working too well for too long now. This is all too crazy."

She sat for a moment with what anyone who would have seen her might have thought was an expression half utterly stunned, half completely bemused. Part of her seriously thought Bianca would show up at that very moment in a more angelic type of caftan, gold filigree pen in her hand, twisting her hair with the pen and telling them in her kitten voice that it all was just an otherworldy joke. But nothing happened. No purple lights twinkling anywhere.

"Why do you always have to think things won't work out? Just try to be happy for once in your life," Erik said in a clearly exasperated tone, taking the letter back from Jenn and pulling out the envelope's other papers. "I for one am more than willing to take this money. So maybe these are forms we have to fill out to get the money, the letter doesn't say anything about us having to go to California."

"I can ask Ken to look at things, he's a lawyer and he's free."

"This is going to make life a lot easier for both of us," Erik said with some finality, realizing as he looked around that some people were looking at them and probably listening to them as well. "I can buy a house in Rosedale, or you can buy a condo downtown, or even something nice here in Riverdale. We can travel. You now have enough of a dowry to marry Ken if he'll have you, and I don't know what else. I can imagine a whole lot of other possibilities. A lot. I just wish my mother and father were still around to see this day."

"Don't forget, we have to pay taxes on this, I am sure, at least Canadian taxes," Jenn said cautiously, also wishing at that moment that she too could see her brother's parents. "That could take a big bite. But you are right, we can do a lot of stuff now. We're going to find out if money can buy any kind of happiness."

As it was, a ball hockey game between a team of yellow-shirted pre-adolescent boys and a group of bigger and more threatening looking pre-adolescent boys in purple shirts was just starting, and Erik was becoming engrossed. Even though the enormity of what they had just read on that fancy cream-colored bond paper was making him almost shake. He almost wished he could join the kids but of course, that was completely impossible. None of those uniform shirts would fit him anymore.

"I was just thinking about something you asked me when we were still in Iceland, when we were in my lab after the eruption," Erik said quietly as he looked directly at Jenn. "Remember asking me whether Hekla would have a caldera after the eruption or not, and I told you no, the magma chamber was too deep? Well, and I suppose you'll attribute this to my whacked scientist mind, but you know, in a way, you and I experienced a sort of reverse caldera when our lives erupted, as it were. You know, you found out you were adopted, we learned who our biological parents were, we met Bianca, we lost Bianca, Tony Fionarello is our uncle, and he's a pretty decent guy most of the time, we got way better jobs and moved here to Toronto, which you have to admit is way more exciting than Minneapolis…"

"Or Reykjavik."

"Or Reykjavik, to be sure. But the magma chambers of our lives blew up, if you will. Instead of leaving a depression, we were lifted up. It really is unreal."

"That's sort of profound, Erik. I never would have thought about a reverse caldera. Still, as nice as our lives seem, and they are, believe me, I think I am truly in love with someone for the first time in my life, my father is almost normal and happy, we live here, we like our work, you have the lovely Amanda, speaking of possibly getting married, and now we have money, but…"

"But what? What more could you want, Jenn Bergquist?"

"I don't know, I guess I at least had a real caldera in my life, I don't know how to explain this, but for a while there, after I found out I was adopted and I got back from that unearthly experience in Iceland and I thought I was going to go back to my same boring job and life filled with a deceit I never knew, no excitement, nothing, going out with one creep after another, I was pretty major league depressed. Can you understand that?"

"I can, but all I am saying now is that the depression caused by this eruption, this volcanologist language is too much, was lifted. That's all I was saying."

"Fine."

"We should get some lunch in a little bit so we can look at all of these forms and then maybe you can call Ken and have him help us out."

"Fine."

"Maybe a gyro."

"Okay, you sound so very enthused. But uh, I want to stay here a while longer and watch these kids. They really go after things with all they've got, don't they? It's very inspiring."

"They are something to see. Although, come to think of it, I don't think Bianca would be so happy to see us so interested in a competitive sport involving a ball."

They just smiled at each other. Without smirks. Neither one was sure Bianca would have known what she would have wanted for them. Or for herself.

But what they had at this moment (barring getting smacked by any errant balls lobbed by the exuberant ball hockey boys) seemed just fine.

Acknowledgements

I'm one person who has come to realize that no one achieves any measure of greatness without support or assistance from others.

While I don't want to be so boastful as to claim any measure of greatness small or large about *Life Erupted,* I do want to thank some people who have supported me and helped me since well before that day in the bitter, cold winter of 2009, when I started my exile in Minneapolis. That is when I decided I could not only edit books for other people and then market their works but that I just might be able to write my own novel.

First and foremost, I must thank my mother, Virginia Phillips. This book is dedicated to her because she supported me and believed in me through many a time of rough trial and tribulation. I hope this book will prove your faith in me to have been worth it.

My boss from my time at the University of Minnesota Academic Health Center, Sally Howard, deserves thanks for teaching me about the merits of discipline and for having me watch her downtown Minneapolis condo with a fabulous view for two winters. Much of *Life Erupted* was written at Sally's house. When I left Sally's condo, I moved into my friend Jeff Mattson's apartment, eventually taking it over when he decided he'd rather live up north all the time and not just on long weekends. Thanks, Jeff. I still miss cocktail hour.

I want to thank Brenda Bredahl, who provided early and valuable criticisms regarding characters and their development, as well as a willingness to listen to me during all manner of woeful times.

Emily Reynolds must be given massive thanks for listening to me so often when I thought I was either on the brink of a fabulous (translate: crazy) new idea or at the edge of losing it. The same for Elaine Fogdall. Similar thanks go to my great friends in Oregon, Jenn Casey and Shannon Rose (so no, those 14 months spent in Eugene were not all unhappy) as well as to my brother Joseph Stanik and especially to my brother Nicholas Stanik. I am grateful to Susan Papanicolaou for her willingness to continually devise creative efforts to get me out of the house and find some measure of entertainment. My former Public Education Network colleague Howie Schaffer deserves much gratitude for always hiring me for a communications project just when I really needed the work.

Zanne Miller must be given kudos and great thanks for editing the book in a most thoughtful and careful fashion. She is truly a writer's editor and a wonderful writer in her own right.

Colleen Killingsworth, who wrote a testimonial, deserves more thanks than I can possibly summon in any one paragraph. She hired me for consulting projects, never stopped encouraging me with my writing, helped me try to find permanent jobs in my spiritual homeland of Canada, told me all the time I was great, and was one of the first to read the book from first page to last.

Thanks as well to the internationally renowned bioethicist, Dr. Arthur Caplan, for providing a testimonial, to Aaron Fahrmann for taking such nice photographs of me, and to my former Science Museum of Minnesota colleague Lawrence Sahulka, for designing a beautiful book.

I also must thank my unofficial "big brother" Ralph Heussner, who hired me for my first job at the University of Minnesota Academic Health Center and has been an unswerving source of support and counsel for me through many a time of trial and triumph.

Lastly, thanks are in order for Jack Ohman, the Minnesota native, multiple award-winning (and 2012 Pulitzer finalist), nationally syndicated editorial cartoonist for *The Oregonian*, who drew the lovely, whimsical illustrations that grace the book.

Biography

MARY STANIK, a Milwaukee, Wisconsin native who has now spent most of her life among those of Scandinavian descent in Minneapolis, Minnesota, is a former spokesperson for the University of Minnesota Academic Health Center, Northwest Airlines and the University of Oregon. She also was a speechwriter in Washington, D.C. for former U.S. Secretary of Education Richard W. Riley during the second Clinton administration. *Life Erupted* is her first novel and book. She lives in Minneapolis.

photograph by Aaron Fahrmann

www.ingramcontent.com/pod-product-compliance
Lightning Source LLC
Chambersburg PA
CBHW050040180626
46810CB00002B/823